RAILDOGS
BY REJEAN GIGUERE

Other books by Rejean Giguere

Jackfish Reborn
Endpoint
Franklin Asylum
Merlin 444
DreamWeaver

Short Story Collection

First Works

www.rejeangiguere.com
@RejeanGiguere

RAILDOGS

by Rejean Giguere

First Print Edition
Copyright 2014 - Rejean Giguere
ISBN 978-1-927047-22-4
Ontario, Canada
www.rejeangiguere.com

This book is a work of Fiction. All characters and events (and some places) are products of the Author's imagination.

RAILDOGS

Prologue

The conversation was obviously over. Dougie Rackman balanced himself against the side of the boxcar as it rumbled down the southbound rail. This couldn't be happening. He tried to focus on something, anything, except the sound of his heart hammering against his ribs.

He felt more than saw the others scrambling around in the dark. Someone banged and scratched against the outer walls. Another let out a short sharp scream.

He looked up, his eyes desperately seeking a glimpse of daylight – a gap that offered the possibility of escape. He could hear footsteps above. The smell of the fuel invaded every corner as it poured through holes in the ceiling of the boxcar. Fumes rose from the pool of gasoline as the shaking train sent the liquid spreading slowly across the floor.

As he examined the number three tattooed on the inside of his wrist, he realized he was as angry as he was scared. He was third in line. This shouldn't be happening to him.

His head snapped upward at the muted roar of a blowtorch...

The Box

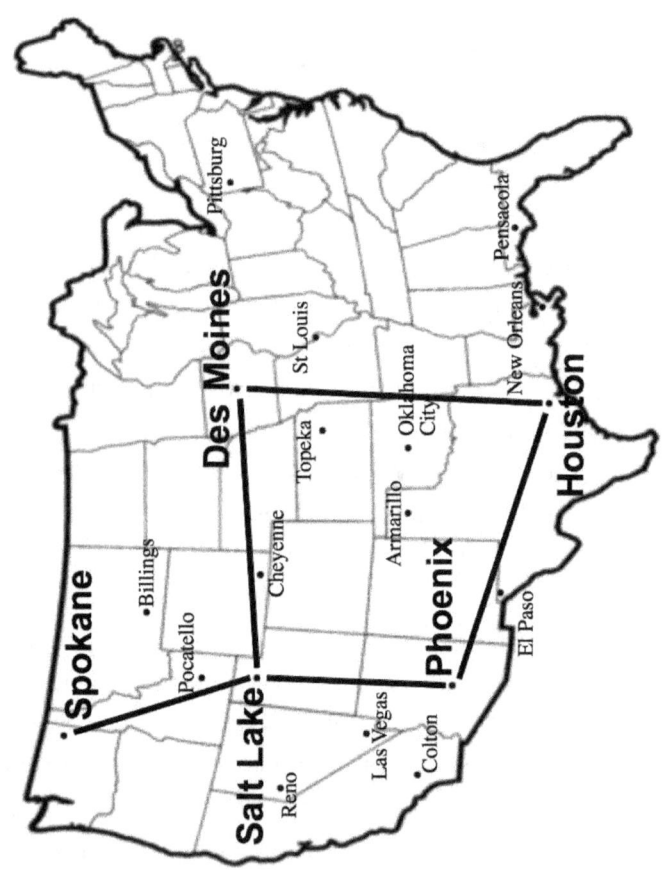

CHAPTER 1

Reno, Nevada

The figure sat unmoving, immobile. Hands on the arms of the chair, a light shawl was wrapped around her shoulders. Anyone walking the grounds would see Sarah Perez sitting in her window on the second floor and think she was some invalid relaxing in the sunshine, enjoying the nice early-summer weather. Anyone who walked the pathways regularly would know she was there every morning and night, absent only during her own afternoon walks.

This morning her gaze was again fixed on something beyond her window. Was it the flocks of birds wheeling across the sky? Perhaps the flowers and shrubs leading to the tree line? Maybe the mountains off in the distance? Or was it something that no one else saw?

Sarah looked young for this type of long-term care home, but at forty-five she had already been here for ten years, and had long ago settled in.

Her lip curled slightly as the sound of a tap at the door brought her back from her thoughts.

"Who is it?"

"Lunch time."

She was pretty sure she heard the orderly mutter under his breath.

"You crazy hag."

She hated the staff, and most of the decrepit old farts and crazy morons who lived here. But for some reason she liked her room and the view. That had been important back in the beginning and it was still true.

"On the table would be fine."

She stubbed out her cigarette and pulled the window closed, her sole concession to the non-smoking rule. Quietly, she moved towards the small table. The staff had long ago given up trying to make her eat with all the others in the dining room.

The orderly dropped the tray on the table and grabbed the pastry before heading for the door, "You won't be needing this."

Her right eye twitched twice. She knew the light shake in her shoulders was anger. Looking down at her hands, she tried to unclench her fists. They had been stealing from her and taking advantage like this ever since she arrived. She hadn't really noticed in the beginning, but back then she was in pretty bad shape. Now she saw it every day, and it just wasn't right. But it had gone on so long that making it stop might take more effort than she had inside her.

Sarah watched him leave with her desert in his hand and looked down at the remaining food. She didn't like it, or hate it. It was a damned necessity, rather bland and inoffensive. It didn't take long to eat and before she knew it she was back at the window staring off at something. Or nothing.

The battle raged in her head constantly these days. In the beginning the demons had consumed her, and she lived pretty much in her mind. But in the years since she had created a balance of sorts. On most days she was living real life, just as much as she was stuck living in her head.

They all thought she was a little crazy, and at one time she would have agreed. Now she felt like she was just biding her time. She knew the years were going by, but she still grasped some belief, some hope, kindled by thoughts of walking away, free of this place. And she still had her son.

No one knew that he was who she was watching for. He would visit when he could, and so she waited for him.

The guilt was heavy at times. She'd had so many plans for them, for him. Then it had all come crashing down. Sarah shook her head and stared down at her fingers as they curled together on her lap. She'd abandoned him too young.

Lately, she had begun to examine this world she'd made for herself. She wondered how he was surviving out there and what kind of person he had become. Was he happy? He never really told her what he did for money.

It was time for her afternoon walk. She had to keep in shape, in case she ever got up the courage to walk out that door forever.

*****

Salt Lake City, Utah

Cliff Turner scratched his head. He knew he was a scruffy kind of guy. He smiled to himself. He was a crafty son of a bitch as well. Running a hand over the two-day-old steel wool on his face, he looked out over the rolling hills of the Wasatch Mountains. "Not bad Cliffy, not bad."

The twenty acres of trees and scrub brush acted as a buffer zone around the modest house. The new place was private, one that no one knew about. It had been months since he had been to the crewhouse in town. He spent most of his time now on the deck that hung out over the rocky valley in back. It didn't matter, day or night; he just sat there and stared. There was something about this place that allowed him to let his guard down.

Was he really having second thoughts about the whole damned thing these days? Was he running out of steam? Or was it his balls? Was he getting soft? He formed his hands into fists, looking down at the white lines etched across the clenched knuckles. He still had his strength, so what was eating at him?

Did he have the answer in the back of his head already? He was finally in a position to consider letting this whole thing go. He was still so much farther ahead than when he started. *Christ, what a trip it'd been.*

Ever since Cliff had a chance to separate himself from the filth of the road, he'd been watching the neighbors who also lived along the canyon road. He'd begun to decide he really liked the way they lived. Lately, whenever it was time to go back at it, he'd been less and less interested. Everything that used to matter; the adrenaline, the power, the honest-to-god brutality, didn't seem to have the same pull as it used to.

Some part of him hated craving the freedom he got from having cash – too much easy cash – but some other part of him was becoming accustomed to this new life. Perhaps that was what was picking at him. He knew he had to keep the process going if he wanted to have it all.

Unclenching his fists, he looked back down, his eyes stopped on the tattoo. The number one was just two inches high, half an inch wide. Just one color, the black brand looked crude. On the inside of his right forearm, the number could be seen by anyone whenever he shook hands.

"You've come a long way Cliffy, a long way."

He knew it was time. He had a gang out there. After all these years it worked well enough that they didn't really need a leader there all the time, but Cliff still needed to make sure his baby was chugging along. Besides, however many doubts he had about the grind, the feeling of power was proving hard to give up.

Power had been everything in the beginning. He'd gotten drunk on it and abused it. Shivers went down his spine at the thought. *Jesus, had he done damage.* Once he had put the gang together it had been a free-for-all. Anyone who got in the way paid dearly.

Cliff smiled at the memories, the high they'd been on. Some days he had the odd twinge at the amount of carnage they had caused, and the pain the poor bastards who crossed his trail must have felt. Maybe he even experienced a little regret.

Right now he had to get changed and ready to head out on the rails again. He snorted. He may be trying to look more like the folks living around these parts, but he still wasn't pulling it off. He looked down at his cargo shorts and loafers. There was something rough and awkward about his look that didn't fit into designer clothes too well.

From the chest in the basement he pulled out a pair of grease-stained coveralls, a black watch cap, and work boots. Stuffing a few things into an old shoulder bag, he checked the mirror by the door to make sure he looked the part. Not good enough. He rolled his lip into a snarl, and nodded. That ought to do it. He knew deep down this was who he was, but still, he felt a little uncomfortable in his own boots these days.

He looked back at the discarded loafers sitting at the bottom of the steps. The thought of giving it all up, choosing comfort over hardship, was becoming more tempting.

His Raildogs were spread out across America, riding the freight trains and preying on the never-ending supply of riders looking for a cheap way to travel the country.

Cliff pulled out his black book, checking to see which members of the gang were current on their dues and which ones he still needed to collect from. If you wanted to make money on his tracks, you became part of the gang and paid your dues. He liked knowing they were out there now, making money and causing mayhem.

Driving down from the hills, his beat up old Chevy step-side truck would be safe for few days somewhere as public as the parking lot at the all-night Wal-Mart in Salt Lake. He climbed on the city bus for the final ride down to the freight yard.

The old loading docks and switching yards were in a run-down section of town where the old carpet and textile factories used to be. Now the boarded up warehouses were slowly becoming condos. He could never figure why someone would want to live in such a place.

To him it was just another day at the office.

*****

Billings, Montana

Bart Forest eased back inside the tree line and glanced left at his partner.

"You ready man?"

"Yeah, yeah."

He didn't know how Danny was going to be able to run beside the train with those stupid brown dress shoes. He reached down and pulled one last time at the laces on his Doc Martens. Good and tight.

Bart really wasn't sure exactly how he got involved with the kid. The kid may be only eighteen, but the dude dressed like somebody's grandpa in a department store windbreaker and brown dress slacks. His bright curly red hair flopped down over his black-framed glasses. The only thing on the kid that didn't stand out was that big old suitcase he carried; it was a dark enough green to blend into the trees.

The two of them had spent the winter hatching a plan that all came down to this very moment. The long row of freight cars was headed their way. The only free ride out of Billings was on the Burlington Northern. Once they got further south there would be other rail lines, but right now this was it. Weeks spent watching around the clock, taking notes, meant they were sure which train to catch.

They knew enough to stay clear until the train started to leave. There was always a chance that someone from the railroad would walk down the train track looking for riders, and they had no intention of getting caught. Shit, they could even end up in jail. Worse, the trip would be over before it began.

The train jerked and the car's couplings slammed together, steel on steel, as the long line of cars rolled forward.

"We gotta go man." Bart pushed away from the tightly packed trunks of the Aspen trees. "We gotta go now!"

"I'm with ya." Danny was up and running right behind his buddy, the two of them sprinting hard down the slope to meet the train.

What sounded easy in the planning was proving harder in reality. The rocks of the rail bed were loose in places and running in the dark was never a sure thing. They had to get close enough to the railcars to grab on, and the sound of the steel wheels rolling on the rails was nerve-wracking. One slip in the wrong direction and the wheels would get you. There were plenty of examples on the internet to drive that point home.

The boys had even seen a story about a town in Brazil that had built a hospital at the train station because of all the people who were injured trying to jump on the freedom train running north to the US.

Bart, a little quicker, ran along side the train, trying to decide which car to jump on. He wanted a grain car because the V-shaped hopper left enough space at each end to shelter under out of the weather.

A steady stream of refrigerated cars left little option. They weren't supposed to be too bad, the little overhang of the cooler unit stuck out on the end of the car above a level area of grating where they could sit with their backs wedged against the wall.

"This one," Bart looked back for a split second, then grabbed the railing on the end of the car. Keeping his legs going, he stayed even with the train for a few seconds as he searched for a foothold on the steps.

He knew he couldn't run with both hands holding on for long, so he jumped into the air and pulled hard at the same time. His eyes locked onto the steps as he flew through the air and slammed against the steel.

It took him a spit second to be sure he'd stopped there and wasn't about to fall off, before he scrambled up to where they would be able to sit. Bart relaxed a second, then looked around, remembering Danny. Was he going to make it?

He watched the kid trying to gain traction as he ran. The friggin' shoes were slipping and sliding while his suitcase acted like a pendulum, swinging him off balance as he ran, but he had a fierce look of determination as he kept pushing.

Bart wasn't even sure why he was hanging with this kid, let alone taking off on a trip with the guy. He didn't need anyone. He liked being a loner. He didn't care that he had no friends at school or in the neighborhood. He didn't think there was a cool one in that bunch of pussies.

Danny ran beside the car, looking ahead and then over at the train as his legs pounded forward.

"Come on Danny, before it's too late." The train was slowly picking up speed.

The kid reached out with one hand and grabbed the rail. As he ran, he swung the suitcase back, and then with one last blast of effort, windmilled it around towards the stairs. The suitcase's momentum jerked Danny off his feet as his body followed and slammed to a stop against the steps.

Bart grabbed the suitcase and pulled, hoping the kid was holding on tight. It took a second for Danny to get his footing and begin to push the suitcase up onto the landing. Shaking, he crawled up and lowered himself beside the case.

The two of them sat there holding on tight as the train shook it's way along the track. It must have been more than ten minutes before they looked at each other and burst out laughing. They'd made it. The laughter went on a little longer than it should have, they both knew they'd been scared shitless.

Dragging his packsack close, Bart reached in and pulled out a couple beers. He cracked the tab on the can of Bud and lifted his hand. "Cheers buddy. Nothing but sunshine now."

He could tell the kid was hesitating. Did he even drink? Finally Danny opened up the beer and tipped it forward in response, "Florida."

*****

Houston, Texas

Trains were stopped, loading, hooking up or moving. The twenty or so sets of rails were all pretty much full. Some trains were eastbound and others westbound, but the Pacific Southern was heading north towards Oklahoma City.

The two black men watched the train closely, waiting until the last second to jump on. They wanted to see as many cars go by as possible before then climbed aboard, hoping to see other riders.

Athletic and tall, Devon wore his shoulder length hair in dreads, for this trip he'd made sure his running shoes, cargos and sweatshirt were all black. His only distinguishing feature was the gold-capped tooth visible when he grinned.

"I want some action tonight Ras man."

Rashad was shorter, thicker and balder. A linebacker in high school, he knew how to use his weight and more importantly, he liked to use it. Devon looked over at his partner, Ras wasn't a thinker or a leader, but he sure was back-up.

Devon saw it first, a flash of something red coming right at them. He moved to the edge of the ditch and started to run. Rashad reacted late, taking off towards the train. The bright color wasn't normal and Devon wanted to be close when it went past.

The red flashed by. Bingo. It was a packsack on the back of a refrigerated car. Devon didn't see anything else, but someone could have been lying down, out of sight. They should have hid that packsack. He smiled to himself.

"People on the train Ras man, run!"

The train was picking up speed.

They make it look easy. It took a flat-out run to keep up, and the rail car with the red packsack was gone, but the two men raced beside the train. One after another they quickly grabbed hold and jumped up on the side of one of the boxcars. They'd clearly done it before.

Catching their breath, they didn't seem disappointed. Devon was patient, "The train will stop again at the north yards, there's always extra cars to hook up. We can move up then."

Rashad leaned out, keeping an eye up the side of the train, watching for anyone jumping off. They rode in silence with no idea what was coming, just understanding that there was going to be some kind of action shortly. Sure enough, the train slowed as it entered another rail yard. Devon knew it could be stopped for a minute, or an hour. Either way the two men wouldn't wait to find out, they both hit the ground running.

Devon slowed up as he neared the car with the red packsack. The switchblade clicked out of the four-inch handle, instantly doubling the length of the weapon. Rashad caught up, already wearing steel knuckles on each hand.

Nodding, they stormed the stairs. Two heads popped up at the sound of boots on steel and Devon didn't slow down. Stepping forward, he kicked the first person square in the face and watched as the neck snapped back and the head banged against the unforgiving side of the rail car.

Still moving, he came down hard with his fist on the head of the target's wide-eyed companion. A quick knee to the head was just instinct at this point, and he relaxed it at the last second, knowing it wasn't necessary.

"Fuck Devon, leave me something man." Rashad stood behind him, fists up, pissed that he didn't get a shot in.

"Don't worry Ras man. These guys'll wake up soon." He couldn't stop himself from grinning at his buddy's anger. "We'll wait until the train is out of town, then you can have some fun."

One of their victims woke up before the train started moving, but he decided to stay put when Rashad gave him an evil stare.

Devon sat on the ledge at the back of the railcar and went through the packsacks the men had been carrying, finding nothing of interest. It was pretty clear that they were bums with no money or anything. That was too bad for them; they were only staying on the train if they could pay their way.

Devon asked a question and Rashad moved closer, waiting to hear the answer. "Where's your money?"

No one answered and Rashad let his right arm fly loose as he punched the closest guy in the mouth.

The second one was quick to speak up. "We don't have any."

Rashad's punch caught him off guard as his head cracked against the steel storage container. Devon's problem was he knew they were telling the truth. Everyone always said they had no money and all you had to do was beat it out of them. But he knew that would get them nothing here. These losers didn't have a cent.

"You gotta pay to ride these rails, those are Raildog rules. No pay, no ride."

The shocked look on the two bums turned to hysteria when Devon grabbed the red packsack and threw it off the moving train. Rashad grabbed the second pack and it quickly followed the first. When someone was really holding out, the sudden loss of their stuff, was usually a back-breaker, but again Devon knew there would be no money this time.

The bums began to struggle when the two black men stepped forward and grabbed them. Devon had the first one's hoodie over his head while his other hand pulled on the oversized jacket. When the bum grabbed onto the Raildog's leg to stop his progress Devon pounded his head with both fists until he let go. Then he dragged the bum to the edge of the car.

The guy was screaming as the countryside rolled by. The steel wheels scratched and squealed over the rails. He held the guy there for a moment, half-suspended in mid-air, and let his situation sink in. He wasn't sure if the guy was appreciating the view like he was.

"Hey Rashad, pick your number."

"Two."

Devon smiled, that was a pretty low number. The bodies always bounced at least a couple times. "I call three."

He gave the bum a twist in the air as he dropped the guy off the car and watched as he hit the rough rock that ran beside the tracks, bouncing once, twice, and then a third and fourth time before rolling to a stop.

"That's ten bucks Ras man."

Rashad held the other guy's face, bleeding and scraped, against the steel plate of the landing. He could feel his victim shake uncontrollably as he watch his buddy thrown from the train. Now the guy started to flail around as Rashad got off the bum's back and half-dragged him, face down, towards the side.

"Over or under," he asked.

Devon chose under.

Rashad didn't hesitate, keeping the momentum of his victim's body going, he pushed the weight out into mid-air, and let go. The body seemed to hover a second before falling fast to the rock below. The bum took an awkward bounce and settled into a heap.

"Sweet mother, I love this job Ras man." He grinned. Devon was wide-eyed and full of energy as they looked back at the bums lying alongside the track. "That looked like two bounces man. You owe me twenty."

He sucked a whistling breath in around the gold tooth. The adrenaline was still pumping hard, surging through his muscles. He was proud of the number fifty he wore on the inside of his forearm. He looked at Rashad, his good buddy wore number fifty-two.

Devon liked the beginning of the month, the guys all got together on the line they patrolled and paid up their dues. Then the boss would throw a party and they'd all have a blast. Nothing like perks with the job.

"Let's get up to Oklahoma," he said. "The boss will be waiting and we got some partying to do."

CHAPTER 2

San Antonio, Texas

Sam Dorson hung out from the side of the freight car. The wind pulled at his hair and with his eyes closed he let the rush of air wash over his face. He still couldn't believe the fucking peace of mind he got from riding the rails.

A trucker by trade, he had seen every goddamn corner of the country before giving it up to run and hide. Since he knew some things about a few women who had disappeared, when he felt the heat getting a little closer on that missing woman case, he'd decided it was time for a change of scenery.

He'd have to think long and hard about how he got on the rails in the first place, where had it been? It didn't matter now. That was twelve years ago. Now he was a Raildog. He looked down at the number two tattooed inside his left wrist and smiled before he swung back into the freight car, reinvigorated and alive.

"Fuck boys, it's another sunny kick-ass day. You up for it?"

Their shouts and whistles echoed in the rail car, sounding like applause to him. Some of the crew had been with him when they left San Antonio and the rest would be waiting in Phoenix.

Sam lived on the rails most days. He controlled the southern section of line running east-west from Texas to Arizona. He didn't want to miss any part of the action that was always going on. He knew Cliffy was getting out on the tracks less and less these days, and he heard one of the Rackman brothers was holed up in Vegas pretty much full time, but he didn't care. He wasn't slowing down for nothing.

The beginning of the month meant the whole gang was on the rails. It was the only time everyone was mobile. Dues to pay, and hopefully there were travelers to collect from. If the people out there knew it was the worst time to hitch a ride they'd stay away, but they didn't, and people were always riding at the first of the month for their own reasons.

It didn't matter how much money he put in his pocket, Sam would be out working his turf and taking advantage of any opportunities that came his way. The big man, over six foot and at least two hundred and thirty pounds of muscle, liked beating people up and making them pay to ride the rail. He really liked when he came across women riders, because that was an entirely different ball game.

Sam drifted back to the open door of the railcar. He knew the train would slow again near Eagle Pass. He watched the landscape roll by, wondering if there was anybody waiting for the train up ahead.

*****

Pittsburg, Pennsylvania

The rain pounded down as the slow moving train lumbered down the rails. Dark, miserable and wet was the only way to describe it. Raul Alvarez crouched against the back of the railcar holding a chunk of blue tarp over the two of them. His girlfriend Maria Martinez was huddled against him, asleep. He shook his head, *shit, how did she do it?*

Raul was pissed at the weather, not just with this rain tonight, but the whole damned northeast. He'd been sent here last fall to set up another route for the Mexican cartel to ship drugs into the northeast U.S.. More and more, the cartel was moving their product directly to major cities and cutting out middlemen.

Raul was an up and comer. This project was a big step for him and he was sure it would lead to bigger opportunities. But right now all he wanted was to get back into Mexico where the sun was always shining, the weather always warm. Shit, in this place he might not see the sun for weeks.

Everything was in place and ready for final testing. The route, the couriers, and the distributors. Raul was heading back south to lay all the details out for the bosses and oversee the first test-runs himself. He had always used freight trains down south when he was a junior couriering shipments of weed into the U.S. and he sure wasn't renting cars or taking planes at this point. He never left a paper trail.

So he was riding from Pittsburg to Cincinnati in the rain and his ass was already sore. *How long was it going to take to get to Mexico?*

He could barely make out Maria's shape in the dark. The hoodie and oversized clothing he forced her to wear turned her into a hobbit. He almost laughed out loud.

He never should have let her come along, but who was he kidding. He wanted her with him from now on, wherever he went. The little Panamanian had a figure that didn't end. Long black hair, dusky skin and sensual lips drew Raul in like a moth to a streetlight. They had been drawn to each other from the moment they met in New York. It hadn't taken long for her to move to Pittsburg, now they were inseparable.

He had been just about to leave his apartment when she arrived to join him on the trip. She looked so serious.

"I'm packed and ready to go."

"Baby, you can't wear that stuff. I told you we're going on a train." She was rocking a tight skirt and high heels and pulling a pair of rolling suitcases.

"I go everywhere in heels Raul, you know that."

"I told you to bring a packsack, what are those?" He pointed at the two suitcases.

"Raul, you know a woman needs her things." This time her lips formed a sultry smile as she fluttered her eyelashes at him.

He had finally won their long discussion and laughed out loud when she'd reappeared from his bedroom wearing two layers of track pants, sweatshirts and a large hoodie, all of them too big for her. It was a good thing they were traveling in the rain, because he was sure he wouldn't be getting any for a while. Her packsack was stuffed with old cargo pants and sweatshirts, which pretty well ensured she wasn't going to be happy.

Raul listened to the pelting downpour drumming against his tarp. The only other sounds were the steel wheels against the rails and the rattle of boxcars as they swayed from side to side through the open country.

Cincinnati, he thought to himself, *St. Louis, and then down to Mexico. The sooner, the better.*

*****

Spokane, Washington

"Raildogs! Gather up." Albert Simms rounded up the posse.

"Al, there's riders up near the front of the train!" A young guy ran down the side of the freight train yelling.

"We'll take this boxcar, load up." The train was about to pull out of the rail yard headed south towards Salt Lake. The men started throwing their packsacks and shoulder bags in the open door of the car. "Mickey, take someone and go get those riders. Bring 'em back here."

He pulled a gun from his waistband and threw it to the younger gang member, motioning to the guy who had spotted the people. "Hurry, show him where they are."

Albert slowly crawled up into the boxcar. Jesus, he liked his life. He ran this section of the northwest rail and loved every second of it. He wasn't a big guy, but everyone knew the number five tattooed on his wrist made him a top dog. A Raildog.

Looking around at the others, he could feel the adrenaline starting to pulse through the car. Everyone knew what was coming next. Albert cracked his knuckles and waited, feeling the rush of anticipation creeping over him.

He could picture what was happening up ahead, he'd done it before himself. Mickey wouldn't piss around. He knew the drill. Storm the fuckers, take them hard and fast, show them who was boss.

Of course how hard you had to be depended on what you found. Sometimes they folded right away, and sometimes they fought back. Albert liked it when they fought back. With his violent nature Mickey would strong-arm them off the train and bring them back by hand, he figured. He probably wouldn't even need to pull out the gun.

His thoughts were interrupted when a body slammed against the steel doorframe of the car. Then another, and another lined up beside the first. He could hear Mickey yelling, "Climb up you pussies. I'm not fucking around."

One of the kids wasn't quick enough and Mickey started punching people in the back of the head. All three began climbing, hand over hand, scrambling over each other. Albert noticed the shiner on one face and the blood coming from the nose of another. He caught his lieutenant's eye and they shared a knowing smile.

As if on cue, the train started to move. Someone lit a propane lantern in the corner and Albert took a last look at the daylight before pulling the heavy sliding door closed.

Although the scene must have looked like a horror show to their captives, it was a comfort zone for Albert. He let his eyes adjust to the darkened interior. Gradually the light from the lantern seemed to grow until he could see into the dim corners of the train car.

The three kids huddled together just inside the door while his crew taunted them. Attempting to scare the shit out of them was more like it.

He pushed off the sidewall. "Get them up."

A kick to the shin of the nearest kid was enough and they all jumped to their feet. It took awhile to get good at walking around in a moving freight train. Albert and the crew had it nailed down, while the kids didn't.

One kid leaned back against the sidewall with both palms against the wall to hold himself upright. The second was trying to use his knees to ride the roll of the boxcar, but he didn't seem able to maintain control because he was standing facing forward instead of sideways. The third one looked sick to his stomach. It was pretty easy to tell he was fighting not to puke. Even in the dim light, Albert could see the kid's face was changing colors as he searched wild-eyed for something to hold on to.

"Where you going boys?"

No one answered. Albert's face changed from casually friendly to frighteningly dangerous as he started forward, "You don't want to answer...?"

He paused, then took one more step forward before the middle one squealed out, "We left Eastport this morning."

"That's better. Now where are you headed?"

The kid swallowed hard. "Through Oregon and down to Oakland."

Albert smiled like he was on some great adventure with them. "So it's off to California for the summer."

No one answered.

He took the last few steps to stand in front of the teenagers. "I sure hope you got money to pay for your ride," he looked around. "Because this here is my rail line."

Still no one answered.

A quick backhand knocked the kid into one of his companions.

Albert stepped sideways to stand in front of the next guy, staring down at him. "Someone better answer me soon, because I'm getting pissed."

"I got some," the kid started fishing for his cash, he looked up with a handful of bills squeezed in his fist. "How much is it mister?"

Albert laughed at the absurd question, reaching out to engulf the kid's hand and money in a tight grip. He squeezed, feeling the smaller hand crumpling in his own, "Everything you got kid."

He squeezed even harder and felt the kid trying to pull his hand out of the vise. Slowly he let the fingers slide free and watched the kid shake his hand in pain. Laughing, he opened his fist to look at the wrinkled bills. *How easy was that?*

The next kid had his money held out in the air, gripping the edge of the bills as if to distance himself as much as he could. He seemed eager to give the cash away. Albert reached over and snatched it.

"How about you puke face, got any money?" The kid shook his head side-to-side, no.

"Really, a trip with no money. You telling me the truth boy?"

"I... I don't have any cash, sir."

Albert usually ate up the sir and mister stuff, but something about the way the kid said it got his attention. He reached over and grabbed the kid by the hair, raising him onto his toes. He pulled hard, almost hoisting the kid off the ground.

"You fucking with me kid?" He lifted up harder on the hair, pulling the kid off balance.

"I got a card. I got a bank card in my bag."

Albert slammed the kid's head backwards off the wall. Then he let go. The kid slumped down to his knees, leaned forward and lost his battle to hold back the vomit. His puke slammed into the floor, splattering in a wide circle.

"Someone go through all their bags. Let me know what you find. I want them off the train before we get to Hinkle."

The crew went to work ripping the kid's bags apart, coming up with a little bit of weed and the kid's bank card. Albert knew the crew was itchy so he made it simple. "You get the bank information first, then you can have some fun."

He didn't consider kids a challenge, it was a bit disappointing that they were so young. Mickey and the guys didn't care so much. They pushed and taunted the boys, hitting them with the odd shot to the face or stomach. Whatever it took to get the account numbers. At first the kids turtled to avoiding the blows, until they were warned that if they didn't fight back one-on-one they would be gang beaten.

The three brutal fights didn't last long.

The first kid to summon his courage and step forward got kicked in the kneecap with a pair of worn out work boots. His face held pure shock as he buckled forward and was met with a knee in the face. Even Albert felt a twinge as the kid's nose flattened and blood flew out in every direction. He was out.

Albert always wondered how the next guy convinced himself to step up, surely they must realize at this point it would have been better to be first and get it over with. The puking one stepped off the wall and got his hands up in a fighter's stance. Mickey took a run from ten feet away and jumped up in the air. Leading feet first, both heels hit the kid in the stomach and drove him into the wooden wall of the car. Mickey bounced up to pummel the breathless kid until he lay on the floor, unmoving.

Usually, the last guy would either collapse in fear, or take the gang-beating, which always ended up being the worst. Or he would get pissed, even though the odds were against him and come out fighting.

This kid was a fighter.

He waited for the Raildog to come closer. When his opponent was in range he struck out with a power punch to the head. Albert laughed at his man for getting hit, but knew the kid would pay.

The Raildog rushed in hard this time, leading with his shoulder and colliding with the kid. He wrapped him up, raised him off the floor, and slammed the kid down again on his back. His victim yelled out in pain as the gangster pinned him. Now in a dominant position, he started punching down into the kid's face, he didn't stop until the others finally pulled him off.

Albert was used to the adrenaline surge from the action, but his crew was younger and he could tell they were still fired up. He looked at his wristwatch, they were halfway to Hinkle, so it was time.

He slid the boxcar door open. Fresh air rushed in and sunlight glared through the opening, Albert waited a second for his eyes to adjust before turning, "It's time to say goodbye boys."

He motioned to Mickey. "Get it done."

There was a quick scramble as the crew collared the desperate kids and dragged them to the doorway. Kicking and screaming they were thrown off the rapidly moving train at long enough intervals that they landed well apart. Mickey watched out the door as the last one tumbled down a small cliff.

To Albert it looked like another good run was brewing. Ten a.m., they'd just left Spokane and still had a ways to go before hitting Salt Lake, already they had cash in their pockets and a bit of stuff to puff on. He reached into his bag and pulled out a bottle of bourbon, spun the cap off, and took a nice long swig.

Turning towards his men he lifted the bottle up in salute before passing it to the right. "Raildogs rule!"

*****

Reno, Nevada

The old guy manning the front desk recognized the tall muscular kid. He'd been there before.

David Perez didn't care if he stood out. It didn't matter that he looked out of place dressed in black, a battered duffle bag slung over his shoulder. He deliberately kept his long dark hair tucked behind his ears to emphasize the piercings on his face.

He never concerned himself much about what other people thought about his look, he'd given up on that a long time ago. He had enough going on with his own shit to bother with others.

"Going in to see my mom," he said.

"You'll have to sign this here book first young man."

David went through the motions of scribbling something down. This was stupid. He hated rules for this and rules for that. Dropping the pen on the open book, he didn't look back at the clerk, as he headed down the corridor. He knew where she was.

"Visiting is only till three mister…" the clerk trailed off as he squinted to read the scribble in the book.

"Yeah, yeah." David waved his hand without looking back. More friggin' rules.

She was waiting with the door open when he got there. She always was. He'd seen her sitting in the window, watching him as he walked up to the building.

"Hi Mom."

She reached her arms around him, as big as he was, and tried to squeeze him, "I'm so glad you could visit. Come and sit with me."

It was awkward and they sat quietly for a bit taking each other in. She seemed to still be in good shape, healthy, and as usual, a little nervous with him there.

He could tell she was always taken back by his growth. He was twenty-five and seemed to still be growing. Of course his father had been just as big.

David knew his visits were important to her and that it went without saying that she was wondering if he had gotten anywhere. He hadn't, but he was almost ready. He'd let her know when it was time, until then he was just happy to see she was okay.

"You're still sitting in your room alone mom." He wanted her to get out and socialize, visit with the others in the home. In his head it was like she was living in a jail cell.

"I'm okay David," she looked over at him. "I still hope to get out of here. These people around here are sick. They scare me."

He couldn't help feeling sorry for her. She'd had so much going for her and then her world had come crashing down. The fact she'd been doing everything for him when it had all happened put a strain on his shoulders. It was a weight that felt heavier every year. He knew that was why he kept coming to visit, and would until he fixed everything.

He let her fuss over him and he worried for her, reminding her to eat properly and get her sleep. He didn't know what else to say.

David didn't notice the desk clerk watching him as he walked down the long driveway. He pulled out his small leather bound journal from his duffle bag, flipping through the pages as he walked from the building. What was the date? He had to figure out where he was headed next.

*****

Colton, California

Bill Dewton used to be a good cop. Until his daughter Cindy left with a friend for a simple weekend in Long Beach, just a couple hours west on the coast and never came back. Then everything in his life went to hell.

The other girl made it back, although she was in pretty rough shape. Bill had been given permission to interview her right away. When it became clear to him that the two girls had planned to ride the freight trains east to New York he'd been floored.

The Long Beach story was a lie.

All autumn and into the winter he and his wife argued. Every time he demanded to know, "Why didn't you know she was going to do this?" She'd turn it around on him. "What did you do to make her leave?"

The insinuation was that he worked her and pushed her too hard. Christ, he'd only wanted his little girl to succeed.

Bill had heard it before, but still wasn't ready when their marriage broke down. He should have known – loosing kids could do that. He didn't know where his wife was now, didn't care. They should have pulled together in the crisis, should have depended on each other, supported each other. He'd always blame his wife for copping out.

He stared out the window briefly, burning to be out on the streets, working a case. But those days were over. He was lucky to still have a job. His boss had put him on a desk. His way of showing loyalty for time served. Now Bill did research for the bullpen and worked his daughter's case on the side.

He didn't get far over the winter, but as spring came the feeling was like he was finally getting ahead. He'd made arrangements to do another interview with Cindy's friend the next week. He felt leaving the other girl alone over the winter had been respectful under the circumstances. She had been awfully drained and mangled the last time he'd seen her.

What he had been able to do was put feelers out with other departments and set up some alerts in the computer system in case anyone else came across anything to do with freight trains and missing people. With all his free time, he spent hours on the computers after each shift searching police files on unidentified bodies, checking prison files and anything else he could think of to locate her, alive or dead.

Around eleven he finally left the precinct, hitting the gym on the way home. The place was simple, free weights and benches. None of those new machines. He was in pretty good shape for a middle-aged guy, once you overlooked the shiny dome. The smell of sweat built up in the windowless basement and hung there. At this hour the place was almost empty, except for the hardcore, and they kept to themselves, deep in their workouts.

As usual, with too much time to fill, he was thinking about freight trains. All winter it had been the same.

Now he worked out, pushing hard, because he'd made up his mind. He was going to have to retrace her steps. That meant riding the tracks himself. He could take the summer off. God knew no one around here would mind, he was deadweight anyways.

He sat down at the bench press. *Get on the tracks and then what?* Shit, what else could he do? He leaned into the weights, pushing, straining. *Find something, anything, that was what.* Sitting here wasn't getting him anywhere.

Bill finished his workout and headed for the showers. Tomorrow. Tomorrow he would put in the paperwork to get the time off.

He stepped out of the gym into the warm southern night. He felt better for some reason.

CHAPTER 3

Wyoming

By the time night had settled in Danny and Bart were well into their adventure. The initial rush of sneaking onto a moving train was long gone, but the small buzz from the beer still hung in.

Once the dark set in it had become hard to recognize anything. Bart was pretty sure they were already in Wyoming. Small towns flew past before they even had a chance to get a good look.

"Shit man. This metal grating is hard to sit on." Bart readjusted his flattened butt on the hard platform for the hundredth time. The realization that they were going to be riding the rest of the night like this was setting in.

Danny was busy tending to a small propane camping stove. He kept one hand on the base of the stove, pinning it to the grating, the other hand holding the handle of the pot. "Hang on bud. This hot soup will make all the difference."

With the pot crammed between them, they tried their best to keep the wind out, sheltering it between their bodies and the wall of the car.

Still cold, bundled in his extra coats, Danny cupped his hands around the pot. Holding it close, he felt the warmth of the container through his fingers, the steam rising up to warm his face.

Bart didn't want the heat outside, he wanted it in his friggin' body. He alternated between blowing cool air over the cup he had been handed, and taking short sips that burned his mouth. He just couldn't wait for it to cool down. He didn't need a reminder of why he was getting out of Montana.

"Christ, I can't wait to get some Florida sunshine."

Finally warmer, Bart watched Danny putting the stove back into his suitcase. *Who the hell travels around with a camping stove?* The curly haired kid looked like the typical geek. At first he hadn't wanted anything to do with him, but loners attract, or something like that.

He really only had his mother these days, and he normally stayed pretty close to their little house on the other side of the tracks near the trailer park.

He knew Danny had a nice home in the newer section of town. The kid's old man was a big shot or something. It was only after they had talked a few times that Bart realized how much they both seemed to be unwanted by the other kids.

One time he asked Danny about hanging with other kids. He'd been only slightly shocked by the answer.

"I don't need nobody," the kid said. "They don't like me because I don't follow their crowd around like a fucking puppy."

Bart knew it was true, but the shy looking kid had put it perfectly. He didn't follow anyone around either. He made his own tracks. Now they were leaving the shitheads behind, all of them.

He stood again to stretch his legs and eased towards the side for a look forward up the track. Something caught his attention. There seemed to be a light off in the distance, but as the train moved slowly up and down with the terrain it blinked in and out.

"Danny, check out the lights up there."

Danny leaned out around him. Sure enough, the lights meant they were nearing a city. That had to mean they were almost through Wyoming.

"Here we come Cheyenne."

*****

Ft. Worth, Texas

Devon and Rashad were waiting for the train to pull out of Fort Worth. They'd moved from the small landing at the end of a refrigerated car to a large half-filled boxcar. If you're travelling for long periods, getting inside was the way to go. Devon wasn't cold but he appreciated the room to spread out and sleep without worrying about falling off on a corner or while bouncing over a series of rough tracks.

They were near the border with Oklahoma. The plan was to hook up with the boss tomorrow around noon. Then the partying could begin. The train jerked once, then twice, and the freight cars slammed against each other as the whole thing started to roll forward.

It was looking like a quiet overnight trip when Devon caught sight of a guy running towards the train from beside a nearby building. The idiot was leaving it late, the train was already rolling at a good clip. "Rasman," he raised his voice. "Get up, we got company."

Rashad jumped up from the corner where he had been sleeping, looking around franticly. Finally he noticed Devon at the door, and realized they were moving. He quickly joined his partner.

"Let's get him in here." Devon wanted the guy. "Hey buddy over here."

The Raildog waved his hands to get the guy's attention. He tried to look concerned, getting down on one knee to reach his hand out beside the moving car.

He knew it was now or never. The guy would slow purposely if he felt danger – if he didn't want to get on with the two of them – but he would pick up speed and commit if he wasn't suspicious of the offer to help.

The guy bore down and leaned his head forward. He pumped his legs faster, swinging his arms hard as he ran. His packsack bounced from side to side, threatening to throw off his balance, but he was gaining on the boxcar. He reached his arm out as he ran beside the accelerating train.

Devon leaned out further, knowing he could reach the guy. There was a second where both their arms grasped at mid-air and then their hands locked and they gripped hard. The guy used the Raildog for leverage, swinging his legs through the air and up into the car.

Devon pinned him to stop his momentum, and held the guy with his legs inside the car and his body hanging over the edge as the train came up to full speed. The guy was suddenly heaving with panic. Devon eased off and pulled himself up off the floor, bringing the guy up with him. "Hey, you okay there buddy?"

"I'm cool. Thanks for the lift."

Devon looked him over. He was twenty-years-old at the most, built pretty solid, but short, no more than five-foot seven. No problem there, that was for sure. The Raildog backed up, giving the kid space, then slid the door almost closed leaving a gap to provide a bit of light.

"Where you going?" Always the first question.

"North to Chicago, got a sexy woman up there," the kid smiled.

Devon laughed. *Not much chance you'll be seeing her.* He looked at his partner and nodded once. He waited for his partner to nod back, then he turned his attention to the new rider as Rashad eased around behind the target. "Okay boy, you want the good news or bad."

The change in Devon's tone had the kid immediately on alert. He watched for that moment when realization set in. Fear spread across the kid's face and the simple things became hard, like just swallowing or maintaining eye contact.

"I'm not sure. Have we got a problem?"

Devon watched as the kid searched for a source of newfound courage. The guy was scared shitless, but he was showing a tough face and flexing his shoulders. He had good street instincts.

"Well that depends on how you take the news," the Raildog paused. "The good news is that if you got money then you'll be able to pay for this ride, which satisfies me. The bad news is that my buddy Rashad here is going to beat you one way or the other. He just don't care about the money."

It was a study of people and the things they did. Devon was amazed that whenever he mentioned a sure beating the money always appeared faster. He expected them to see it differently. He was still waiting for the one who said, "If I'm getting beat anyways no sense giving up the cash." But sure enough, the kid pulled his wallet out and started forking everything he had into the gangster's waiting hand.

Looking down Devon wasn't pleased or pissed, a hundred and fifty bucks was better than nothing. He felt suddenly tired, it had been a crazy few days and there were more to come. Turning his back on the kid, he walked past Rashad looking for somewhere to sit down. His normally impassive friend's small smile didn't hide the intensity in his eyes. Devon could see his anticipation and knew he didn't want any part of this next scene.

Rashad got closer to the kid and started speaking in a low voice. Devon couldn't make the words out, but his partner slapped the kid up-side the head a few times and kept talking. He watched as the big guy started to herd the kid backwards, around the corner of the skids. *Thank god.*

Sounds of a struggle and a few echoing slaps came from the dark corner. Then a sound like a punch connecting. More whispering, then quiet. Devon didn't venture forward and no one came out of the corner until the train slowed going through the rail yard in Texarkana.

Rashad appeared pulling the kid by the back of his jacket. He headed straight to the door and squeezed the kid out through the opening. The kid never even struggled, and Devon pictured him cartwheeling as he hit the gravel.

He watched as his buddy came over to sit on the next skid. No words were exchanged. Their friendship meant he was expected to mind his own business. The two men swayed slightly as the train lumbered off towards Oklahoma in the dead of night.

*****

Salt Lake City, Utah

The old train yard was over two miles long. Mostly it was sidings running side-by-side, full of heavy traffic. A couple lines ran alongside the loading dock attached to a run down stone building that still stood as a reminder of days past. At one time goods were loaded from these decayed and crumbling docks.

Since these days most of the cargo came from overseas in shipping containers, loading docks were rotting across America. Cliffy used this building as a meeting place.

At forty-five, Cliff knew he looked a lot older, shit, he felt it too. He also felt the respect from the others, he knew he deserved it. He nodded to a couple of the boys as he headed towards the building. The Raildogs were his idea. His creation. Fuck, he had the central U.S. in the palm of his hand. He wasn't kidding earlier when he'd been thinking that he'd come a long way.

Each of the five bosses had a tattoo numbered one to five on the inside of their right wrist. They each had a section of line, with at least twenty soldiers working their piece of the rail at any given time. In the beginning the five of them had ridden the lines from one end of the country to the other, working together, taking whatever they wanted.

As the thinker of the group, Cliff eventually realized a few things. One; they could cover more ground if they split up and took sections. Two; the best place for them was the central states. Sure, everyone wanted to go to New York or California, but that was Cliffy's point, everyone had to go through the middle to get there.

There were four big names in the rail business. Two of them, the Norfolk Southern and the USA CSX Transportation Company worked the Eastern seaboard. The gang learned to stay clear of those lines because of the security hired to patrol the yards. Besides, there were too many stops and starts where the cities were packed close together.

The other two companies were the Burlington Northern and the Union Pacific, both operating in the central and western states. These outfits were too big and spread out to properly patrol or keep things under any kind of real surveillance.

What Cliffy realized was that all the lines going east or west had to come through a few choke points. He based the territories on them. Cliff had kept the east-west line running across the north between Salt Lake City and Des Moines for himself. He also took the number one tattoo.

The other four guys had lines that completed the box. Sam Dorson, number two, took the east-west line that ran across the southern states, from Phoenix to Houston. The two Rackman Brothers, tattoos three and four, formed the sides of the box. Dougie had the north-south line between Houston and Des Moines, and Bobby had the north-south line between Phoenix and Salt Lake.

There was a lot of traffic from Canada down to California as Chinese and other Asians used that line to sneak into the

U.S.. The fifth Raildog, Albert Simms, took care of a branch off the square that ran north out of Salt Lake up to Spokane and Seattle. He plugged that leak.

Now anyone moving anywhere on the rails was bound to come through their box, it was just a matter of time. It took a while to get a handle on things, but eventually each boss had crewmembers working under them that allowed them to keep a presence on the rails all the time.

That the fucking thing was still running like clockwork was amazing. Each of the bosses was paid dues by his members for the privilege of working the line. Cliff had twenty soldiers that paid a couple hundred bucks a month apiece for the privilege of making free money. That was a cool four grand a month he was making these days off his plan and it had been like that for years.

The real money was in the bonus riders you stumbled upon, the people that were out there travelling with all their possessions. Someone's heartache was someone else's score. His guys all made money, or they wouldn't keep getting back on the trains. They sure wouldn't keep paying dues. They robbed whatever cash they found, held some victims hostage while the others cleaned out their bank accounts, and ran up any credit cards they discovered.

The only prerequisites needed for the work were a penchant for causing pain and no moral conscience to think of. That part had been easy for Cliff, at least in the beginning.

"Hey guys. How's everyone doing?"

"Good Cliff."

He didn't waste a lot of time collecting dues, he liked getting that out of the way. He did take a second and make some notes in his little black book. "You guys ready to roll?"

The crew was off the dock and heading towards the freight trains before Cliff managed to climb down himself. He liked traveling in numbers, something that always worked. Everyone knew the schedules, so he wasn't surprised when his crew led him to the right train. This one was heading out after midnight, running east towards Des Moines.

The crew took over two boxcars and waited. Cliffy sat with his legs hanging over the side even after the train eventually started moving. He stared out at the passing buildings, lost in thought.

*****

Reno, Nevada

Sarah sat at the window in her room looking out at nothing in particular. David wouldn't be back for a while now, and that left her sad as usual. She lit another cigarette, watching the smoke drift up from her hand. Idly, she took a puff here and there just to keep it lit.

She should probably open the window so they didn't bitch about the smell, but fuck them, they shouldn't mess with her stuff.

She was pissed. Someone had taken the designer house magazine she kept on the little table. It was years old, but it reminded her of another time, another place. It had to be that bitch cleaning the rooms. It must have happened when she was out for her walk. They all thought they could just walk in and do anything they wanted. One day she'd show them. She'd get hers.

A bird landed momentarily on the windowsill and broke her train of thought. It was gone as quickly as it came and she went back to contemplating David's situation again. She had no idea what he did, or where he was most of the time, for that matter. He seemed to not want to tell her anything.

The boy had saved her back then. Gotten her help and then found her this place. She had money and the bills were taken care of, she'd even encouraged him to use it; he'd not taken a cent. Did he work? Have a girl friend? Where did he go when he left here?

How did ten years go by and she not know these answers? For some reason they never talked about it. There was one thing they discussed occasionally, but David seemed unable to help in that one area, although he promised he would. She wondered if it would ever happen.

In those early years she had been so caught up in her own world of pain that she forgot about him. Had he finished school? Did he have any other clothes that weren't black? And what was that whole black thing anyways? By the time she returned to the real world she felt she'd lost the right to question. Besides, she had to admit she was just happy he came to see her at all.

The grey twilight was giving way to black outside the window, but Sarah continued to stare. She didn't want to turn on a light, because then she'd see her own reflection in the glass. So she sat in the dark and looked out into the night.

*****

Pocatello, Idaho

The rough character walked slowly alongside the tracks, unconcerned. This was his turf. He was early to catch Albert and the crew coming down from Spokane but he couldn't help himself.

He was a newbie. He'd been a Raildog for six months now and only got his tattoo three months ago. He didn't care what time the others came through, he just knew he couldn't afford to miss them. The gang had given him a whole new lease on life. Shit, it gave him more money in six months that he'd had in the last two years.

He ignored the northbound train leaving the yard. It had only stopped briefly before continuing on towards Washington. There would be another one later, but that didn't matter either, he was watching southbound traffic.

He stood waiting, looking down with pride at the number ninety-two tattooed on his inner wrist, when a sound behind one of the buildings caught his attention. Action? Interested, he jogged over to the building and looking around the corner.

Standing quietly, he listened hard for a moment. When he didn't hear anything, he turned to walk back. He wasn't prepared when something hit him square in the face. Then everything went black.

Over the next couple of hours he drifted in and out of consciousness. It was like waking to hell. He had visions of trees blowing in the wind and a madman with a blowtorch.

He didn't want to wake up. The smell of burning flesh made his stomach heave up into his throat. He didn't dare to look down. The sight had to be gruesome. He heard someone screaming and crying. "Yes, No, I don't know." Then he realized it was himself and the crazy fucker would raise the torch up again.

Please god, he thought to himself, *I've said everything I know.*

"Oh, I'm sure you've told me everything," the psycho replied.

Did I say that out loud? Jesus, he was losing it.

He watched the madman adjust the yellow flame until it became a finer blue. He wasn't an expert, but for some reason he knew that meant the flame was even hotter. He couldn't help but feel the real questions were coming now.

He was sure it was important not to pass out, and he struggled against the ropes as his tormentor moved in close.

"Does anyone hear a Raildog if he screams in the woods?" The flame sliced into flesh.

CHAPTER 4

Pocatello, Idaho

Albert stood at the opened door of the boxcar and let the rushing wind wake him up. The morning sun warmed his face as he watched the outskirts of Pocatello roll past. It was one of the few towns with rail yards big enough that the Raildogs expected the trains to stop in on the way to Salt Lake.

The open spaces changed to side roads lined with farms, which gave way to industrial areas and warehouse districts. They were close to the yards when his phone began vibrating in his pocket. He turned from the wind to block the sound and took the call on the gang phone. "Five."

"It looks like we got a bunch of cop cars in the yard. There's flashing lights everywhere."

His lookout farther up the train wasn't giving him much time to think. Could be nothing, but it could be something.

"Okay, we all get off before the yard. Right side, in the valley near the bridge."

Riding the same section over and over meant you knew where everything was and you had time to plan escape routes at every station. He turned to the others in the car, "Pack up boys, we might have a problem. Everyone off at the valley coming up on the right."

The crew whipped their stuff together and they were all hanging off the side of the train waiting for the valley in less than a minute. As the train started slowing into the yard they knew the speed wouldn't be too fast for jumping. Albert strained to see the track ahead as he watched the ground flashing by, looking to pick the best spot.

The track crossed over a road that turned and ran beside the line for a couple hundred yards before it turned away and the ground came up level with the track again.

"Jump on the slope and roll down to the road."

The train crossed the bridge and the bank appeared. Albert looked at the others once and pushed himself off the train.

He let his feet hit the ground, already pitching sideways to roll out of it and save his ankles, a skill he learned long ago as an All-State quarterback, before he started drinking. As his elbow hit there was no time to think about where his life would have went if he hadn't blown out his knee, then his shoulder hit, then the back of his head that was tucked in with anticipation. One roll, two, then his hands reached out to stop his momentum.

Albert took a quick look back, the others were in various stages of tumbling and cartwheeling down the bank. A few newbies stopped suddenly when they finally slammed into the road. The experienced didn't let themselves roll that far.

A quick scramble back up the bank and Albert checked that they hadn't been seen.

"Mickey, get up here. Go find out what's happening." He watched the younger guy take off along the shoulder of the track towards some old buildings.

The wait seemed to take forever. Forty-five minutes later Mickey slid back over the side of the bank. "Shit Albert, it's bad."

"What's going on?"

"It's one of our guys, that new one Dirk, or Rick, or something. He's been fucked up. They had him in the meat wagon, but I heard someone talking."

Albert realized Mickey had stopped, his face was strained like he was visualizing something. "Well out with it. What happened?"

"Someone tortured him in the woods over there," Mickey pointed. "And dragged him into the middle of the yard. Left his body between the tracks."

Mickey seemed to stall again, but forced himself on. "He was burned bad boss. Someone used a blow torch on him."

Albert knew who it was, Dickson Wallis. The new kid was number ninety-two in the gang. Tortured, why? Who? When? "When did it happen?"

"They're saying sometime late last night."

Albert had to think. He needed to call Cliffy and let him know what happened, but he had to act here first. He wasn't going to let this thing go. You didn't fuck with Raildogs and get away with it. That had always been a priority.

Since the beginning, the different parts of the gang had always kept in touch. Whenever it was necessary, the guys would travel to another section of line to help another crew. Cliff had been right about that. He'd said that eventually they would have a hundred men on the tracks to throw at a problem if needed.

He only had five guys with him on this trip, a few more were waiting in Salt Lake, but the rest were back in Spokane to start the month. That made Albert feel a little weak. The guys in Spokane were going to start boarding freight trains in two's and three's over the next few days to ensure their members were spread along the track from top to bottom.

He was going to have to change the plan.

"Mickey, you take the crew and try and find out more. I want the fucker that did this." He thought for a moment, "I'm going to catch a train back north and rustle the boys together. We'll meet you right back here on the slope tomorrow."

Albert leaned in close and caught Mickey's eye. "I want you guys to find whoever did this and hold them until I'm back."

"If I find out who it is, they'll be here, I guarantee it."

Albert nodded, "Alright, get out of here."

He leaned back against the grassy bank. The sun still wasn't straight up yet, but he could tell it was gonna be a hot one. He had a couple hours to wait until the next northbound freighter would be through. *Just another twist in the adventure.*

He let his eyes close for a while.

*****

St Louis, Missouri

Maria seemed to be enjoying the third day of their trip better than the first two. Raul watched her soaking up the sun as they sped through the countryside. Her legs hung over the edge of the railcar as she moved her head to an unheard tune. The wind had whipped her hair around her face until she finally gathered it up and tied it into a ponytail. He could tell by the smile on the edge of her lips as she relaxed that she seemed happy to be out of the cold and rain of the days before.

The east coast was nothing but a river of concrete, too congested, too many buildings, and way too many other gangsters piled into the alleys and bars for him. You had to stay on guard everywhere you went.

The welcome sun had him stripped down to a t-shirt, showing off the HPL or Hermanos Pistoleros Latinos artwork that stretched across his shoulders. The gun tattoo at his waist, and the string of bullets tattooed up the inside of his right arm told a story. He had earned his rank the hard way. The gang had been formed as a defense organization for Mexicans stuck in prison. They may have gone into prison violent and angry, but they came out skilled and vicious. Raul wondered what the hell could you expect after putting someone in that environment.

With the sun blazing, he'd pulled his bandana low over the eyebrows, acting like a visor. He never bothered to hide what he was. It got him respect in some places, and brought him trouble in others. So be it, it came with the territory.

He could see Maria was still staring at the passing scenery, lost in thought.

"What are you thinking Maria?"

Thank god she was over being pissed about her clothes. Two nights of bad weather had shown her his reasoning, but she still wasn't letting him off the hook.

"I still don't understand why we had to travel this way. I really don't. We could have just taken a plane. Or driven my car."

"It's the safest thing Maria. We can't drive, we can't fly. The feds would be on us right away. If we drove your car, it would only take one cop to pull us over and we'd be in deep shit," his patience on the subject was getting short. "Once we get south you can enjoy yourself again."

"Are you crazy?" She opened her arms wide to show off her baggy clothes, "I won't be going out anywhere in this."

"You look sexy in everything you wear," he grinned at her.

"Well, I don't feel sexy." She crossed her arms and stuck her bottom lip out to make her point. "But you'll figure that out soon enough."

Raul laughed. He reached into his pack and pulled out a small bundle. As he unrolled the material it became her favorite red dress wrapped around a pair of high heels.

"See sexy, I know what you need. We both like you hot." He hadn't climbed up the ranks by not anticipating solutions to potential problems.

With a surprised look, Maria reached out to snatch the clothes, but he quickly rolled everything back into a bundle and put it in the bag. "Not here."

She moved over, closer, and leaned against him. Raul went back to thinking about the work he'd accomplished back east and the first test runs that were coming. He checked his phone for messages. Nothing. That was fine. They'd just cleared St. Louis and were on their way towards Kansas. He was looking forward to turning south.

*****

Cheyenne, Wyoming

Bart and Danny drifted in and out of sleep. The train had been stopped for what seemed like an hour. It was dark, late, and a bit cold. They hadn't dared sleep up until this point and the parked train seemed like the perfect opportunity.

The shouts jarred them both wide-awake. They couldn't see anything, but the voices sounded like trouble. Drunks maybe, but definitely rowdy. Their boxcar was on a siding on the south side of the rail yard, almost right underneath the I-80 overpass.

Bart saw them first, four or five guys walking along a train on the main line. It took a second to figure out what they were doing. Quietly he said, "They're looking for someone."

The gang was almost right even with them and they could make out the voices better.

"Anyone in here?" A guy climbed up and checked a car. "Nope."

"How about this one?"

Another jumped up to check the next car. "Not here either."

The group continued along the train checking cars until one of them yelled, "Bingo!"

The boys exchanged looks. Danny knew instinctively this wasn't going to be good. Watching, they saw the gang climb into the boxcar, seconds later two guys were thrown from the train.

The two men were surrounded in no time flat. The boys could see the pair trying to talk their way out of the problem, but the gang was clearly out to cause havoc. Suddenly, a gang member jumped in from behind and hit one of the pair hard on the head, then the pack reacted.

Vicious kicks and punches came quick and hard, the two men were easily overcome, soon lying on the ground as the kicks kept coming. The gang began yelling, "Raildogs rule."

Bart turned away. He couldn't believe the bastards were still kicking the guys on the ground. Danny was glued to the scene. He watched mesmerized, fear and adrenaline pounding through his veins.

This was real? Who did this stuff? Why? Bart hadn't expected to see anything like that. Suddenly it dawned on him. *It could have been them.* He noticed that Danny didn't take his eyes off the group until he was sure they'd moved on.

His heart was beating against his ribs like a jackhammer. He watched Danny turn towards him, "What the fuck are Raildogs?"

*****

Cliffy and part of his crew were eastbound on the northern line of the box heading for Cheyenne. He sat with his back against the wall thinking about his bones. They were hurting more and more with each passing year, pounded by the rough ride.

He used to ride these lines like they were nothing. He could stand for hours and the swaying and rattling wouldn't bother him at all. Now he felt it. The wear and tear was adding up.

He felt alive though. The crew was amped up and ready for trouble, he was easily reminded of the pro's that came with the job. His phone vibrated, it could only be someone in the gang. "One."

"Five. Thought you should know." There was a pause and Cliffy got a sinking feeling in his gut. "Ninety-two was tortured near Pocatello, up in Idaho."

"What do you mean tortured?"

"Blow torch it seems. I heard it was really bad. We were suppose to meet him today, we were heading down the line."

Cliff didn't like it. Didn't like it one bit. No one fucked with the gang. Then he remembered that a few guys had recently disappeared or gone missing. No dues had been paid. No warning, or heads up. Everyone assumed that they wanted to quit and simply walked away. It happened. Sometimes one of them would get picked up by the cops for something else they'd done. No one thought anything of it. Cliff suddenly had doubts.

"What are you doing about it?"

"I'm leaving some of the guys here in Pocatello to find out more and try and locate the asshole. Right now I'm catching a train back north to rustle up the rest of my guys and we're all coming back here. Should be back tomorrow. Hopefully we get the bastard."

Cliff liked the plan, leave some guys on the ground to keep the attacker there, bring in more men to flush him out if the first group couldn't find him.

"Let me know what happens."

He didn't like uncertainty, preferring things in order. Was this a one-off? Had the guy brought it on himself? He opened up his little black book. It helped him keep tabs on his own crew, but also listed the other bosses and their crews as well. Ninety-two had only been with them six months, so maybe he had a past that was catching up. He was also the newest member and unsure of his place, therefore he could be the weakest.

Either way, the guy was gone so it didn't matter. For some reason Cliff's bones were suddenly aching more. He put the phone away and leaned against the wall, trying to ease the kinks out of his back.

*****

Colton, California

Bill Dewton was trying to show respect by not hurrying his witness. He sat in the living room attempting to interview his daughter's friend while her mother played chaperone. He needed to take it slow, despite his impatience to get at the answers.

"I know it's terrible to bring it back up and make you live through it all again. I was hoping you would understand how I feel with her still being missing," He wasn't above adding a little guilt to the situation if it got things moving.

"No I want to help. She's my best friend." The poor thing looked like she was trying to stick on a brave face. It wasn't working – her bottom lip quivered.

Okay, Bill knew he had to get this right.

"Look, instead of me asking questions that you might not like. Why don't you tell me your story and I'll ask about that as you go along." He knew that approach made people feel less worried about what might be asked and made them feel comfortable.

"Well. We lied. I'm sorry." She looked at her mother and back to Bill. "We learned people caught free rides on the freight trains and thought it would be fun. We knew you guys wouldn't let us go to New York.

"We caught a train in the yard here in town and made it all the way to Vegas." The girl stalled a moment, "Or at least that's what we thought. These guys came out of nowhere and jumped into out boxcar. We knew we were in trouble right away. They were cheering and whistling."

This was all new stuff. The vein on Bill's forehead bulged slightly. He took a deep breath and forced the anger back down. All he'd been told previously was that something happened on the train and this girl had jumped off, while his daughter stayed on. The implications of this new information were overwhelming. He noticed the tears on the girl's face and managed to stay quiet. Blinking, he motioned her to continue.

"The train started going again and these guys seemed to be waiting for something, like they were going to do something but not yet," she explained. "Four of them had Trish in the corner and were grabbing at her and touching her, there were only two left watching me."

The girl looked up and her tears were running freely. "I'm sorry, but I had to get out of there. The ones near me were watching what was going on in the corner because Trish was screaming, so I ran for the open door. It turned out we were on a hill and I fell twenty feet or so before landing on some rocks."

Her mother jumped into the conversation, putting her arm around her daughter, "She's lucky to be alive. She wasn't found until she crawled out herself. It took her two days."

Bill felt bad for her, but not as bad as he felt as for his daughter. "We can thank God for that. I won't ask too many more questions. And again, I'm sorry to bother you, but was there anything you remember that was different about those guys?"

"I've gone over it again and again. I feel so guilty for leaving her," she met Bill's eye. "I could only see the two guys that were watching me. I was worried they had guns or knives, or something. I did see that they had numbers tattooed on their right wrists. I don't know if that helps."

Neither did Bill, but it was the first real lead he had. He held his face still, trying not to betray any excitement. "Where on the wrist? What kind of number?"

"It was on the inside of the wrist, about two inches big," she held her fingers apart. "They were hard to read, but one guy's looked like a seventy, and I think the other might have been eighty-one."

A few questions later it was obvious there was nothing else. Her mother was clearly getting agitated. Bill knew when to quit. He wished them peace and thanked them for their help.

Driving back to the office he knew he finally had something. Tattoos usually meant gangs. Was this a gang? What were the numbers? The sooner he added this information to the search criteria and attached it to the messages he had out to other detachments, the better.

He stayed focused on the tattoos, but inside his heart was crumbling. He knew now that she was gone. Unless they planned to keep her permanently, they would have gotten rid of her by now. Since she hadn't come home, he assumed they had made sure she wasn't going to be found.

The rail lines went through remote and isolated areas, crossing canyons, mountains, and bridges over rivers. There were endless dumping grounds. Endless.

Bill felt his own tears running down his face. It wasn't over, not by a long shot, but the scales had surely been tipped. He was still going try to find her alive or dead.

Pulling into the parking lot, he looked up at his office on the second floor. How long was he going to be here tonight? However long it took to not have that shot of straight gin he was thinking about. He knew she was really gone.

And someone was going to pay.

*****

Eagle Pass, Texas

Sam Dorson and his crew kept quiet while the train was stopped in Eagle Pass. They didn't want to alert anyone, or scare off any potential marks, before heading west for El Paso. They kept the door of the boxcar opened a little, and once in a while someone looked out, checking up and down the train.

Just when Sam started getting a little discouraged, the lookout pulled his head in, excited. "Women, getting on up ahead of us."

Sam jumped to the door and looked up the rail. "Shit. Lets go."

The men peeled out of the boxcar and started running towards their objective. The three women were almost at the train when they noticed the men running towards them. They seemed to hesitate and then climbed up into the nearest boxcar.

Sam was on a rush, his senses were wide-awake, the anticipation thrilling. This was his game, his score. Women. He'd paid for them initially as a truck driver, then realized that truck stop girls and hitchhikers could disappear without consequences. Here it was much easier, uninterrupted hours alone in a boxcar out in the middle of nowhere.

The men got to the car just as the door slid closed.

"Open up bitches," Sam yelled.

"Don't piss us off," one of the others joined in.

"Get it open," Sam encouraged the crew. "Before the train starts moving."

The girls were showing some brains. They'd jammed the door with something and the crew struggled to move it. They just had to climb up there and put the muscle to it. Two men were up along the ledge trying to pry the door loose. Two more joined them, but the women's block was holding strong. Probably freaked out, thought Sam. They should be.

This was the reason he rode the tracks from the beginning. He assumed these ones would be Mexican or South American. That was what you found here in the mid-south. It was also why he had wanted this section of line. It provided an endless supply of people slipping into the U.S.. It was the women he enjoyed.

Then the train started to move. *Fuck!* It jerked a few times and clanged as it rolled forward. Now he had a problem.

So close, yet he was going to have to wait.

"Last chance to open this door bitches. You'll pay if I have to work my way in."

The door stayed shut.

"Alright boys. Get on the next car, we'll get them at the next stop, maybe sooner." He didn't care where he got them, just that they were his.

Sam was last to climb aboard. He looked ahead at the car with the women, smiling. He wondered how old they were.

CHAPTER 5

Denver, Colorado

The ride between Cheyenne and Denver hadn't been over soon enough for Danny and Bart. There had been some hair-raising moments as they'd waited for the freight train to finally start moving.

"How the fuck long are we going to be here?" Danny kept looking up the track.

"It's already been too long," Bart watched the other side of the train.

Danny had been sure the gang in Cheyenne would have seen them. They hadn't, and when the train left and they cleared the city, the boys had visibly relaxed.

The train worked its way through the foothills around Denver. They could see the lights in the distance, and before they pulled into the city the night broke and daylight cleared away the last flickers of fear still haunting their trip.

Danny leaned over his suitcase, checking his homemade maps. "Hey Bart, we got to decide here between going south or east."

Bart didn't have any maps. Danny had been into figuring all that stuff out. He thought about it a second. "Where's this train going?"

"I'm pretty sure this one turns east and heads towards Kansas. Eventually it ends up on the east coast." The kid reeled off his research, most of it gained on the internet.

Bart was still trying to get a clear picture. "What other options are there?"

"We can get a train south through Colorado and the top of New Mexico into Texas. It's a lot more wide open, less cities but..."

Bart caught the hesitation and turned. "What's the but about?"

"Well, this line we're on is less used, which means fewer trains and maybe some longer stops. I'm not sure."

It was probably thoughts of the gang back in Cheyenne that made them pick the south route in the end. They would travel through fewer cities and populated areas.

As their train pulled into Denver they were ready, watching for cover along the track. In this case there was a bridge running over the track. Going slow enough, they jumped off and hid behind the bridge pillars until the train moved on.

They worked their way across the rail yard, moving behind buildings and crouching in fields until they reached the south end. When they were sure which track was the one heading south, they holed up in the trees running alongside the South Platte River to wait.

Bart was back to feeling the excitement of the trip. Jumping off and on trains brought a certain thrill that he'd never experienced before.

Danny, on the other hand, was deep in thought, "You know this will be a tough train to catch, the thing should be moving pretty damn fast by the time in gets to here."

Bart looked down at the track and followed the steel lines back to the yard. Danny was right. To make sure they had chosen the right track, they had walked more than a hundred yards down from the rail switch where the tracks separated.

They settled on walking back a ways, getting as close to the station as they could, while still being able to see if the train turned. From there they could run beside it and get on the back half of the train while it was still moving slow enough, instead of a hundred yards or more out of the station.

Their worries were unfounded, after a number of trains rolled by, and three hours more of their time, a train made it's way slowly through the yard before it turned to head south along their track. It moved slowly enough that they were able to walk beside the cars. The boarding was easy and this time they managed to climb under the sheltered end of a grain car.

Bart stuck his head out, keeping an eye out as they left the rail yard. It wouldn't be long before they were in Florida.

Danny leaned back against the steel bulkhead lost in his head; still back in Cheyenne watching the gang do its dirty work.

*****

Texas

Sam didn't mind the heat. That was a good thing, because even with the door open the inside of a boxcar could get hot as an oven. Sometimes when the cars were partially full, they would move the freight around to help the air circulate, other times they just threw stuff out of the moving car to make room for the air to get in.

He had a hard time with not stealing the stuff in the cars, after all it was sitting right there. Cliffy always made a good case though. They might make bigger money, but the exposure wasn't worth it.

You also had to move anything you boosted. That meant dealing with an outsider. If they got rolled the cops end up involved, serial numbers could be traced, and security camera's checked. All that exposure jeopardized the whole gang. They didn't need it.

Cliff was lucky that it had worked out like he said. They made enough off the travelers, and most of the victims were the type who wouldn't even call the cops. Even if they were straight, they didn't want to explain why they were illegally riding a freight train.

The train slowed and shook as it rolled over a bridge and Sam glanced at the open door. He wondered what the women in the car ahead were doing. Then he heard the faint squeal of a boxcar door opening somewhere. The sound didn't last long, like the door was only moved a bit.

Shit! Sam jumped up and sprinted towards the door. Something blue caught his eye and he looked down. Three bundles were rolling and somersaulting down the bank. Two blue and one yellow. The bitches had jumped off the train. *Fuck.*

He turned, looking for his man who was supposed to be watching for the women. The Raildog popped out from between the two cars and started working his way along the edge to the door.

"They jumped you asshole, where were you?"

The gangster clung to the side of the rocking boxcar while trying to explain, "Well, it was too windy to have a smoke," he noticed the look on Sam's face and stopped talking.

"You had a job to do shithead," Sam shook with anger. "Get the fuck off my train."

The gangster stopped edging towards the door, struggling to comprehend what he was being told. "What do you mean man?"

"Let go. Get the fuck out of here. Don't make me come out there, or I'll make it worse."

The gangster knew the stories. He'd seen the results of Sam's temper more than once. He looked down at his feet balanced precariously on the thin steel ledge, and then out at the passing countryside as the train gained speed.

Sam watched as the man picked his spot and pushed off the train. He kept his eyes on him as he hit the bank rising up alongside the tracks. He watched as the gangster slammed against a rock outcrop, his momentum coming to an abrupt halt.

Sam was so pissed he didn't notice he was squeezing the edge of the door with all his strength. Bastard. Three women lost. He shook his head. He had already made plans about what he was going to do with them, had already visualized every minute of his enjoyment in his head. Now he was left with a long trip to El Paso without any company.

He wanted to hit something.

*****

Las Vegas, Nevada

Bobby Rackman didn't feel he had the luck of the Irish today. Sitting in one of his usual spots in the Bellagio. The blackjack table in the corner offered a good view of the action on the casino floor. He was almost through his daily limit of play money. It was a good thing it was the beginning of the month. His crew should be starting to filter in one at a time over the next couple days.

Bobby was born to be a gangster. He and his brother Doug had been in trouble early and often. How neither of them ended up in jail was a mystery to anyone who knew them. They said, of course, it was the Irish in 'em.

The two brothers grew up as true Boston Southies, terrorizing D Street, working their way up from stealing cars to strong arming local businesses. Rumor had it they got big enough the mob came calling. They wouldn't give in, but they couldn't stick around either.

The two brothers had run across Cliff and Sam back in the beginning. Tough enough to defend themselves, that first meeting had been a stand-off. A train ride, and two bottles of whiskey later they had teamed up. They all had something in common: The desire to make money the easy way.

Ten years down the road Bobby didn't need to ride the rails anymore, but he wasn't letting go of the gang either. It was there if he needed it, and he felt he deserved the dues he was paid. He believed that they'd built a business together and that the five of them were like CEO's, earning dividends on their hard work

That was his logic in staying off the rails but keeping close tabs on the crew. Besides, he'd always been able to make money in the casinos – at least most days. He sure wasn't hurting for cash, he'd been investing the whole time and he had built up a nice little nest egg.

That early score of thirty thousand dollars in a suitcase carried by a South-American family had a lot to do with his early investing success, but it didn't matter where it came from, as long as you had it.

Bobby didn't waste time watching for the crew, they knew where to find him. He didn't realize how easy he was to spot. Red hair and freckles on a six-foot six-inch guy stood out no matter where you were standing.

The blackjack dealer flipped a ten for a total of twenty and Bobby watched his cards being swept into the discard pile and his chips disappear into a slot in the table.

*****

Hinkle, Oregon

Albert Simms was still sleeping as the train slowed. There were only a few stops on this section of line, this one had to be Hinkle. Waking, he took a second to orient himself. Then he remembered his tortured crewmember and his reason for heading back to Spokane.

He still had a few hours more before he got home. Fumbling around in the pocket of his jacket, he pulled out his phone and dialed. An unknown voice answered, "Eighty-nine here."

"Its five. We've got problems. Get all the guys in Spokane together and meet me when I get in. I should be there in three hours tops."

"Yes boss, see you there."

Albert put the phone away and leaned back, he wanted some more sleep and closed his eyes to try inducing it. If he had been more alert he would have noticed the guy who jumped on one of the boxcars behind him in Pocatello. Then he would have been watching at this stop to see what the guy did.

Instead, a figure was moving towards Albert's car, catching him off guard when he climbed up into the freight car. Even at this point Albert felt safe, he ran this section of rail and he was tough enough to defend it.

"Get the fuck off this car, it's taken." He didn't bother to get up, just gave the intruder the finger.

He couldn't believe it when the guy set down his bag and slid the door closed. It was dark outside, pitch black inside. Albert had a sudden surge of uncertainty. He jumped up, confronting the intruder.

"You not hear me fucker? Get the hell out."

Albert's eyes began to adjust to the darkness. As he tried to locate the guy he heard the sound of something spraying. The heavy mist hit his eyes, nose and mouth as he walked into it unawares.

The pepper spray was like a punch in the face. Albert recoiled, "Holy Christ!"

Through his blurry vision he noticed movement, and then something jammed into his leg. The electricity shook his body, his nerves fired like a thousand needles jabbing at him, his muscles strained as his breathing locked up.

Albert fell over backward, fighting with every fiber to not go over face first. That always hurt. As he laid there the thought hit him, *Why is this guy doing this?*

Was it hours or minutes later?

Albert realized he must have passed out. He could just make out a figure in black hunched over a small lantern by the door, a shoulder bag open on the floor beside him.

He went to move and found he was tied upright against a skid of boxes. *Shit this isn't good.* He could see his attacker rise up, the light behind him throwing him into outline as he turned. Albert lost all sense of normal, his heart began to jump as his knees went weak. All he could see was the gleam of the steel blade in the lantern light.

Then the figure stepped in front of him.

"Hey buddy, easy. *Jesus.*" He blinked. His voice felt tight. "What do you want, I can help you man."

The laugh echoed in the confines of the boxcar. In the silence that followed Albert heard a low voice, "I got all the help I needed from that asshole in Pocatello."

Albert tried to push backwards, but the skid wasn't moving. He struggled to understand what the guy's intentions were as his shirt was cut off with a few well-placed slices. He wondered what kind of predator this monster could be when his dirty jeans were torn off and he was left standing almost naked in the cold dark.

He shivered when the guy moved in close and whispered into his ear. He tumbled the words around in his brain and tried to understand. Then he screamed at the top of his lungs in sudden pain.

He looked down, terrified. Afraid to look, afraid of what he would see.

His tormentor had shaved a slice of meat off his thigh and left it there like it was a chunk of bologna. Lightheaded, he thought he was going to pass out again, he watched the blood start to well up and begin seeping out over the whitened edges of the skin. An involuntarily jerk made the hanging piece of flesh wobble back and forth.

He choked and looked up at the ceiling, trying to hold down the puke that was forcing its way north. *What the fuck was happening?*

Suddenly, he realized the guy was on the other side of him, whispering again. He wanted to hear the words, to understand the message, but he kept focusing on the action that came with the words.

He didn't know how long he screamed. He had to – but couldn't – look down. His mind didn't want to see the picture, but he forced his head to turn anyway.

He didn't recognize his own voice, "Oh God, no."

He had to understand what was happening: maybe if he understood he could stop this guy. *What was the voice saying?* The guy stood beside him filling his ears with a story.

There was no scream this time. Albert chose the easy route, and passed out instead.

The next time he woke, he was groggy and confused, until the sight of the little lantern by the door and bag on the floor snapped him back to the horror in a hurry. His stomach was already heaving again and his head was swirling when he looked down.

Albert closed his eyes, and then opened them again.

Both his legs had strips of flesh hanging off them. His tormenter had worked his way around each leg, slicing down, creating flesh strips about four inches wide. One row circled each of his thighs with a second row around his calves.

It was the sight of his shin bones staring back at him that finally got his stomach heaving and he leaned his head forward just in time to vomit all over the floor.

He struggled to catch his breath while spitting the last remnants out. Albert knew he was really in trouble. *Fuck.* This guy was going to kill him.

"Please man, listen to me." He struggled to get the words out. "Why? Why me?"

When he blinked the guy was right beside him again and Albert couldn't stop shaking. He must look like a scared dog about to piss right there on the spot. The guy started talking, this time slowly and louder. He was telling a story that took Albert a long time to recognize. Suddenly he knew what this was about. It didn't make things any better.

He tried to place the story, the events his torturer was talking about. It had been so long ago. At least now he knew why it was happening. In some weird way that made it easier to understand. You do the crime, you do the time.

He almost chuckled to himself. Obviously there wasn't going to be a lot of jail time applied here. This street justice was something Albert understood.

He tried to scream and realized he didn't have anything left. He looked down with more fascination than horror as he watched the guy slice a long curling strip of flesh off his bicep, then another off his forearm.

What a strange angle for the skin to hang. It reminded him of cleaning fish when he was a kid, trying to slide the knife between the meat and skin.

Albert woke for the third time as the guy sliced into his cheek. He let his head fall forward. He was weak now and seemed to be having trouble holding himself up. He couldn't avoid seeing the carnage on his body, as his head hung down.

A hand grabbed a fistful of hair, lifting his head before the knife sliced into the other cheek – then let it drop again. Albert was staring at the strips of skin hanging from his chest. He could hear the blood drops hitting the floor. Curious, he pressed his tongue towards his cheek and wasn't horrified when it went past his teeth and into open air.

Christ, he must look bad.

The sound of the door opening and a rush of fresh air made him turn his eyes even though he couldn't raise his head. He saw a figure jumping out of the train car. That was when Albert realized the train was slowing. *Was he home?* Somewhere in his head he knew he wasn't going to make it. But still he struggled one last time to breathe and stand up straight, before giving up and slumping forward against the ropes.

CHAPTER 6

Topeka, Kansas

The afternoon sun beat down on the long freight train as it pushed out into the open spaces of the midwest. The train shook a bit more on these older rails, but that was fine with Raul.

He leaned back against the train car, his legs stretched out in a sitting position with Maria on top of him. The steady rocking of the train was enough for both of them. She straddled his legs and let the vibrations move her up, down, and around.

He was intoxicated with her, she made no effort to move and he was so close. He knew that one of these bumps or corners was going to set him off and he relaxed, just enjoying the moment of anticipation.

Maria's eyes stayed closed as the train's momentum rocked her back and forth. A couple of bumps and she slammed down on him. They had been riding like this for twenty minutes and that was the last straw. Raul leaned his head back further and moaned.

She joined in, rubbing herself against him and closed her eyes, enjoying the pleasure for the second time. Finally, she slumped forward against his chest, her head on his shoulder.

Raul held her, letting her rest. He knew she was stressed out, but they were through the tough part now. The big cities were behind them and he knew the track from here a lot better than the jungle of lines back east. They would turn south now, heading for New Mexico and down into El Paso.

He had no idea he'd just crossed into the Raildogs box. He was cruising now, the border was next and then he would be able to relax with his woman for a few days before meeting the bosses. He let his eyes close and enjoyed the smell of Maria's hair.

It would be good to be home.

*****

Oklahoma City, Oklahoma

The boys all called him Dougie. Doug Rackman liked being a leader. It fit his cocky attitude well. He was the number three in the gang, ahead of his brother Bobby's number four.

He liked his section of the line from Houston up to Des Moines with Oklahoma holding the middle. That gave his boys a good shot at anyone leaving or heading for the east coast. Beginning of the month was party time for his crew and Doug did like to party. He would meet up with the gang, collect his dues of course, and then get them all shit-faced for the night. It was a small price to pay to keep an eye on things.

He took another look at his watch. He liked the gold case with its silver dial. It was the only thing he wore on the tracks that hinted at cash. Normally, he kept a low profile, and grubby clothes worked best on this job. He tucked the watch back in his pocket. Where was the six p.m. freight from down south? He had crew coming in on it.

Like his brother, Doug's red hair and freckles made him easy to find, even easier when he was hanging around the old steel mill next to the freight yards. Someone from the gang was always there, it was a message drop as well as hangout. Dougie and a handful of others were waiting to meet the guys from down south before heading north to Des Moines.

His house up there was away from any tracks. Just like Cliffy said, it gave them somewhere to get off and hide out when needed. The first big scores they'd got in the beginning were used to set up each line with a house.

None of the places were anything fancy, but it was something none of them had ever had before. Doug figured he was only in the house half the time. He preferred being on the rails or staying at one of his girlfriend's places. First of the month though, he was there to party with the crew like clockwork.

"There they are." One of the guys hanging near the fence spoke up.

Doug looked up as Devon and Rashad came walking down the track.

"Hey boss. What's up?" Devon and Doug touched fists.

"Not much. Been waiting around for you losers."

Devon held out a handful of cash, payment for him and Rashad.

"So, any action on the way up?" Doug asked.

"A couple bums, then a kid with a buck and a half. Nothing big."

The guys all understood. This wasn't a big-hit game, although one of those was always nice. This was about one hundred or two hundred at a time. People on freight trains usually didn't have much, but whatever they did have they kept in their pockets. Get enough of them and they added up. That was the game. Get as many as possible. The big hit was just the bonus.

"Hey that's enough to pay your dues for next month too." Doug smiled at the look Devon gave back.

"Don't think so boss. See you next month."

The boys all laughed and Doug jumped off the ledge where he'd been sitting. "Alright, lets get out of here, the train north won't be here much longer.

*****

Colton, California

Bill Dewton crouched low in the bushes. He couldn't believe what he was doing. The leave approval had come in and he'd quickly jumped on it. With a month off he was now waiting for a northbound freighter.

He was jumping a train. Illegally. He wasn't taking chances either. He had his forty-five in a shoulder holster and a concealed knife strapped to his leg just above the ankle. The train started to jerk, clanging as it rolled forward. He'd studied the cars, trying to figure which one was best to ride on and had picked out a couple.

Bill took a quick look up and down the track and jogged out to run beside the train. It wasn't going fast but he sensed it was picking up speed. He looked at the cars and selected his target.

He slipped once, then twice, and realized that running on rocks while you were looking sideways was a challenge. Widening his stance for stability, he placed his feet forcefully as he ran, reaching out for the metal railing.

With one hand on the car, he looked down for a place for his feet and realized he hadn't been thinking about that when he was watching the cars go by. Seeing a small metal ledge, he sped up his feet and leaped while using his arms to pull. Slamming against the car, he fumbled, his feet scrambling to find something solid.

Breathing hard, Bill realized his adrenaline was pumping, and he smiled. There's one of the rushes the riders must like.

He pulled up hard and dragged himself onto the landing, where he sat and collected himself.

This train car held storage containers that were double-stacked one on top of the other. The one on top was forty-feet long and the one on the bottom only twenty. That meant a ten-foot overhang at each end. Bill hoped that cover above his head would do.

He had a lot to think about and too much ground to cover. Where was he going? Where to start? His daughter's steps headed north. He sat down for the ride lost in his thoughts.

Six hours later, as he watched over the side of the car he noticed the buildings in the desert landscape. Vegas was coming up. Bill got his stuff together and prepared himself.

The train slowed as it neared the city limits, crawling through the outskirts. He was beginning to think they weren't stopping, they were almost out of the other side of town when the train slowed almost to a stop.

As quick as the freighter slowed it started to move again, the cars clanking against each other. Suddenly, two kids came out of nowhere. Running beside his car, they jumped on, one after the other. Bill's first thought was that they'd done that before.

His second was; *Shit, what now?*

The kids were exhausted but still seemed focused on their mission. The first kid looked quickly at his partner and received a nod of the head. He turned to Bill, "We want your cash old man. You don't want to get hurt."

Old man? Shit he was only forty-six. Sudden anger flooded through him, he could feel his shoulder muscles flex. The vein on his forehead throbbed. He reached into his coat and came out with the gun, "Who are you fucking with kid? Move one step and I'll blow your fucking head off."

The second kid quickly took a step backwards and pushed off the train. He landed hard but he was out of the situation.

The first kid turned and looked at the ground going by as the train kept moving.

Bill could tell he was calculating, "Don't even think it kid. I don't miss this close. Ever."

"What the fuck you want man? Just let me go." The kid was cocky, even when scared.

Bill wondered what to do, then it hit him. "Roll up your sleeves, both arms."

The kid hesitated then did as he was told. Sleeves were peeled back, and the kid stuck out his arms. Bill didn't see any tattoos, so he was pretty sure this one wasn't part of the gang. He was a piece of shit though.

"You know anything about guys with tattoos on the inside of their wrists?"

"Sure man, everyone does." The kid stopped there.

"I'm a cop kid. So either tell me what I want to know, or I'll drop you off at the next station." He paused. " Now if you tell me what I need, I'll probably let you go."

He could see the kid think it through and knew the moment when he decided he couldn't see a bad side. "Everyone knows the Raildogs have those tattoos."

"Who the fuck are the Raildogs?"

"Bunch of guys, maybe hundreds, they control a big section of the tracks man. You don't fuck with them."

The two of them stood there staring at each other while he put it together. Bill could tell this one was a small-time thief, not what he was looking for. "Okay kid, off the train if you want." The kid didn't hesitate and ejected off the side, landing running, taking a few stumbling steps before catching his balance.

The way the kid feared these Raildogs was something. So there was obviously a gang out there. Doing what? Working the rail lines? How many people were there out there to prey on? How many people used freight trains to travel? Now he had more to think about as the train headed north towards Salt Lake City.

*****

Reno, Nevada

David looked up at the window as he approached; she was sitting there as usual. He wondered if she actually saw him or was she staring off into another place in her head. He waved up at her and she quickly waved back. Okay, she was watching.

David Perez walked through the front lobby of the care home for the second time in three weeks.

He signed in with another scribble and made his way through the hallways. She was waiting inside her room, the door open as always.

"Hello mom."

"I can't believe you're back so soon David. I'm blessed." She reached up to pull his face down for a kiss.

They settled into the pattern of awkward silences and intermittent questions that always formed their time together. "I can't stay long Mom, but since I was in the area I wanted to come by."

"That's alright. Any time together makes me happy."

After another period of silence David stood up. He walked to the window, looked out, and then pulled on his black jacket. "I think I should go Mom."

"Okay." She fussed over him again, hugging him tightly. "Thanks for coming."

He headed for the door. Silently, he dropped something on the little table against the wall. Sarah looked down at it momentarily before closing her door.

*****

Nebraska

Cliffy wasn't enjoying the ride. The crew had already made some easy money and the cash had everyone in a good mood. The beatings they gave out had everyone pumped on adrenaline, but none of it helped him.

Something about number ninety-two's torture didn't sit right with him. Who does that? Only a friggin' psycho. It had been too long since he last talked to Albert. He should have heard something earlier this morning, but nothing.

As if on cue the phone started to vibrate. It never rang. It could put a guy in a bad spot to have it ring out loud at the wrong time. He checked the number.

"One." Cliff waited.

"Forty-five, sir. Sorry to call." The voice sounded apologetic.

"You're not supposed to call me. Where is Albert?"

Cliff had his black book out trying to figure out who forty-five was. Some guy named Mickey.

"He's dead. The guys in Spokane got ahold of me. Said his body was on a train that came in last night."

"What happened?" Cliff was getting itchy, anticipating what was coming next.

"It's fucking crazy. He was skinned alive. Someone took a knife to him while he was tied to a skid. It was right out of a fuckin' horror movie. Insane."

"Where's the body?" Cliff needed to know who was involved.

"Yardmen seen our guys around the boxcar and they had to hightail it. The cops will have him now."

Cliff felt his heart drop. What the hell was going on? More importantly, why? "Where are you now?"

"In Pocatello, trying to find the guy that attacked ninety-two."

"Forget it. He's gone. Get the crew together in Spokane and watch the phone for me. I'm coming up there."

"Yes sir."

Uncertainty twisted his stomach. Something wasn't right, and he suddenly had problems. He needed to get up to Spokane and sort out the crew. This Mickey was taking the lead, which was good. He'd been left in charge in Pocatello, Albert must have seen something in the guy.

They hadn't made it to North Platte yet, so Cliff could get off and change trains when they arrived there. He wondered if he should just get off the train and walk away, but he didn't think he could.

*****

Reno, Nevada

Sarah watched out the window as David walked down the lane. She hated seeing him go, but everything was different this time. This time he'd left a surprise. She kept taking her eyes off the window to look down in her lap.

This changed everything. Somewhere in her head she knew it. Like a piece of precision machinery, once one piece moved then all the others followed in perfect sequence. She looked down at her lap again. Her hands shook slightly.

Finally it was happening. The only thing she knew that could save her was happening. She knew it was a block in her head, probably one she put there herself. It was holding her down like she was buried under sand. There was no getting around it, no way to medicate it. That day long ago something had clicked off in her head, and she'd been waiting all this time for the switch to be turned back on. Finally.

He was long gone now but she continued to watch. David had known all along what she needed because she'd made it clear. She hadn't really believed he would, or could help, but then she looked down in her lap again.

How did he do it? What had it taken for him to accomplish it? On one hand she suddenly felt guilty. Why should he worry about her problems anyway? He'd suffered enough already because of her. Even when she was ruining his life she was still using him. *God have mercy.* She looked down again.

She opened her hand carefully and stared at the flower. It wasn't anything special like a rose, but it signified everything to Sarah.

She held the flower gently in her left hand and ran a finger around the petals one at a time. Her finger traced the stem from top to bottom and back up again.

For the first time in a long time anyone walking the grounds would see that she wasn't staring out the window. They wouldn't be able to see that she was reading.

Sarah scrutinized the note that came with the flower. It was so simple and quaint. Yet she was soaring inside. She read the words one more time.

"Here's your first flower mom."

CHAPTER 7

Colorado

The Florida-bound teens huddled in the dark. Bart looked over at Danny who was passed out cold under the sheltered end of the grain car. The kid had changed into jeans and a hoodie that would have been better if it hadn't been such a bright orange that stood like a sore thumb. Adidas had replaced the fancy dress shoes. Now at least he didn't look like such a geek.

The kid had changed a lot since they first became friends. Danny approached him one day while he was sitting alone on a bench outside the school. "Hey, cool jacket."

He'd liked that. He knew he looked like a thug and the jacket looked tough.

"You belong to a gang?"

Bart had looked closer at the kid with his curly hair hanging to his shoulders, white tennis shirt and blue shorts. He even had white socks and sandals to match. What would this kid know about gangs? He'd laughed, "Naw, I go alone, nobody brings me down."

He came back again and again to how they'd started this strange friendship. Him and the geek. Looking at the kid again he wondered about that close call back in Cheyenne. How would the kid have faired in a real fight? Bart hoped they didn't ever have to find out.

They had spent the first part of the night stopped for three hours outside of Denver. He hoped they hadn't made a mistake taking the southern route. Now they were slowing again. He stuck his head out of the end of the grain car and realized they were entering a siding in the middle of nowhere again. He couldn't see any lights in either direction.

"Danny!"

Bart watched the kid move in his sleep and start to come around. He could tell the moment when Danny remembered where he was, jolting awake, "What's going on?"

"Nothing man, we're stopped on another siding in the middle of nowhere. Want to check out some of the train?"

Danny seemed to jump at the thought. It took a second to get their bearings in the dark and become comfortable that there wasn't anyone around.

It was dark enough they could hardly make out the graffiti as they walked alongside the train. They passed ten or more grain cars and then a few low-riders with storage containers.

Suddenly they were beside something different. They stopped and looked up. Then slowly they turned to each other and realized they were both smiling.

"You thinking what I'm thinking?" Bart watched Danny hesitate and look around. *Shit, there isn't anybody here kid.*

"You bet. Let's get our stuff."

*****

Topeka, Kansas

Raul hadn't slept since they'd stopped in Topeka. He didn't get where he was by being reckless. For now he settled for keeping an eye on Maria as she slept cuddled in a ball under the tarp.

He was on full alert. The freight yard was a big one. They were lucky to be on a rail where he could look across the rest of the yard and keep an eye out for trouble. The question was, how long would they be stuck here?

Looking around he could see there were other tracks running parallel to his, but it was the main set of rails on the other side that kept him on edge. He tracked any yard workers closely, making sure they weren't paying any attention to them.

He knew that sitting on a stopped train in the city was just asking for trouble. It wasn't the railroad cops that were a worry. They'd just move you along. It was the drifters, the thugs, and the gangs you had to watch out for. Not that he was scared. Raul had fought plenty of times in the past and would again in the future. Sometimes the fights were for show, or to improve someone's position. Sometimes they were to the death. It wasn't new, it was just the way it was.

He expected to someday die in battle. It wouldn't be pretty, but he would go till he dropped. He knew the numbers, he watched those above him in the chain of command, he kept track of how many were alive, and how many had disappeared.

Understanding the consequences, the numbers game, that's what kept Raul wide-awake in the dark of night. Now, his headband down low, just over his eyes, he crouched down with his arms resting on his knees, watching for anything that moved, examining every train entering and leaving the rail yard.

At one point he took a walk alongside the train to get a better look at the yard, but didn't notice anything out of the ordinary.

Suddenly, he heard a noise that stood out as different. Above the constant squealing of metal on metal, of rail cars slamming, together he heard something else. Music?

With head cocked in the direction of the sound, his heart rate picked up speed. He couldn't control his body's reactions, muscle contractions or adrenaline, but he could control his mind. He had fought hard as a kid to teach his brain to think, and now he used that strength.

No panic – there wasn't even an actual threat yet.

He retraced his steps back to their boxcar, contemplating waking Maria. Then on second thought, she might get all worried. It was better to leave her to sleep.

Climbing back into the car to keep out of sight, he listened. The sounds were getting closer. The rap music was filtering back in his direction. "In da club … feel like drinking … baby."

It had to be a boom box, they should be in sight soon, so he kept still, waiting to see what was coming. Then he heard the first voices and started counting. One, two, three at least. When he heard them all laughing he upped the count to six or seven.

Leaning back, Raul tried to become invisible. He watched as the group came into sight. Young guys, all of them. They were drinking from beer bottles and stopping randomly to spray paint the sides of the odd car.

It sounded like they were looking for trouble just by their cockiness. A couple of the kids were roughhousing and another smashed his empty bottle against the side of the train.

A lot of violence happened on the spur of the moment, right place – right time, or, wrong place – wrong time. These guys didn't need to be looking for trouble, but if opportunity presented itself, like here in the dead of night, six or more against him and Maria, someone might get ideas. It might even look like fun.

Another train was pulling in, momentarily distracting him. He glanced over to watch the train roll up and slow to a stop before returning to watch the young kids causing shit.

*****

Pocatello, Idaho

The train had been sitting in Salt Lake for an hour. It was everything Cliff could do to not get off the train. His forty-five years felt more like seventy right now. He thought hard about just walking off and heading out to his new homestead. He had enough stashed away to get by for years, but he would have to stretch it out.

He was that close. Another five years maybe, or a couple nice scores along the way and he'd be set for the rest of his life. The couple grand a month from dues was nice, but once he left the tracks permanently he might run into problems trying to collect. You were only the boss if you were still influencing things, still keeping a tight grip.

Either way, Cliff waited it out and eventually the train headed northwest towards Spokane. Just thinking about the place had him conjuring up wild visions of what must have happened to Albert.

He shook his head. "Fuck Albert, I hope you were already dead before the knifework started." But he knew he hadn't been. This time the violent shudder that ran up his spine made him reach out and grab the wall of the boxcar for balance.

He could use a drink right now, but didn't think that was too smart. He watched the small town of Pocatello roll by. Was it all a coincidence? He kept wishing it was, but he had a bad feeling that stuck with him. There was something going on, and Cliff had no idea what.

It was almost like someone was purposely leaving their bodies to be found that kept him thinking. They'd lost gang members before. It was bound to happen. Sometimes when you ran into another gang and there were more of them than you, you didn't always win the battle. Some guys had just disappeared, probably dragged off the tracks and left hidden somewhere. A couple of times bodies were found that showed signs of beatings.

Cliffy sometimes liked to see himself as a general, and you knew you were going to lose pieces in a war, but you kept going and just added new ones.

This time around it was like the Raildogs were being sent a message. Someone wanted them to find the bodies, to know what had happened. Who was the message for? And more importantly, who was delivering it? He had caused a lot of pain in a lot of places in his time. There could be a lot of people looking for him.

*****

Utah

Bill Dewton cursed for the hundredth time. He wasn't settling in very well to travelling by freight train. He wanted to get some sleep while it was still dark, but the constant up and down over the hills bordering Nevada and Utah kept shaking the train.

He had never suffered motion sickness, but this was getting him pretty close. He hunkered down, closed his eyes and tried to drift off, but before he could his head would begin swirling. His eyes would snap open and he would suck in gulps of fresh air until he cleared his head and he would be able to start thinking about sleep again. The train was going over the top of a hill when he caught the beep of his cell phone.

Someone was trying to call him, but the reception was crappy at best. It showed two missed calls and a text message. But then he was heading down into another valley and lost service again. Fucking phones, he shook the damned thing, never working when you need them.

Now each time the train crested a hill, he tried to return the call. The text message had changed his mood. The Pocatello police had entered their dead man into the system and hit Bill's alert. He read it again.

We have a body here in Pocatello with a number tattooed on the inside of the wrist. Found near the train tracks.

Bill was almost bouncing with anticipation. He was awake now and eager to call back. Realistically, what help was a body going to be? Still, he was excited that the new information he'd entered about tattoos and trains was already showing results. Now the only question was, how was he getting to Pocatello. He groaned, knowing he was stuck on this train until Salt Lake.

*****

Topeka, Kansas

Dougie Rackman always had a lookout on point when the train was moving, but when they were entering or leaving a city he liked being at the door watching for himself. He knew that if just one friggin' idiot missed something you'd land in shit.

Cops, yard police, hell, it could be just a bunch of hard-cases looking for fun. You needed to be on top of things and he did that as a rule. That was how he noticed the group walking alongside the tracks before the train came to a stop.

"Raildogs!" Everyone in the car turned to his voice,

"Rally up boys, we got a rumble." Dougie smiled broadly, like a dog baring its teeth.

Electricity surged through the car. Muscles flexed in anticipation. Crooked grins grew more menacing.

He rolled his shoulders to loosen up and dropped a few quick squats to get the blood moving. It looked like even numbers, six on six, or close to that. He chuckled, he'd out his six guys against any other six out around.

Doug jumped before the train stopped. He didn't hang back and that was why he was a leader. Rashad never missed the action, he was in the air beside him. They hit the ground running, headed right for the other group.

Devon and the rest of the crew hit the ground behind them, some landing better than others, and they surged forward.

As they got nearer, he realized it was a group of kids, not men, but that wasn't his problem.

Momentarily stunned at the sight of the charging Raildogs, the kids stopped, jaws hanging open. Then the first one of them reacted and they started to spread out into a defensive position.

Dougie fought not to laugh out loud. Perfect, he thought to himself. This was what he wanted all his opponents to do. Scatter. His men had been taught well and this was a situation they would eat up. They understood gang mentality, and the gang stood together.

He went at the biggest one, Rashad with him. The guy must have thought Doug was going to stop at some point, but he hit the guy on the run in a full tackle and knocked him off his feet. They landed in a heap, and he pushed off the kid, rolling away.

Rashad came in hard behind him, kicking the guy in his exposed ribs as he lay there sprawled on the ground. As their victim's body curled forward in a fetal position to protect his ribs, Rashad kicked him full in the face. Doug watched the head snap back with a sickening crack.

One down.

He turned to take in the rest of the action. Devon was sitting on another kid's chest, dropping bombs in with his fists while someone else helped him by sitting on the legs. His men always fought in groups of two or more. They'd been taught to take their opponents out one at a time, and make sure they stayed down.

The kids were trying, but two were already out of the fight, another one was being kicked by a pair of Raildogs every time he tried to get up, a fourth took off running up the tracks. The dust settled a bit and only two remained. They stood in the center of the circle as the Raildogs took a second to catch their breaths.

Doug liked these odds a lot better, six on two. That was more like it. They could have taken their time with these guys. No money was on the line, but there was still a lesson to be given. Unfortunately, the train would probably be moving again soon and they had a party to get to.

"Okay boys, finish this up. Train's gonna be moving soon."

He reluctantly headed for the parked train, knowing what was coming next. The two kids kept turning, attempting to square off with his crew surrounding them, wondering who was going to come at them first. He grinned, they were in for a surprise. He didn't turn when he heard the shouts of, "Raildogs rule".

The gang jumped forward and five men closed the circle. The kicks and punches were too much for the two kids and the blows slowly reduced them to mounds on the ground. Doug knew it wasn't any better down there as the sound of kicks took over.

By the time he jumped up into the open doorway of the boxcar to sit and watch his guys, they were already on their way back. They climbed up into the car fist bumping and high fiving. None of them gave a thought about the bodies left abandoned in the yard as they started replaying the fight.

Doug kept an eye on the crumpled forms on the ground until he felt the train start to move below him.

*****

Des Moines, Iowa

A figure sat hunched on the top of a garden shed, tucked under a large tree. The darkness kept him well hidden, yet gave him a clear view into the back yard of the house next door.

He watched, as he had for the last three hours, while the party raged on. It hadn't been hard to find them when you knew where to look. He'd waited at the rail yards and watched them arrive. Keeping a distance, he'd followed them to this house. Finding the shed and big tree in the next yard had been a sign. It was meant to be.

It looked like fifteen, maybe twenty guys drinking and toking up a storm. The figure kept watching like he was searching for someone in particular. When the limo pulled up in front of the house he eyed it between the buildings.

The women climbing out of the long car looked ready to party in their short dresses and high heels. He could see things were going to pick up. He was going to be in for a long night, but some how he kept still and waited.

Later, when two men came out on the back deck he focused in.

"Been a good month Doug, but I'm pretty beat."

The figure leaned forward in the dark.

"I know what you mean, but for ten years it's been going like clockwork."

"You sticking around long? We should get out together."

"No I can't, heading out in the morning." The first one laughed. "Might miss the big score." They clanked their bottles together, then turned for the house.

"Let's get back to the ass."

The figure crouched on the shed smiled. That was the news he was waiting for. He could get off the shed and find somewhere to rest up for what was left of the night. He was revved up. He'd be leaving with them in the morning.

CHAPTER 8

Reno, Nevada

Sarah Perez walked the grounds with an urgency in her step. She'd been energized since David's last visit. She stalked down the pathway without noticing the blooming flowers or hearing the chirping in the overhanging trees.

If any one noticed, they'd see the extra bounce in her step and the slight crack of a smile on the edges of her lips once in a while. She stopped and looked up at her room above. Then she noticed a figure move by her window.

"Bastard." She muttered to herself. She'd known someone was in her room whenever she was out. She wasn't supposed to notice, but one time she'd found things moved and now made a point of placing things in specific positions. It helped to track what had been touched.

The good feelings she had been enjoying vanished and she turned for the building. She entered her room, closing the door and just stared. It wasn't a game, but she needed to know what he'd done.

One particular daytime staffer was always around. She was sure the creep was in her room every time she was out on her walk. It freaked her out, but he was too chickenshit to be a threat.

Walking around the room she took inventory. He'd been in her clothes drawers, into her perfumes and powders, and the bed had been sat or laid on. She tried to picture the idiot in her stuff. What was he doing? It was a violation, and it really pissed her off.

She didn't like the one who brought the food, or this asshole either. Christ, she didn't like anyone in this place. Sarah double checked the lock and then slid the bed away from the wall. Reaching in under the mattress, all the way into the middle of the bed, she struggled to bring out the little wrapped package.

Taking it over to the chair by the window, she sat down. She found herself giddy as she looked down. Gingerly, like she might damage the contents, she slowly unfolded the silk handkerchief to reveal the flower.

She realized she was shaking as she reached down to gently wrap her fingers around the stem and took a second to steady her hand. Bringing it up in front of her face, she tried to appreciate the color of the petals, but her hand started to shake again.

Suddenly there were teardrops landing in her lap. Looking down through blurry eyes, she saw she was squeezing the stem so hard it was flattening in her fingers and the flower head drooped to the side.

Sarah found her composure and wiped at her eyes. She placed the flower down delicately in the small silk square and slowly wrapped it up again. With her hands clasped on her lap holding the package, Sarah fought down the excitement.

Don't let me down David.

*****

Colorado

Bart threw his pack up on the locomotive. Danny's suitcase followed.

"You got to get rid of that case man. It's going to bring us trouble."

Danny had already thought about that, he realized it didn't look too cool. Cheyenne had woken him up. He'd be getting some other kind of bag as soon as he could. "I know man. I know."

Danny was stoked by the thought of riding in a locomotive. The long freight trains sometimes had a second locomotive in the middle of the cars that was run remotely from the front end of the train.

It should be empty, and a hell of a lot more comfortable than the steel decking of a rail car. Danny got to the door first and yelled in triumph when it opened. The two kids couldn't believe their luck. The inside of the locomotive was warm, and there were a leather sofa and plush driver's seat.

"Right on man. Jesus, this is cool." Bart seemed beside himself.

Danny was as amped up as his buddy was, "Awesome man. Awesome."

An hour later the boys had made the engine their own. Bart commandeered the drivers seat, feet propped up in the corner between the dash and the front window. Danny was cooking with his little camp stove sitting nicely on the counter.

"What do we do when we hit a station?" Danny was trying to think ahead.

"No big deal." His partner shrugged his shoulders. "We just stay down hidden until we leave. Easier in here than on the back of a rail car."

Danny figured he was probably right. If something else happened they'd have to deal with it then. Looking around at the inside of the locomotive he couldn't help but grin. First class travel, that's what this was. He wondered about Bart now that they were on the road. The guy looked tough, but was he really? What could have happened back in Cheyenne?

He hadn't been in a lot of fights, the few in public school had mostly involved bullies picking on him, and he hadn't done much to defend himself. This was a whole new ball game out here on the road and he was starting to think about what he'd have to do if they got attacked. Like a lot of things he did, he was running through all the possible scenarios.

Bart let out a long hoot and faked pulling on a horn. As Danny watched him he couldn't help but feel that his friend was more of a joker than a gangster. Based on the violence he'd seen so far on this trip, they were probably going to get the chance to find out how tough they were sooner or later. The more he thought about it, the more he worried about what was ahead.

"Hoot, hoot, next stop Florida." Bart laughed.

"Yeah, sure Bart. This soup is ready to eat. So get your ass over here"

*****

Missouri

Maria kept reassuring Raul she was alright when he woke up from his sleep to check on her.

The truth was she wasn't alright. It was daytime and they were miles away from the station where they spent the previous night, but she was still scared.

She'd been confused when he shook her awake in the dark of night. One thing was sure, she wouldn't ever travel on a freight train again.

He said he wanted her ready in case they needed to run or hide. Her brain kicked in when he pointed out the gang of thugs nearby. First she heard the music. Then the shouts made their way over to her, and she'd frozen with fear.

They had stayed out of sight while they watched the fight. Some guys calling themselves Raildogs had beat the shit out of this other group of guys. She'd never seen anything like it. Brutal.

The only good thing was it didn't last long. Then the gang climbed on a train that was moving out of the yard. She had been making ready to move when Raul had stopped her dead. "Don't move Maria." His hand stayed out in the air, palm open, right up her face. "Not an inch."

They had waited silently, keeping an eye on the bodies crumpled on the ground. When their own train jerked into life, the relief was like a blanket smothering her.

Now the next day, they were flying along the track, sun beating down, and Raul was relaxed enough to catch up on some sleep. He didn't seem to have a care in the world.

Maria, on the other hand had a lot.

She couldn't rest and didn't want to alarm him, but the scenes in her head wouldn't go away. She was worried about what lay ahead. Were they heading for trouble, or was he really going to be able to get them all the way to Mexico safely?

She sat there with her arms wrapped around her legs. Raul had been tough the first time she met him. She'd watched him beat two guys down right there in front of everyone in the bar that first night. His strength had impressed her.

She was new to New York and it turned out so was he. He sat by himself at the bar nursing a shot after the fight. Ordering two for herself, she'd banged them back.

He'd turned then and taken a closer look at her. "Easy woman. You in a hurry?" he asked.

Maria had deliberately batted her eyelashes, and placed her hand on his thigh while she stared him in the eye. "Well actually yes, I am in a hurry."

Raul completed the turn and faced her, smiling. They hadn't been apart since.

Now swaying with the motion of the train she let the scenes from last night slip in again, and for the first time she had to wonder, was she making a mistake?

*****

Spokane, Washington

Cliffy felt the train slowing down, finally he was in Spokane. This was a good test, he would see how the crew was handling the situation. Was anyone taking control? Calling the shots?

Riding at the door, watching for anything, he noticed a guy in the bushes as the train pulled into the station. He seemed to be talking into a cell phone. A quick surge of adrenaline caught him off guard as he thought about the psycho. Was he waiting?

He didn't wait for the train to stop, he was off and moving away from it while it was still rolling. He didn't get far before two guys headed his way from behind a building. They must have anticipated him jumping off early, or they were warned by the guy in the bushes on the cell phone.

Stopping, he gauged the threat, watching them as they approached. Instead the guy put his arm out, wrist up, so Cliff could see the tattoo.

"Hi there, Mikey's the name. This here is Philly." The first one was clearly in charge.

"Good to meet you boys. Wish it wasn't like this." He stuck out his hand and they both took it, tentatively.

"Okay Mikey, show me the crew."

An hour later, after meeting the other men in an abandoned warehouse off the yard, Cliff pulled Mikey aside.

"You know how things work right?"

Albert's lieutenant outlined what he had been told. What he'd been responsible for, and who ran the other sections. "Albert told me to keep it to myself."

"And did you? Did you tell anyone?" Cliff watched the younger man's face for any sign of a lie.

"Nope. I knew it was a privilege."

They sat there silently for a while and Cliff made a decision. "Okay Mikey, I'll give you the crew. You get the monthly dues. You need to replace the men you lost. And you need to do whatever you have to get hold of the section."

Mikey nodded vigorously, obviously trying to hide his pleasure at being chosen.

"I want to hear from you daily for the next while. You got any problems with that?"

"No boss, I look forward to learning what ever I can from you."

With the serious stuff out of the way, Cliff wanted to unwind a bit. He felt a little better about the section and felt more at ease. "Let's have another drink. I've got to get back on a train tonight."

*****

Pocatello, Idaho

"We don't get officers from out of town come up this way very often." The sheriff's face was carefully neutral.

The two lawmen sat across from each other. Bill had arrived before noon in a rental car, driving straight from Salt Lake City. The sheriff was checking him out from across the desk.

No one liked outside interference in their cases. Bill would feel the same way if someone came in asking questions about a body on one of his cases. He'd hold back until he was sure about the guy's intentions.

"Hey, I'm just glad you guys caught the alert I set up in the system." He decided to work the friendly angle.

The sheriff shuffled some papers around and pulled one out of the stack to read over a second time. "What's your interest in numbered tattoos?"

Bill was about to start to give this guy all the expected answers to his questions. Then he decided to cut to the chase. Fuck it, he had too much to lose by dickin' around. He looked at the floor between his shoes. "Look, my daughter disappeared on a freight train last fall."

This seemed to take the sheriff by surprise as he stopped shuffling papers and looked up.

"The only leads I have are the freight trains and stories about a gang with numbers tattooed on the inside of their wrists."

The silence got heavier as the two men sat there. Finally Bill added, "I'm doing everything I can."

The rawness in his voice seemed to change the tide and the sheriff transformed from defensive to concerned.

He dropped the papers on the desk and folded his hands on the top of the pile. "Okay, tell me what you want. We'll do our best."

Bill drilled the sheriff about time, place, and anything else that he could think of. Finally it came down to his last requirement. "I'd like to see the body if it's still here."

"It not a pretty sight." The sheriff's face twisted at the thought. He straightened up in his chair blinking his eyes as if to change the picture in his brain. "I'll drive."

At the morgue Bill braced himself as they pulled the metal tray out of the locker in the wall.

"No one has claimed him yet. Only reason he's still here." The sheriff pulled the sheet back and both men took a reflexive step backwards.

It was involuntary, but the inhuman sight made you want to escape. It was only after he was able to conquer this initial instinct that Bill stepped forward. *Jesus, what a mess.* The blowtorch had created openings to the bone and beyond as it raked along the body. It must have been pure horror. The autopsy report said the vic was alive for most of it.

Bill tried to ignore the melted spots and concentrate elsewhere. Really he just wanted to see the tattoo. He leaned forward to get an angle on the wrist that lay on its side, facing in. He could see the numbers, but had to twist his head to make them out. Ninety-two.

It was rather crudely done. Some kind of homemade instrument. He had to be happy with that. At least he knew what to look for now, and he'd confirmed that the tattoos did exist.

"You know the perp torched the whole body and this tattoo is the only thing untouched." The sheriff stood a few paces away, hand over his nose.

"You mean like a message? Maybe." Bill thought about it. "Who's the message for?"

His phone rang and he nodded he was done to the sheriff as he stepped away to take the call.

"Dewton."

"You the guy from Colton with an alert out for tattooed wrists on the rail lines?"

Bill's hand squeezed the receiver, "Yes, what have you got?"

"Jim Stevens, Spokane city police. We got a fucking nightmare up here. Some guy was cut to pieces and left in a boxcar that came in last night."

Bill waited, until he realized the cop was done. "You mentioned a tattoo?"

"Shit, sorry. I keep getting distracted, I'm seeing the guy like it was a minute ago. The tattoo was a number five on the inside wrist. The only part of the guy that wasn't cut up."

Bill knew this was important, he just didn't know why. Was it the number five? If there was any kind of organization to this gang wouldn't the numbers start at one? If they did, then number five was close to the top. Number ninety-two over here in the cooler meant it had to be a large gang.

Why was someone leaving the tattoos to be recognized in the first place? It was like someone wanted them found.

"Okay, I'm in Pocatello right now. I can be in Spokane later today. Can I call you on this number?"

"No problem. I assume you're going to explain all this when you get here."

"Sure thing. See you later." How he was going to explain, he didn't have a clue.

Bill left Pocatello with a copy of their file in his hands and adrenaline pumping in his veins. He was finally getting somewhere, even if it was finding bodies that were already dead. He set the cruise control on the Malibu he'd rented from Hertz and looked down the highway towards Spokane.

*****

Missouri

The wait for the train in Des Moines had been a brutal few hours for the Raildogs gathered in the freight yard. Epic hangovers were everywhere, and from the smell of it, Dougie was sure someone had puked.

It wasn't any easier two hours later crossing into Missouri, as the swaying train tossed them around. Devon and Rashad were heading south with the boss and a few others had decided to come along. The five men sat or laid flat out in the boxcar with the door closed to keep the blinding sunlight out of their blood-shot eyes.

Dougie knew he'd find a second wind by afternoon and let his eyes close as he tried to think of something other than his pounding head. Four hours maybe and he'd be in Oklahoma City and then he knew a woman that wouldn't mind him crashing at her place for a while.

Something just barely caught his attention. The little noise wasn't that loud, he didn't even open his eyes. Laying there, he tried to separate the different sounds of the train and the wind outside and listened more. There it was again, a little noise, like something sliding, filtered out to him from the corner of the boxcar. Then nothing. He'd almost dozed off when he heard it again.

Doug's eyes sprang open. He didn't move, just stared at the car door across from him. He recognized it now, the sound was like someone's feet sliding along the outside ledge of the boxcar.

The hair on the back of his neck started to stand up and Doug felt a sudden stab of fear. He was rolling over to stand up when the noise outside changed. He heard the chain rattling and understood. *Shit.* "Guys, get up!" He charged for the opening.

The rattling of the chain became louder. Then he heard steel against steel clinking as the links hit something. There was a brief pause and then a loud click.

Doug slammed against the door, trying to move it. Wrapping his hands around the inside handle he leaned into it. The door slid a fraction of an inch, then stopped. The crack was barely wide enough to see chains looped around the outside door handles. His eyes meticulously checked each link of chain before settling on the lock that hung at one end.

"Hey, out there," He rattled the door. "There's people in here. You can't lock us in."

Silence. Doug knew someone was out there, he hadn't heard any shuffling to get back away from the door. "Come on man. Let us out, okay?"

A voice came back, deep and slow. "Don't think so."

It had to be some shit disturber. "You don't want to fuck with us whoever you are. This is Raildogs you're fucking with."

When there was no answer, he yelled again, "You hear me out there."

"Don't worry yourself asshole. I got it right. It's Raildogs I'm looking for."

Then he heard the shuffling feet moving away from the door. Gotta hand it to whoever it was, it took balls to be out there all that time clinging to the side of a boxcar while the train was moving.

Christ, what now? Doug was trying to assemble his thoughts when he heard the guy outside climbing up the ladder at the end of the car. Footsteps followed along the top. There were short flashes of someone visible through the air holes and corner joints.

"What the fuck is going on Doug?" A grim faced Devon was clearly getting agitated. The others were working at the locked door trying to pry it open. They looked desperate.

"I don't know. The guy seems strange to me. Could be a nut case." Doug touched the drop that splashed onto his arm from above. *What the hell?* He smelled the gasoline before his hand got to his nose.

"Hey man, what the hell is going on? Are you crazy?" He shouted up at the ceiling. His heart was pounding and his palms were starting to sweat. The guy needed to answer back. But he didn't. Doug raced to the corner and using the frame as leverage, climbed up to get close to the top of the car.

He pressed his face against the ceiling. "Listen to me man, we can work this out. You want money? I can get some."

He could hear footsteps on the roof. The stranger moved to his corner and got down close. "I don't want your money."

"What you want man? I can get you anything."

"I want you to remember asshole."

The conversation was too quiet for the others to hear, but it did seem to go back and forth. Then everyone heard Doug talking back to the guy. "No way, not me man. I was just there, that's it."

Now the liquid was pouring into the boxcar faster, splashing down to the floor. Doug climbed back down from the ceiling, looking over at his guys. The fear was plain on every face. He felt trapped. What could he do?

The conversation with their assailant was obviously over. Dougie Rackman reached out and balanced himself against the side of the boxcar as it rumbled down the southbound rail. This couldn't be happening. He tried to focus on everything, anything, except his heart pounded against his ribs. He could hear the others scrambling around in the dark, banging and scratching against the outer walls, someone let out a scream.

He glanced upwards and ran his hand through his hair, his eyes darted around the boxcar. He could hear the guy moving around up above, the smell of the gasoline was everywhere as it poured through the holes in the ceiling, pooling on the floor. The constant vibration of the car rattling along the rail line just spread the gasoline further.

Doug looked at the number three tattooed on his arm and realized he was as angry as he was scared. He was third in line, this shouldn't be happening to him. Then he heard the muted roar of a torch and he snapped his eyes straight up.

Fuck no. This can't be happening.

A blue curl of flame crept down from the top. The bastard's gasoline pouring through the roof had left paths down the walls soaked in liquid. A firestorm raced to engulf the boxcar. With nowhere to go, the Raildogs jumped around, trying to avoid the flames on the floor, but the gasoline spread further as the train sped along.

And then as Rashad retreated from the encroaching fire, he surprised himself by backing into the gasoline soaked wall.

Doug watched him come off the wall over a puddle of flame and saw the moment when Rashad lost it. He was standing surrounded by curls of blue licking at his legs when he went up in a fireball. Lunging at the man next to him, he dragged that guy down too. Now both of them were in flames, screaming and frantic, pushing and trying to get up.

Doug turned to see who else was screaming and realized it was himself. He backed against one of the few pieces of wall that wasn't in flames. The smell was revolting. He'd never smelt burning flesh. The smoke was getting thick as he sank to his knees.

Once he realized the walls were on fire he knew there was no chance. They were never getting out of here. He watched Devon slam repeatedly against the door even as the flames burned through his clothes.

He slumped down to the floor, coughed a few times and shook his head. He didn't have any fight left, no screams either, he was struggling to breathe. He thought about what the guy had said. Fuck, so long ago. Doug wanted to laugh, he'd said it may times, payback was a bitch.

It was daytime. *Didn't anyone see the flames?* He slumped over dead, his body hard to see in the suffocating smoke, as the flames started to claim his leg.

*****

Missouri

A figure crawled down the boxcar's ladder, the screams didn't last long, but that wasn't important. Getting the job done before the train pulled into Topeka was. With a mission at hand, timing was everything,

Working his way along the outside of the cars towards the back of the train, he looked back a few times at the flaming boxcar. Now he took up position on the last car and waited for something to happen.

Either the engineer was going to see the flames first, or someone was going to phone it in. The flaming boxcar could probably be seen for miles. He shook his head as he thought about farmer's fields along the track. There was probably a string of fires behind them.

Would the engineer stop right away? Or keep going for the next station? You couldn't plan everything. He wasn't too worried, attention would be on the burning car and no one would notice anything happening at the back of the train.

With Topeka in sight the train started to slow. When he saw the flashing red lights off in the distance heading towards the rail line he knew it was time to get off. The figure jumped into a passing ditch going a little faster than he wanted and rolled a few times before coming to a stop.

Angling away from the tracks, he worked his way through the fields, keeping the rail in sight. He had to get to a station and find a train back up to Des Moines and then east to Salt Lake.

No one noticed as he slipped into the train yard, nor did they see him checking his little book for information on which trains went where, or see him pause to scribble a few words in the back of the book.

CHAPTER 9

Spokane, Washington

Cliff was back at the freight yard. He'd spent the night talking and drinking with Mikey's crew. Now he just wanted the southbound train to leave so he could sleep the night off on the way back home.

He hung out in the vicinity of the train, keeping out of sight. Spotting the unmarked police car driving through the yard before they saw him, he quickly ducked between two boxcars, putting himself on the opposite side of the train.

Crouching, he peered under the train as the car drove by, stopping further down. Curious, Cliff moved around to get a better vantage point on the cop car. Getting out of the vicinity would be smart, but with everything that had been going on he wondered why the cops were in the yard.

The cop who climbed out of the car in a suit had to be a detective. Cliff was confused when the other one got out. He wasn't dressed like a cop, wearing hiking boots, jeans, and a leather bomber jacket. Who was this guy? Undercover?

He couldn't stop himself, inching closer trying to pick up what they were saying.

"They pulled him off here," the detective said. "What was left of him."

"The one in Pocatello wasn't on a train, he was by the tracks," hiking boots replied.

Cliffy retreated back the way he came. He'd heard enough. These cops weren't here randomly, they were discussing the torture of his crewman. Who was the guy who knew about ninety-two down in Pocatello? How did he find out about Albert up here?

His head hurt. He'd had too much booze the night before to handle a problem like this. Something was definitely going on. He'd been sure someone was hitting the crew, but now there were cops involved and they seemed to know as much, or more, than he did. Shit, what the fuck was happening?

The train jerked forward and Cliff jumped back in surprise. He was so amped up about the cops that the train nearly scared the shit out of him. He shot another quick look under the train at the cops and then back at the rail cars as they jerked and banged together as they started moving.

Reaching up, he grabbed the handrail as it went past, his feet sprang into action as he gauged the steps and jumped aboard. He dove flat on the floor of the boxcar, but now that he was inside he could see the opposite door was open on the other side. Shit. He hadn't seen that coming.

The boxcar rolled by the two cops who were looking absentmindedly at the rolling train. Cliff kept his eyes open for the one in street clothes, hoping he wouldn't be noticed, but the guy locked eyes with him and the two men stared at each other, their heads swiveling while the train picked up speed.

Cliff kept staring into the daylight for a second after the face was gone, his heart pounding. Would they stop the train? Call right now and have it stopped? He didn't think so. There were too many trains out there with people on them to be stopping them every time they saw someone. They could have it stopped at the next station though, and that was an issue.

The train wasn't up to full speed yet, still within the city limits. His heart slowing, he made a quick call, he wasn't staying on this train. It might get stopped somewhere ahead. He'd catch the next one. He just had to slip back to the station and wait. There was always another one.

He flexed his muscles to loosen up, he hated rough landings and looked carefully for someplace to jump off. What he really wanted was to be sitting on his deck back home sipping on a beer. Hesitating just a second, he leapt off the moving train.

*****

Spokane, Washington

Bill heard the train rattle, he turned to see the boxcars rocking, the steel knuckles slamming as it started to move. His eyes idly traced the passing graffiti and examined the open doors on the boxcars. Suddenly, something caught his eye and he zeroed in. Someone was staring back at him from the moving train.

He couldn't see the guy well, he was laid flat out on the floor. He would've thought it was a bum except for the intensity of the stare. It was like the guy knew they were cops and he was watching them as closely as Bill watched back.

"There's someone on that train." He turned to the detective.

"Nothing new there." The detective didn't seem too concerned.

"We going to stop it?" He wanted to talk to the guy on the train.

The detective raised an eyebrow as if he though Bill was kidding. "We can't do that. Christ, it's just a bunch of kids and people with no money riding the trains. What? You want to hold up the line? Have trains stacked up from here to who-knows-where. Just to kick some bum or a couple kids off? Ain't happening."

Bill let out a sigh. He knew the guy was right. Still, he wasn't going to forget that face. He'd like to run into it again. Something about him had been dangerous looking. He pictured his daughter getting onto a train with that guy and it sickened him.

It was easier now to feel like he was going to vomit when his stomach was already empty. Arriving later than he thought he would the day before, he had made plans to meet the detective this morning. He skipped breakfast purposely because he knew he'd be in the morgue at some point.

He shook his head. The fresh memories from the visit to the morgue that morning weren't needed, nor had he summoned them. Some things just stayed with you awhile. He would have to just add this one to the stack of nightmares from past cases.

The detective had said they'd found a wallet in the jeans left behind in the rail car and so this body had a name, Albert Simms. One thing Bill was sure of, the guy had paid a high price for whatever he'd done in life. He tried calculating in his own head. Would he have wanted a blowtorch or a knife used on him? What a bizarre decision to have to make.

After what he'd seen in the morning, Bill was thinking that the knife was probably worst. It had taken something out of him to witness the damage. In police work you got a bad case every once in a while, you didn't usually get mutilated bodies one after another. Your mind could only deal with so much at a time. No wonder war vets had problems. The non-stop horror in those situations would grind you down.

Since the body had been lying down when he saw it, some of the skin flaps that had originally been hanging downwards had actually flipped back into place. But most of them had been hanging open, hardened with rigor mortis. In some spots you could see clear down to the bone where the knife had carved away the muscle and meat. In other places the wounds were flayed open until you could see the veins and layers of cut muscle.

Out of habit Bill started counting the wounds, stopping at forty. There were too many. They went up the front of the legs and chest, down the back and into the meat of the calves. Little ones crisscrossed down the sides and insides of the legs and arms. No doubt a bleed-out. Christ, it would have been a bloody mess.

"Okay detective, how about a ride back?" Bill wasn't sure what he was doing next, but he did have two confirmed tattoos, and he had two bodies.

As they left the rail yard, both their phones started ringing. Turned out all the station equipment hurt the phone reception. People had been trying to get a hold of both of them.

"Dewton."

"Detective Roberts, Topeka, Kansas. Good day there."

"Hello, what can I do for you?" Bill wasn't sure where this was heading.

"Well, we got some bodies up here. Your alert in the system about tattoos and rail lines came up. I figured you might help us solve this thing here."

"Do you mind telling me what's happened?"

"Shit no. We got a boxcar full of burned bodies. Looks like someone chained the door and then poured gasoline over the boxcar and set her up in flames."

"Jesus." Bill was shocked.

"You can say that again. Anyways, one victim who died of smoke inhalation was only partially burnt. He has a number three tattooed on his inside wrist. That what you're looking for?"

"You got it." Now he knew where he was going next.

It took a few minutes to catch the caller up to speed. Then they made arrangements on where Bill could get a hold of him.

"You should know. The other vics had tattoos as well, but we can't make anything out of the mess that's left."

After closing out the call Bill turned to the detective. "Think I can get a ride to the airport and have your guys take care of my rental car?"

"Sure Bill, no problem."

On the way to the airport he reviewed his notes. Things were happening too fast. Suddenly bodies were dropping hard. Another low one, this time number three. He felt like he was running behind and needed to get caught up. As he thought about it, he realized he needed a live gangster to talk to and made a mental note to add that to his search criteria.

He wondered what Kansas was like. He'd never been there.

*****

Amarillo, Texas

It was early evening as the freight train slowed for Amarillo. Bart and Danny hung precariously off either side of the train watching the sights while acting as lookouts.

When they slowed further, Bart realized they were stopping and really started paying attention to their surroundings. Carefully he examined the run-down buildings separated from the track by a battered fence.

The train was still rolling when he noticed a figure slouched against the fence. The guy on the ground looked drunk or high. The train finally stopped about a hundred yards past the guy. He turned to Danny, "Better keep an eye out. There's some guy back there leaning against the fence. Looks drunk."

Danny moved around to look out the other side, nodding, and went back to watch his own side.

Ten, twenty minutes later Bart stood up straight, his adrenaline starting to surge, "Shit, we got company." He wasn't sure what to do.

He could see three young guys walking up the track, they must have stepped through the fence somewhere near the back of the train. Now they were almost even with the guy passed out against the fence. Bart wasn't sure what to expect and jumped slightly when one of them gave the drunk against the fence a vicious kick.

The drunk startled awake and looked up at the three with his head cocked to the side. Bart couldn't hear the words, but the voices sounded threatening. Then the three closed in, encircling the guy. He suddenly felt his own anger rising, "Aw, don't do that. The poor guy's hammered."

Danny tried to push in beside him. The gang was throwing the odd kick and punch. The kid rubbed his sweaty palms together.

"I can't watch this happen. Those fuckers aren't that big and there's only three of them." Bart jumped off the train car and headed back up the track before Danny could stop him.

Bart had been drunk and alone once when some jocks had pushed him around and given him a few bruises. He wasn't going let it happen to this guy. He started to run, picking up speed, hitting the three guys from behind. They didn't even hear him coming.

With both arms out, he clotheslined the heads on the left and right, and body slammed the middle one. Bodies bounced off the fence. Bart used the element of surprise to his advantage. Coming up swinging, he clocked the one on the left good. The guy went over backwards just as he'd been trying to get up.

Danny stood frozen, watching while Bart landed another good shot, then the third guy grabbed him from behind. While he was held in place, one of them got up and drove his fist into Bart's face.

When two more came running out of nowhere to join the scrap, things changed. Bart was fighting a losing battle, even as he got the guy off his back. There were three of them in good shape, and the one on the ground that was pissed and bleeding. The first one was still out cold.

They backed off, forming a semi-circle. The only thing moving was the drunk, as he crawled away from the forest of legs surrounding him. The troublemakers focused on their new target.

"Hey, assholes," Danny strode towards the group with his hands held out at his sides.

The distraction was all Bart needed and he swung at the nearest thug. The others backed up a second and spit their force. Two went at Bart, while two attempted to intercept Danny.

Never a fighter, instead of squaring off and looking for an opening, Danny walked right up to the first one and reached for his head with both hands.

Out of the corner of his eye Bart saw the guy let go with a punch that caught Danny square in the face. The blow seemed to just bounce off. His partner now had the thug's head firmly in his grasp, pushing backwards, using his own momentum until the guy went right over.

Danny followed the guy to the ground, hands wrapped in fistfuls of wiry hair. When Bart got another chance to look, Danny was smashing the guy's head into the gravel. Once, twice, three times. Then the thug's buddy tackled Danny, knocking him away from his unconscious partner.

As he rolled and tumbled with his new opponent, Danny managed to get ahold of an arm. When they stopped rolling, he twisted and turned the arm at an impossible angle. The guy screamed and Danny took the arm another six inches until he heard a snap. He let go quickly, and the arm hung at an unnatural angle, twisted and contorted.

Bart had one of his attackers down, the other was kicking at him. Approaching from the rear, Danny kicked the attacker hard in the back of the leg, as the guy folded backwards he grabbed two handfuls of hair.

The closest immovable objects were the round metal fence posts. Danny swung the guy's head sideways. The first attempt drove his victim's head into the fence post, then a second, and third, hollow tone rung out as the guy went limp and Danny dropped him to the ground.

"Shit man, you're an animal." Bart watched his buddy start to shake.

"What do you mean?" Danny wasn't sure of anything at that moment.

"You beat those guys stupid man. Wow." Bart really was impressed.

"I don't know how to fight. I just knew I had to help." Danny looked around at the crumpled bodies, the grubby bum, the leaning fence, he was lost for a moment.

"Sure, you don't know how to fight. Sure." Bart laughed.

The sound of shuffling on the gravel made them turn. The drunk was a little more with it, lifting his hand. "Thanks guys. Fucking assholes."

Bart assumed he meant the attackers. "No problem. We thought you needed a hand."

"Where you going?" The bum looked up at them through squinting eyes.

"We're on this train, so we're probably moving shortly." Bart looked up and down the track.

"No. Trains sit here all night. They load in the morning and then head out. See it all the time."

Bart didn't know what to say to that. It looked like they were stopped for the night. "Fuck, that sucks."

"You guys need anything? Booze, Pot? I can help you out there. I owe you that."

Danny shook his head, but Bart was all in. "We could use a few joints for the road, and I'd like a beer." Then he looked back at the train, "but we don't want to go far from the track."

"It's okay." The guy struggled off his ass and wobbled towards the back of the train, "It's not far, just over this way."

They let the guy walk ahead of them a bit to see if he was actually going somewhere. When it seemed he was, Bart looked at Danny and raised his shoulders in question.

"I'm not sure, what about out stuff?" Danny asked.

"Let's throw it under that tree on the side of the track in case the train leaves. We won't have to carry it."

Quickly, Danny climbed up into the locomotive and rustled up Bart's bag and his suitcase. Placing them against the fence, they ran to catch up to the swerving drunk who was using the fence to help himself walk.

*****

Texas

Sam Dorson was in a foul mood. The train must be having some kind of problem. It had pulled onto a siding in the middle of the afternoon, and they were still sitting there as it became dark. And they couldn't just jump on another one flying by on the main line.

He figured he and the boys were stuck until the train was fixed or someone decided they were ready to move again. Sam kicked his foot at a rock on the sidehill and looked around at the others sitting or lying in and around the boulders.

This hadn't happened before, not in the ten years that he had been on the rails. Shitty luck. It would have to happen out here at night with nothing around. That wasn't what was pissing him off the most though, he kept thinking back to the women they'd lost in Eagle Pass.

Imagine the time he'd be having now. Stopped here on a beautiful night with three young ones. That would have passed the time quite nicely. He kicked another rock, harder.

If there was anything that kept him going, it was the thought of what was going to happen to the next woman that they did get their hands on. Well, first it would be his hands, then the boys would get their chance. He didn't know who it was going to be, just he was going to enjoy it.

Sam kicked a third rock, this time with a slight smile playing on the corner of his mouth. He was a patient guy, there would be another one. Shortly, he hoped. Patience did have its limits.

El Paso has always been good to him, he just needed to get there.

*****

Las Vegas, Nevada

The sounds of the casino's nightlife all merged together in a pounding rhythm. Lights twirled on the ceilings, different colors flashing out in sequence. The sirens and bells of the slot machines rang out. You could just stand there and be entertained.

Bobby was out tonight for one thing only. Women. He usually gambled in the mornings, there were fewer people in the place. When he felt like some tang, he would go out at night, drop some cash and take his pick. *Hey, somebody had to do it.*

These days he had a lot of friends in the clubs and casinos. He tipped well. That, he'd found, got him attention and service, two things he liked. With a little extra to spend, from the dues paid by his crew, he was feeling good and ready to try some black jack.

But he wasn't in a hurry. He chatted with the waitresses and slapped a few friends on their backs. He would gamble a bit first, but at some point tonight he'd get down to business.

A woman walked by wearing a tight little leopard print dress that stopped well above her knees, a set of long lean legs led his eyes to the matching four-inch heels. Who cared, because it sure looked good.

Another woman, one he knew, walked up and put her arm around his waist, "Hi handsome, looking for some fun tonight?"

He was, but not with her. He wanted something new. But he liked having something ready to go just in case, "Not tonight sexy, but we do have to get out sometime."

"You know where to find me." She smiled as she slid away, disappearing into the crowd.

He laughed out loud, he sure did. Then the lure of the table started to pull at him and he aimed for the green felt. He was hearing the dealer's voice before he even got there, "The man scores a twenty-one." Bobby smiled as he pulled out a chair and put his chips on the table.

CHAPTER 10

Salt Lake, Utah

Locomotive number 65652 pulling thirty-five freight cars neared the outskirts of Salt Lake. Cliffy was thinking about sitting on the deck with his feet up on the railing, watching the sunset. Then his cell phone rang.

For a second he looked at the thing like it was a foreign object. His elation at being home was soon swallowed up. He didn't even want to answer it. Somehow he knew this was bad news. Real bad. "Number one."

"Ah, yeah, boss, sixty-two here. We got problems," said a shaky voice.

Cliff stalled long enough to pull out his book and flip through until he found number sixty-two. Brent Coney. Cliff had never heard of the guy. Expansion could be a bitch and now he had to deal with it. "What's going on Brent?"

"Ah, someone locked the crew in a boxcar." He hesitated. "Then they lit the thing up with gasoline."

"What?" Cliff's mouth reacted before his brain could think.

"They were burned alive inside the boxcar. It's all over the news and everything."

Jesus Christ. He looked around his boxcar and tried to imagine. Then it dawned on him, "Who was in the car?"

"Sorry, Sir. Number three for sure, and maybe four others."

He couldn't believe Dougie was gone. They'd been together since the beginning. With Albert down as well, that meant the gang was down to three of the original five. This was crazy. Cliff had been on the road for almost three days now, he was tired and his reactions were slower than he would have liked. He took a second before deciding what to do.

"Okay, Where did it happen and where is the rest of the crew?"

"Between Kansas and Topeka. We're all at Doug's place holing up until we could get ahold of someone."

Cliff knew where the house was. "I'll be there soon as I can, probably tomorrow afternoon. I'm leaving Salt Lake now."

The train hadn't even pulled into Salt Lake and he was already thinking about where he had to be to catch the eastbound. Now he had to get to Des Moines, which is exactly where he'd been heading three days ago when this all started.

Cliff was angry at having to change his plans again. Firmly, he pushed aside random images of the inside of a burning boxcar that were trying to invade his brain. He couldn't imagine burning alive, but then he couldn't imagine the torture that the other two guys had gone through either. None of it was making any sense.

No fucking sense at all.

*****

Reno, Nevada

Sarah steeled herself for the next five minutes. The cleaning lady was about to do her room. In other words, the old bag was going to walk in and walk right back out. She never did a thing.

She would point out items of concern, the dirt on the window or the dust in the corners, but the woman never listened. The cleaner knew Sarah would keep the place clean. All she ever did was walk a broom from the door to the window and back, spraying some air freshener on the way out.

There was no use saying anything. She had tried that, and the old bag had a vicious mouth. She'd warned Sarah to mind her business and not report a thing. So she kept quiet.

She waited until the door slammed shut and then leaned her head back in the chair. Concentrating, she forced herself to stop shaking. Starting with her head and shoulders, then the rest of her body, she focused until her feet finally settled on the floor.

Her patience was shot. She looked back at the bed, she didn't need to get the silk handkerchief out again, just knowing it was there was enough. For the first time in a long time her mind was thinking about the future, and she realized that this place wasn't part of it.

All the little things were standing out clearly now as she took a series of deep breaths to relax. With her eyes closed she could see the flower, as if she was holding in front of her face.

She wasn't seeing the softness, or the way the petals rippled and curved. Her mind was seeing the meaning behind the object. The implications were enormous, the hope it brought was intoxicating.

Sarah moved past her anger at the hired help, looking at the endless possibilities that lay ahead. She was starting to feel alive.

*****

Amarillo, Texas

The drunk continued to lead them along the tracks, until they came to an intersection where two sets of tracks crossed over each other. One set went north/south, the other east/west.

The drunk turned and went along the other track until he came to an abandoned building set back from the rails. The place looked empty until the boys heard the music.

Danny slowed up a bit while he scanned the outside. He didn't have a choice but to follow when Bart and the drunk marched up the stairs. He was surprised to see so many people inside the building. A couple of girls and five guys sat around a picnic table. A small fire burning in a rusted barrel appeared to be for light more than anything else.

The group around the table looked at the newcomers suspiciously while they questioned the drunk. His story about being attacked and the help he got changed the mood in the room immediately. He told the group that Bart and Danny were there to buy.

"What you looking for?" One of the men at the table asked.

"We have about ten bucks and would like a few joints and a few beer if that's alright?" Bart took the lead.

"Hey man, no problem. You help Ricko here, we help you."

The guy put a six-pack on the table and a small pile of weed, at least enough for a few puffs. "Thanks a lot there buddy, Danny you want a beer?"

"Sure." Danny grabbed one and moved aside to take a drink. Idly he turned, looking around at the place they'd ended up in. The inside walls were sprayed with graffiti, like people had been hanging out here for years. The sofas and rugs probably come from a dumpster. Obviously this place had been in use for a while. A music system blasted, some rap he didn't recognize echoed through the hallways and empty rooms.

Danny caught a flicker of light from somewhere down a hall. There were other people in the place, lazily he wondered what was going on down there. He left Bart talking with the people at the table and casually followed the light towards the back of the building.

There was different music and the sound of more voices coming from that direction. Danny was curious, but he wasn't sure if he was allowed to just walk around anywhere he wanted. He looked over his shoulder and one of the guys at the table noticed him.

"Hey look, this one wants to see the needle boys." The guy waited while everyone turned to Danny, "Hey buddy, you don't want to see what's in there. But go ahead make your day." Then he laughed. "Make my day."

That was all the kid needed to hear, his feet started moving even though he wasn't sure what he was going to see. Pausing for a second to take a breath and prepare himself before the last step, he stood in the open doorway and looked in.

The dude on the end of the table moved quickly to cover his leg with a blanket. But the other two just sat there and looked at him defiantly while Danny sucked in his breath in shock.

He held the breath while he forced his brain to think. *Holy shit*. What the fuck was this?

Danny knew he was still holding his breath, but couldn't make his lungs open and close. This was the freakiest thing he'd ever seen. His stomach moved and he realized he might puke. His mouth was hanging open and it must have bothered one of them.

"Hey what the fuck you looking at? You got a problem?"

Danny finally let his first breath out and sucked in some new air. Blinking rapidly he tried to settle his pounding heart. "Sorry there buddy, I... I never seen anything like this before." He was lying, he was sure he knew what it was, but he never expected to see it in person.

He summoned up his courage. "Is this Krokodile?"

All three of the men in the room had patches of scaly brownish skin. Danny knew that was where the drug got its name, the user's skin started to look like crocodile skin. This was a drug that was ravaging Russia. He didn't know it had come to America.

They said the drug started killing you from the inside of the body at the injection sites and your flesh started to die from gangrene. These addicts were rotting from the inside out. When the disease finally hit the outside skin there was nothing left underneath and you could see right into the body. When the stuff was made in labs they took out the hard metals and left pure stuff behind. The problem was the homemade stuff still had the garbage and corrosive stuff inside because the street producers didn't have the labs and proper equipment to get it out. Then these guys shoot the crap right into their veins.

One of the men had an exposed sore on his arm, an open hole ran from his wrist to his elbow. Danny stared at the exposed bones surround by slabs of skin hanging off the dying area.

He felt light headed, he wasn't sure he could look much longer. He actually reached out to grip the doorframe for balance.

"Yeah, it's Krokodile. Have a good look kid. Learn a lesson." The guy with no forearm answered his question.

Danny had no doubts. He'd learned something. Humans were sick. How could you do that to your body when you could see what it was doing? Shit. They said that in Russia most people starting on the drug were dead within two years. He was close to hyperventilating and not sure where to look next.

The third guy with the blanket helped him decide as he pulled back the cover to expose his leg. Danny yelled out as he jumped in shock, "Holy fuck!"

Bart heard him and came running down the hallway. He stopped by the door and looked in around his buddy.

"What the fuck is going on here?" Bart looked around, "I said. What the fuck is going on?"

Danny took a second to explain how Krokodile was made and what it did to the users.

Bart kept his hand on the doorsill as he was locked in a stare he couldn't seem to break.

These guys were walking zombies. What other name was there for it? They were half dead. Alive and dead at the same time. Bart looked like his stomach and brain weren't co-operating.

"Sorry to bother you man." Bart stumbled away from the door swallowing hard then taking a long haul from his beer. Danny backed up and nodded to the three guys before he turned to follow. *Had he really just seen that?*

When Bart looked back, Danny swigged the rest of his beer and nodded towards the door. He was getting out of this place as soon as he could. What a crazy nuthouse. You could get killed in more ways than one in this world.

Bart thanked the guys in the front room for the stuff, and shook the appreciative drunk's hand again, and the two of them stepped outside.

The fresh air helped Danny clear his head as they started walking along the tracks.

As they watched a slow moving train leaving the yard, Danny noticed Bart's arm raised in the air, and realized he was waving at someone on the train.

*****

Amarillo, Texas

Maria had finally fallen asleep. Raul leaned out and watched the yard go by as he let the night breeze wash over his face. They were moving slow, almost out of town.

He was getting close to home. He could feel it in the hot dry air. It smelled like home. From Amarillo it would be a straight run down to El Paso and the border. Raul was feeling more confident the closer he got. He was getting into his old stomping grounds.

He should call ahead, but he preferred keeping things to himself as long as possible, that was how you stayed alive. He decided he would call from El Paso and get someone to pick them up. Things were going okay so far and Maria was holding up surprisingly well.

The trip was a pain in the ass for her, but as far as he was concerned she was showing her worth. Obviously she could suck it up and do it the hard way if it came to that. He knew he was going to give her the good life, but he liked knowing she could cope if necessary.

The train banged and rattled over some kind of bump. Then, as he stood there watching, the train went through an intersection, clanging over the other rails.

If he'd been sitting down he wouldn't have seen them. He froze as he stared at a pair of young guys standing alongside another set of rails. They watched the train go by. One of them seemed to notice him. So for some reason he raised his hand in salute as he drifted by. An arm lifted in response and held there. Raul watched them until they were out of sight.

Finally the train started to pick up speed as the edge of town appeared. There were a lot of people around the tracks these days. He smiled as he looked up at the stars. "Mexico, here I come."

*****

Las Vegas, Nevada

No one would've noticed the dark figure in the alleyway. Standing patiently in the shadows he blended in while waiting for the woman to arrive. He'd selected her carefully on an earlier scouting trip. She was desperate and she was disposable.

The smell of the alley was bad. Vegas was all shine and glitter on the main street, but don't step into the shadows or walk along the back alleys.

Before she entered, the woman hesitated at the alley entrance. When she was close to his hiding place he stepped out of the shadows, making her jump.

"It's okay, it's me." He tried to ease her concern.

"Why we have to meet here? Christ, it's disgusting." The woman was attractive, new to the game and yet to show the effects of years on the street.

"You want this money?" He pulled an envelope from inside his jacket.

That changed her tune, quickly she became more interested and willing to listen.

"Okay then, this is what I need you to do."

*****

Topeka, Kansas

Bill contemplated the detective's disorganized desk. He wasn't going to visit the morgue this time, been there and done that with burn victims. He waited for the file folder to land on the desk. He'd asked ahead of time for pictures of the tattoo. He leaned back and studied the photo. Obviously, he had another one.

The three was a little larger than the other numbers he'd seen, but it was just as crudely done. This gang was either the most unlucky group of guys, or they were in some kind of war. From Bill's point of view it appeared they were losing.

He spent the better part of an hour bringing the detective up to speed. He didn't have much, but fed him everything he knew. "I'd just like a live body to talk to. These corpses aren't helping much."

"You still think you can find her?" The cop asked with a careful tone.

Bill looked down at his hands that were spread palms up on his knees. "No I don't," his eyes watered a little. "But I have to keep trying."

"Okay, what next?"

"What do you know about the bodies?" He didn't know exactly what he needed, so he would have to settle for collecting as much information as possible and sorting through it later.

"Not much. Like I told you, it was ugly. The papers managed to grab a photo of the only guy who wasn't too burnt. We got a call from family. They ID'd the vic as Douglas J. Rackman."

"So we've got names for two out of the seven guys I've seen in the last couple days. Not good, but something." He took a second to gather his thoughts. While on the plane Bill had been thinking hard about those five who burned in the boxcar. What next? "Can you get me access to a computer, or someone to do some searches for me?"

"Sure."

Standing behind the department's civilian clerk, Bill and the detective watched her do a variety of searches. He had an idea, "Can you run Rackman's name?"

"We already did that," the detective answered, "he's got a short record from way back, but not much else."

"Look for family members and known associates." He waited for the woman to finish the search. They all scanned the list that appeared.

Bill pointed at the screen, "There we go. He's got a brother, Bobby. Run him please."

The screen changed again and a picture of Bobby Rackman appeared. He didn't have much of a record either, mostly stuff from the past and one arrest for aggravated assault three years ago. Bingo.

Any arrests in the last fifteen years had to include photos of tattoos. "Check the brother for tattoos."

Three. Crossed axes on his right shoulder. Twisted barbwire around the left bicep and more importantly, a number four on the inside of his left wrist. "Blow up the wrist shot if you can."

The picture got bigger, but the tattoo didn't look any better. Christ, did they make them with the sharp end of a coat hanger? The thing was ugly, but the number was clear.

His blood was pumping now. He was on the trail. The juices were flowing and he felt like he was catching up for the first time. Now he should be able to get ahead of the game. This Bobby was in danger. He had to be one of the targets. If the numbers started at one he obviously was high up in the gang.

That last arrest had been in Vegas, "He still live in Vegas?"

A minute later, and on another website, the woman had his answer. "Says here he has a house there. So I expect that yes, he is there."

"You better get on the phone to someone down there," Bill told the detective. "I'm heading to the airport. This is my chance to get ahead of it."

"Good luck Bill."

*****

Las Vegas, Nevada

"Yes sir!" Bobby slapped the table. The dealer busted and he scored on all three hands he had been playing. Tonight he couldn't miss. From the looks of the pile of chips sitting in front of him, he was up an easy five grand.

While the dealer reshuffled the cards he looked around and there she was again. To his surprise she was leaning against the bar, staring his way. Then she smiled and turned slightly to show off some ass. And what an ass it was.

He had noticed her floating past just out of his line of vision while he'd been playing earlier. Last time he'd looked up to see her walk away into the crowd, this time she was standing still.

Maybe this time she was looking him over. Bobby liked it. She arched her back a little. Showing off now. She was definitely his type. Her short red halter dress was nice and tight, the ties behind her neck left most of her back bare and showed lots of cleavage in the front.

He wasn't admiring the dress, his eyes were just rolling over the curves that went on forever. She was nice rolling hills from the calves, up the thighs, across the ass and into the hollow of her back.

Pushing some chips into the pot, he looked back up to find she wasn't standing at the bar anymore. *Damn.* That was the one. He could feel it. He looked around a bit but didn't see her. He lost the hand and refocused on the cards again.

At some point he'd had enough. Even when you're winning, if you do it enough, you can get tired of it. Just over seven grand was a nice night. Gathering up his chips, he stood up to leave, stretching a kink out of his back. As he turned he came face to face with the woman.

There she was, inches away. She must have been standing behind him, watching over his shoulder. Bobby felt a charge run through him. She wanted it as much as he did, he could tell by the glaze in her eyes. Her perfume reminded him of somewhere or something captivating he couldn't place.

"Hey baby, what's your name?" He flashed his best Irish smile and tilted his head sideways.

"Roxy."

Bobby put his arm around the hot piece, guiding her away from the table. The bar would be better. He ordered a couple drinks each and slammed the first one back.

"Am I ever glad I ran into you tonight. What's your plans?"

She raised her eyebrows and moved in a little closer. "I'm looking to find me a stud and get the hell out of this place."

Bobby had no problem with her rubbing against him. He loved it when it happened so easy. It wasn't the first time. He just let them know his intentions and they either went with it or didn't. "Well, I say we finish these drinks and get the hell out of here."

They walked arm in arm under the brilliant lights that turned the strip into permanent daylight. His hand riding on a rounded firm back end gave a little squeeze. He laughed to himself, he had this cat by the ass.

"Where we going?" The woman looked up.

"My place baby, that alright?" Bobby was all one-track mind at this point.

"It's nice outside tonight. We should do something wild." There was a look of mischief on her face.

"Where we going sexy?" He was intrigued and excited at the same time.

She seemed to ponder, then excitement flashed across her face, "I like trains. Can we find some trains?"

Bobby couldn't believe it. Trains? Shit, he knew them inside out. "Sure baby, this way."

At the next corner they made a left and headed to his old stomping grounds, the freight yards.

CHAPTER 11

El Paso, Texas

Raul leaned out the side of the grain car, trying to see what was ahead of the train. It had been slowing down steadily for the last ten minutes. He was on full alert as they entered the outskirts of El Paso. Even though he was close to home, this was the heavy zone. He and Maria would encounter a lot more border patrols and police from here on in.

He wasn't really worried, he had well-established routes across the border. Crossing here was an option, but he knew the layout of the border better closer to Arizona and it was a quick train ride west to get there.

Having been through here before, he knew they needed to get off on this side of town and he directed Maria to get her stuff together. If they were jumping off, it had to be done before the train stopped.

Maria had everything together except the large tarp, "What do I do with this?"

"Tuck it under the grating, someone else will find it. We're almost there."

When he spotted the trains parked on the siding, he knew they were at the yard. He checked either side of the car and picked the side with gravel dissolving into grass instead of the wide patch of gravel roadway on the other side.

"Come on Maria, jump here." He grabbed her arm and helped her down on the metal steps beside him.

"I can't jump off the train, its still moving." Maria pulled back against his pressure on her arm.

Raul couldn't debate it. *Jesus, woman.* He pulled a last time and she relented, stepping down just in time for Raul to push her off the moving train.

Maria shrieked as she left the platform. Then her feet hit the ground, and since she wasn't ready, both feet bent at the ankles and she fell forward. Her body made it halfway across the gravel and onto the grass. She slammed down hard and bounced into a roll.

Raul jumped with the bag, his feet moving before they hit the ground. He stumbled slightly but his feet caught up to his momentum and he was suddenly running. He put the brakes on and headed back towards Maria as she stopped rolling. Reaching down, he grabbed her by the arms and pulled her to her feet.

"You pushed me." Maria sounded hurt as she rubbed her shoulder.

"I was just helping you take the first step. We didn't have time."

"You pushed me off the damned train." She stood there with her arms crossed, her bottom lip stuck out. She looked pissed.

Raul threw the bag over his shoulder and curved his arm around Maria's waist, urging her forward. "Okay sexy. Sorry I was so rough. Let's get out of here."

Reluctantly she started to walk with him. "Where are we? Where are we going now?"

"We're almost there baby, one more small train ride and we cross into Mexico."

He felt her stiffen under his arm, she wasn't impressed with another train ride. To be honest, he wasn't either, but that's the way it was. Raul led her around behind an abandoned warehouse as he angled along the side of the yard, looking for the westbound tracks.

Finally he came to a long train pointed in the right direction. These trains on the southern rails were long. There weren't many stops between Florida, Texas, New Mexico, and Arizona so the trains that took the route were heavily loaded, and with the land mostly flat, the rail companies could extend the number of cars.

Raul started walking west, looking for the right car to get on. There were boxcars ahead that would be better than the storage containers they were currently walking past. "Come on Maria, just a little farther. Those boxcars up there will be comfortable to sit in.

*****

Las Vegas, Nevada

Bobby walked alongside the train, pulling Roxy by the hand he gently pinned her against the side of the car.

"No. Not here. I want somewhere nice." She grinned up at him before pushing him off and heading further down the track.

Bobby found a few more spots, but the broad didn't like them either. It was like she was looking for something. He didn't know he was right. The large orange florescent x spray-painted on the building was the mark she was seeking.

The woman turned from the odd artwork towards the train and saw an open boxcar. "This looks like a good spot big boy." She leaned against the doorsill of the car.

It was about time. He nestled up to her as she tilted her head back. Fuck, she smelled good. He lowered his lips to hers and ran his hands around her hips, gripping her ass through the tight red dress.

She reached down and took his crotch in her hand, squeezing and running her fingers back and forth. She used her body to turn him until he was now leaning back against the car, the doorsill running across the middle of his back.

Bobby wanted to get her up into the car, it would be a little more comfortable there, but she started to go down to her knees and he held off. She settled on the ground, opening his pants. Bobby was getting harder, "Yes baby, right there."

She didn't answer, just reached in and took him out of his pants. Her touch felt electric and he felt himself spring further to attention. She stroked him with her hand before leaning forward to take him in her mouth.

Bobby closed his eyes and leaned back, "Oh baby, I like that." He concentrated on the feeling of her mouth. With his hands in her hair, he started to slowly rock back and forth against her. He moaned. It felt so good. He was about to moan a second time when he felt something slip around his neck and pull tight. He had a second to think of an ambush before his body reacted. He kicked forward, knocking the woman to the ground.

Bobby's hands grabbed at the rope around his neck. He had it, but couldn't do anything. He was pinned against the ledge of the boxcar, bent over backwards. As he struggled with the rope he saw the woman get up and back away. She didn't seem to want anything to do with helping him.

"You're good to go. Thanks." A quiet voice came from above Bobby's head. The woman nodded and fled down the rail yard.

Fucking bitch.

Now he fought harder, trying to wedge his arm between his body and the boxcar so he could turn around and see his attacker. He wanted a go at him, but the bastard had him pinned good. Worse yet, he was getting light-headed from the lack of oxygen and knew he was going to pass out.

*****

Bobby woke to the rumble of a train. His brain was sluggish, but his vision confused him even more. He was looking at the stars in the night sky. Then the sound of the train seemed closer, so he struggled to look. Only his head wanted to move. Holding his head up, he looked down at his body and realized where he was. He screamed into the gag in his mouth.

Tied spread-eagled on the train tracks, he faced upwards with his spine strapped to the steel rail. He put his head back down on the rail while the stars stared back from above.

The sound again, closer still. Bobby brought his head up again. There it was, a train moving slowly through the yard. He tried desperately to figure what track it was on, swiveling his head left and right. He couldn't keep his head at that angle for long, reluctantly putting it back against the rail for a break.

Moments later he started to scream again. The fucking thing was coming right at him… Didn't the driver see him?

Bobby moved his head up and down trying to get someone's attention, anyone's.

The train was thirty yards away.

Twenty.

He fought to keep his head up, staring at the locomotive, trying to see the engineer, searching for a face in the window.

He couldn't know that the engineer had seen him, but couldn't identify the pile of rags alongside the rail.

Bobby didn't see the figure hiding beside a nearby building either.

He couldn't know it was the last second when the engineer recognized what he was looking at. But what could he do? You didn't stop these things on the dime.

All Bobby knew was the train was coming and he had to watch for some reason. He couldn't turn away. He looked up when it was yards away and watched the large front end of the steel monster coming. He thought he heard brakes, he did see wheels, and the last thing he knew was pain.

His brain had a second to register the impact… then there was nothing.

*****

El Paso, Texas

The trap was set. The friggin' train had finally started moving in the middle of the night and Sam and the boys were in El Paso by morning. They found a westbound freight on the next track with a long run of boxcars.

He'd had the crew jam rocks into the sliding door grooves on all the boxcars except one. Then they all climbed into the final car leaving the door slightly ajar, jamming it so it wouldn't open any further. It made it darker inside.

Sam had used this setup before. Anyone looking for a ride would try the doors on the other boxcars and end up at this one. They wouldn't be able to see inside the car and would climb in unsuspecting.

When one of the boys peeking out of the car said a couple had just come onto the track and were walking in their direction Sam got excited. "Get away from the door. Everyone get in the corners, stay quiet."

The stretch between El Paso and Phoenix was a long one. A woman to play with would be perfect. He didn't know what she would look like, probably not much he figured. They usually weren't. That didn't matter one bit to Sam. He liked the sense of control, he liked knowing he could do whatever he wanted, anything he could think of.

The people had to be getting close. Sam's heart pounded, his palms were wet. He closed his eyes, focusing, trying to listen for footsteps on the gravel, anything to indicate they were near.

The anticipation was excruciating. He felt his jeans bulge, how many times had he been in this situation. Knowing you were about to have a piece of ass you could do anything you wanted with, but not even knowing what she looked like. He pictured a bunch of women, different nationalities and sizes. What was this one going to be like?

The sound of feet on gravel caught his attention, he stared out of the dark corner, watching the silhouettes at the door as they stopped.

A grin played across Sam's face, maybe she was going to like it.

*****

Las Vegas, Nevada

The figure leaned against the wall killing time. He glanced at the slumped body of the woman he'd used as a lure laying behind him. The body wouldn't move, but he had to make sure. Mostly, he watched the limp body of the guy tied down on the track.

He straightened a bit as the guy woke up and realized his predicament. He knew the precise moment when the guy tied to the track realized the train was coming. The target looked frantic, but all he could move was his head, snapping it up to look around.

The hidden figure assumed the Raildog was trying to place the sound which was coming from everywhere in the dead of night. You wouldn't be sure where it was coming from until it showed itself. The light came first, sweeping ahead of the train, followed by the squealing of steel wheels on steel rails.

The figure looked from the train, to the body on the track, and back again. He watched the distance close. He thought he caught sight of the engineer rising off his seat, then he heard the brakes start to scrape and grind on the wheels. It didn't matter. It was way too late.

He watched the train roll towards the body and slice it in two. Not very neatly. Blood and guts exploded out, splattering across the rail yard while the bones were smashed and ground apart. A section of the body got hung up underneath the train and dragged along the track, but for the most part two pieces were left on each side of the rail.

Knowing the train was stopping, and that authorities would be on the way soon, the figure turned and bent over to pick up the slumped body. Turning behind the buildings, he stayed out of sight as he approached a different train facing south. He dragged the body into a corner of a boxcar and climbed back out.

With a sense of purpose, the figure marched down the yard until he found a train along the tracks pointing north. He had to keep moving. He needed to get to Salt Lake.

After riding the tracks a lot over the years and he knew the system like the back of his hand. He spotted his freight train, right on schedule it started jerking while the engine pulled the slack out of the linkages and the cars rolled forward. He jogged alongside and hopped aboard with ease. Looking back at Las Vegas, the last thing he saw as his train moved out into the darkness were the lights of the cop cars moving towards the station.

*****

Las Vegas, Nevada

Bill Dewton couldn't believe his damned luck. "What do you mean he's dead?"

The detective was almost apologetic. "We got the heads-up yesterday afternoon from Kansas. The guy was killed last night. What could we do?"

Bill was pissed. He'd done everything he could to get there ahead of things, but he was still running behind again. *Fuck.* "You guys seen the tattoo?"

"Yup, a number four, just like you said."

"Damn. This guy was my only hope at getting some fresh intel. I wanted to talk to him." Bill's face showed what he was feeling.

"I did get something for you though."

He perked up, his head came up to stare at the man, "What do you got?"

"A live body. Had the yard checked out, top to bottom, and we came up with another one of them. This guy is number thirty-six."

Bill leaned back smiling, his relief evident. He shook his head, laughing. "You were holding back on me. Where is he now?"

The detective smiled and got up from his chair. "He's waiting in interrogation four. Let's go."

Bill went in himself and spent the better part of an hour working the guy over. "One more time, tell me again."

"I told you everything man," his witness waved his arms in a big circle. "They have a square shaped territory, the sections run into each other forming the sides. That's the box man."

Bill kept at him, "How many in the gang?"

"I told you, I don't know. I've seen guys with tattoos as high as seventy. There could be more. Each section boss recruits his own crew, and they call the big boss who must keep track of the tattoo numbers. I don't know." The gangster was scared and willing to answer anything. The cops outside telling the witness he was the prime suspect didn't hurt one bit.

"You said they have houses?" Bill was trying to get at the money.

"All the bosses do. One on each section."

"Where's the money coming from?"

"I keep telling you. This gang is all about the money. That's what they do. We rob people on the trains. Sometimes they're travelling with lots of cash. We catch people and hold them while we clean out their bank accounts or credit cards. Everybody pays dues to the bosses every month."

Bill shook his head. Considering the time frame, ten years, maybe more – how much money had they made in that time?

When he had squeezed as much as he could out of the witness, Bill left him in the interrogation room. The locals would look after him now. He had to sit somewhere and think. This gang was big and had been around a while. Now suddenly they were going down like flies. Whoever was behind it had to know the gang well. The perpetrator obviously knew which boss held which section, and even though other members were getting killed in the same action, the perp seemed to be focusing on the low numbers.

He had taken down numbers three, four, and five. Bill figured he wouldn't want to be number one or two right now. He replayed the interrogation in his head. Albert Simms was number five, taking care of an offshoot that ran up to Spokane.

Bill scratched out the box on a sheet of paper he snagged off the side of a desk. If Simms was on a section stretching off of the box to the north, Bobby Rackman was on one side and his brother Doug on the other. That left the top of the box and the bottom. Which number was on which section?

He sat back in the chair. What now? He realized his daughter's case was slowly taking a back seat to this bigger puzzle, but he had to assume that solving the disappearing numbers game might get him the right answer in the end anyways.

What Bill needed to do was get to one of the two sections, either top or bottom, and try to get ahead of the action for once. He stepped over to a computer. He needed to check the sections and figure out where the stops were. He had to get in place before another lead died.

CHAPTER 12

Cheyenne, Wyoming

The sudden vibration of the cell phone broke through Cliffy's daydream. He rubbed the stubble on his face and realized he was probably getting dirty. Came with the territory, but still. Lately three days on the road felt like ten.

He lifted the phone to his ear like it was a nasty chore and took a breath before answering, "One here."

"Thirty-six, sir. We have a problem in Vegas." The deep voice was serious, to the point.

Cliff didn't need to hear any more. He leaned his head back against the rough wood. He knew what was coming. It had to be Bobby. He didn't want to know how, he knew it was going to be bad, "What's going on?" He decided to play it slow.

"Number four is dead boss. He was tied down to a rail line and a locomotive split him in two."

Cliff cringed. His hand pushed in on his gut, attempting to smother the uneasy feeling. He liked Bobby. They'd visited from time to time, drinking and spending some money at the casinos. Bobby was like him, not spending as much time on the rails these days. He was ready to give it up as well. He wouldn't be now.

"He didn't deserve that." Cliff didn't know what else to say.

"No, he sure didn't. We'll try and find the bastard that did it though." The voice was determined.

"Okay, I'll get back to you soon as I can." Cliff clicked off the phone and stared at it for a moment. *Good luck with that.*

With his back against the boxcar's wall, he sat opposite the open door watching the countryside whizz past and felt the energy draining out of every pore. His shoulders slumped and all of a sudden he felt old.

Did he want the fight? Was it worth it anymore? The better question was, was he still hungry for it? It was obviously a fight for the whole line. Cliff leaned his head back against the wooden wall as the train shook along the track.

The answer was no. He knew it and was just taking his time acknowledging it.

Cliff looked down at the cell phone, the only connection he had to the gang. His hands shook as a wave of anger flooded through him. He wanted to end things on his terms, not this way. Somebody forcing him out wasn't sitting well. But then, there was always a new dog on the block. He'd once been one.

Knowing he'd left this way was going to stick in his gut for a long time.

Cliff reached his arm up in the air and threw the cell phone out of the moving boxcar. His initial regret was quickly replaced with relief. He sighed and slumped forward, resigned to turning his back on the whole thing.

Everything seemed easier once he made the call. No more decisions to make. He'd get off in Cheyenne. It wasn't that far ahead. He could catch a quick freighter going back towards Salt Lake and get the fuck off the tracks.

As soon as he said it to himself, he knew it was over. Suddenly life on the tracks lost its appeal. He thought of the future and didn't see a freight car there at all. Just the sight of the valley spread out below his back deck.

It was strange how something he put so much time into for so many years could mean so little now.

It had been one hell of a ride. The gang had been going full steam for the last number of years, but it had been harder in the beginning. Trying to take over their sections and build up crews had taken a few years and there had been some close calls.

Running into other gangs when they didn't have the numbers required balls-to-the-wall guts, and the will to punish those who resisted. They had really wanted it, and that was usually enough to carry them through.

The original crew had been serious stuff. The Rackman brothers, Albert, Sam and himself. *Shit.* Cliff realized he should have called Sam before throwing away the phone. The guy at least deserved a warning.

Cliff saw images behind his eyelids, the past was spread out in brutal color, mostly red. Once they had tasted blood, there had been no turning back. He knew it was all a work of art. But it was time for a new canvas.

*****

Las Vegas, Nevada

Bill got out of the taxi near the train yard. He'd ditched the Vegas detective as soon as the guy mentioned phone calls from the FBI interested in a series of dead bodies in train yards. They were looking specifically for the guy who had set up the search criteria in the computer system.

For some reason Bill didn't want to be part of their circus. He'd seen that before. It was invigorating to be back on a case, but right now he didn't want to bother with the layers of bullshit that came with command structure. Fuck that.

What he wanted was to stay on this trail and get to the bottom of whoever was knocking off this gang. He couldn't get his daughter back, he was sure now that he'd missed that chance, but he could make sure the whole gang was down. That's what was driving him.

He was going back on the track. On one level it didn't make sense. Why not fly, or drive, to a section of the box and wait for someone to show up.

On the other hand, being on the ground, on the rails, put him in the middle of the action. He could run into other Raildogs, or he might help someone along the way. It was just like undercover, sometimes you had to get in there and get dirty.

No one would be able to trace him now. He walked towards the northbound freight train. That's where he wanted to go. Number one was supposed to be out of Salt Lake, he'd start there. He climbed up into a boxcar and sat down near the door. His breathing was steady and his eyes were alert. Bill smiled to himself, he was back in the game.

*****

Fort Worth, Texas

Neither of the boys slept much once they got out of Amarillo. Bart was horrified by what he'd seen. Forget about the assholes out to cause shit and pain that you had to watch out for. It was the needle using junkies that shook him to the core.

He'd spent the night muttering to himself. Was that real? Did he really see people with parts of their bodies hanging open, rotted off, and dying before his eyes? He wasn't sure if it was the open wounds or the bizarre calmness of the scene that threw him.

He'd looked over Danny's shoulder and saw the men playing cards. But it was the holes in the shoulder and arm of the card player that caught his attention. His eyes snapped back and forth between the gruesome sight and the cards until his brain couldn't sort either out.

How many people were on this drug? Bits of Zombie movies flashed through his mind. It was damned near the same thing. He shivered violently.

There was a change in Danny too. Actually, he didn't know the kid well enough to be sure it was a change. He watched him sitting on the edge of the car in the train's wind stream, his curly hair flapping and twirling.

He sensed Danny was more confident in some way. It was like the kid was coming out of his shell.

As the train slowed to enter the Fort Worth freight yards the cars started to bump and clang together. He got up to look outside.

They wanted to go straight through, continuing towards Houston, but the train slowed to a stop. Bart looked around slightly agitated, his fingers fiddled with the lighter in his pocket. He was starting to hate stops along the way. He just wanted to get to Florida, the quicker the better.

"You hear that?" Danny asked.

"What?" Bart turned his head.

"Some yelling coming from up there. Sounds like a fight." Danny leaned out as far as he could. "I don't see anything though."

Bart listened carefully, and sure enough, he could hear something. "Shit, I hope they're not coming this way."

Danny gave a strange look. There wasn't any fear on the kid's face. "We got to check it out."

"You crazy? I'm not going anywhere. The train might leave." Bart was scared as well, but wasn't about to admit that.

"Suit yourself," Danny jumped to the ground and started running down the side of the tracks. "Watch my stuff."

He was shocked. The shy kid was going into the night looking for trouble. What else could you call it? Bart sat down to wait.

Almost a half hour later he was beside himself. The train hadn't started to move and Danny hadn't come back. The yelling had stopped and that was about it.

Then Bart saw him coming out of the dark. Holy shit! The kid was covered in blood and he couldn't tell if it was his or someone else's. "What the hell happened?"

"I helped some guys in a fight." Danny had a shiner on the left eye and a cut above the other. His lip looked swollen.

"They were out numbered. Want to hand down my suitcase?" The kid stuck out his hand.

Confused, Bart grabbed the suitcase, handing it down, "What are you doing?" He didn't understand.

"I'm changing plans man, I'm going to join with these other guys." Danny looked him square in the eye.

"What other guys?" Bart couldn't relate, "You're leaving me?"

"I just helped two Raildogs fight against five really tough bastards. They were impressed and said I should meet their boss. They said I could become a Raildog." The kid was almost bouncing on the tips of his toes.

Bart was speechless. He had to be kidding right? "Why would you want to do that? Who the fuck are they?"

Danny shifted his weight from foot to foot. "There's over a hundred in their gang and nobody fucks with them. They got cool tattoos and they make all kinds of money. They do whatever they want. I want that."

Bart stared at him. He couldn't believe this was the same kid who left Billings in dress shoes. *Hey, do what you want.* He thought. *No big deal to me.* He didn't need anyone, and he sure as fuck didn't want anything to do with any gangbangers.

"Okay Danny, cool. Wish you luck man."

He was surprised when Danny came closer to the edge of the boxcar instead of leaving. He looked up at Bart intensely, "I need that hundred 'n fifty bucks you got."

"Fuck you. That's my money. You got your stuff, I got mine."

Danny's eyes closed to slits and he glared at him, "I told these guys you had some. They told me I got to take it to show them I'm serious about the gang. So don't make me hurt you. Cause I will."

Bart looked into Danny's eyes. He didn't know this guy, but he had seen him fight. The kid had been unfazed by pain and relentless at causing damage to those guys back in Amarillo. Bart knew he wouldn't win. More so, he was pretty sure he'd get hurt.

Danny cut through, "Bart! I want that money." The kid's face was getting hard as he grabbed the ledge of the car with both hands.

"Okay, okay." He fished out the cash. It was everything he had. "This is rude Danny, you're being an asshole."

The kid ripped the bills out of his hand, "Really Bart. They wanted to come down here and beat it out of you themselves. I told them we were friends and that if anyone was beating you, it was me."

Bart was beyond words at this point, he didn't know what to think. He pushed away from the edge of the car and out of Danny's reach.

He watched his short-time friend walk away into the dark. He wasn't as comfortable traveling by himself, but he wasn't turning back either. There had only ever been one destination and nothing had changed for him. When the train jerked into life and he knew he was getting out of Fort Worth, he stood at the edge of the car and watched.

As the train picked up a little speed and he felt safer, he yelled out at the top of his lungs, "Danny, you're a fucking asshole."

He wasn't sure if the kid heard him or not, but he felt better.

*****

El Paso, Texas

As Raul walked Maria along the track, he kept his eyes open, sweeping side to side. He wasn't taking any chances, looking under the cars at the other side of the train every ten paces or so.

They were almost to the line of boxcars when the train jerked a few times and started to come to life. The slow rolling started at the front, working down the train as each car began to move.

He looked back, making sure there was no one behind them, then took another glance under the cars. Sure that no one was around, he hustled Maria forward. "Come on woman, run. We need to get to those boxcars."

Looking ahead he could see that most of the doors were closed, but the one closest to them was open a crack. "Look inside Maria." Raul kept his eyes going, ensuring no one came up on them.

"Is it okay?" He kept pushing her.

Maria couldn't see in the dark boxcar as she walked beside the moving train. The floor in the vicinity of the door was lit up by the sun. She didn't see anything suspicious. "I think so."

Raul reached down and lifted her into the moving car. Then he threw in their shoulder bags. He climbed up to join her inside the door. Pausing, he tried to shove the door open wider, but it wouldn't budge.

Standing up straight, he took a breath as he waited for his eyes to adjust to the darkness. Then he saw something move. Instinct took over – he reached for Maria. He had her arm as he turned for the door.

He didn't care about the landing, just that they got off that train. Pulling her hard, he lunged out the opening. He was in mid-air when he felt her jerked out of his grip. Something had her and he knew he wasn't going to be able to hold on.

She was ripped from his hands as he flew through the air, and he twisted, trying to look back. Maria was screaming his name with a look of horror on her face, her arms stretched out towards him.

Raul saw the men holding her legs as he hit the ground hard. His back slammed into the dirt and he bounced into the air as he rolled over and over. He struggled to stop and look up at the train.

He stared at the guy hanging out of the boxcar. The big motherfucker had a smile on his face as he waved goodbye. Raul locked the image into memory. Then he pounded the ground with his fist and yelled.

He looked back up at the train in time to see two bodies jump off further up the line. He didn't hesitate, moving towards them while he pulled his phone out, "Come here you bastards."

*****

El Paso, Texas

Sam heard the man ask the woman to look inside. He watched her squint as she tried to focus. *Good luck honey.* She'd never see into the dark corners he was sure of that. Then the guy was lifting her up as she climbed into the boxcar.

Well, well, well.

She was priceless. Foxy and built to go. It was everything he could do to stay still. Sam watched the bags land beside the hot piece and then the guy climbed up.

Timing was everything. He nodded to his guys and two moved carefully along the back of the car. He watched the man try to push open the door before turning to focus on the interior.

Sam saw the moment the dude recognized that something was wrong. The man was wary and he'd seen something. He was lucky his men were already moving, because the guy grabbed the woman and jumped for the door.

Unfortunately for the couple, his men jumped at the same time. They grabbed onto a pair of sexy legs and the man had no chance, he'd already committed and made his move.

Sam jumped up, "Don't touch her."

He reached the door in time to see the man sprawled out on the ground. He had to make the call quickly. Would this guy call the cops? Sam didn't want the train stopped, he wanted lots of time with this one.

He ordered two of his guys off the train. "He doesn't make any phone calls to the cops."

The two leaped off the train and rolled into the passing ditch. When Sam was sure they were up and moving he closed the door the rest of the way and ordered the lights up.

The two lanterns brought the boxcar's interior to life. The woman huddled in the corner, half turned to the men gathered on the other side of the lanterns.

"Stand by the light sexy." Sam felt the power.

When she didn't move, he told her again. "Listen hottie, stand by the lantern or I'm going to let these guys loose, and you don't want that."

Sure enough, the woman moved away from the corner to stand beside the light. She crossed one arm in front of her chest while the other hand hung loosely by her side as she stood immobile.

Sam heard the whistles and rude comments beside him, but he was too engaged in taking her in.

"Oh baby, you are so good looking." He moved towards the lantern, grinning from ear to ear. "My, my."

*****

Salt Lake City, Utah

David Perez sat outside the post office. The package was already addressed to his mother in Reno. The cardboard box looked insignificant enough. He looked around while he sat there on the bench.

Salt Lake wasn't much different that any other city, this one seemed clean to him. That was one of its characteristics he supposed. He didn't care much for cities, over time he'd come to like the quiet of the countryside more.

He took the time to wrap the contents with care. First one and then the other. When he was sure the packages were well wrapped, he placed them carefully inside the box. Then he took out a piece of paper and the pen he'd borrowed from the post office.

David thought about the words carefully. This was important and he knew it was going to have an effect on his mother. He finally wrote the words and folded the piece of paper. Tucking it into the box he sealed the outside and walked back into the building to return the pen and tape.

He stood for a moment holding the box at the edge of the deposit slot, then he let it go. The box disappeared and he turned for the street. He'd give anything to see his mother's face when she opened it.

CHAPTER 13

Texas

Danny and the two Raildogs rode in silence. The adrenaline had long worn off and the dead of night gave them nothing to see. Danny was trying to deal with the stream of emotions tearing through him.

He felt on top of the world. The gang would give him power, something he never had. Deep inside he knew he had a lot of hate built up, and these guys were going to let him unload it. Even better they would back him up.

Running his tongue against the cut on the inside of his mouth he studied his travelling partners. The other two guys were older, but he had faired pretty well in the dust-up and helped them both out before it was done.

"Where we going now?" Danny didn't care, but still he wanted an idea.

"El Paso or Phoenix, wherever we run into Sam."

Danny looked down and visualized a number tattooed on his wrist. The thought psyched him up to the point he picked up a sliver of steel off the floor of the boxcar and started scratching into the skin of his wrist.

He'd make the box first, and when he was initiated into the gang he'd put the number inside the box. The little drips of blood didn't really register. He ignored the stream of red as he continued to jab at the skin.

Danny was separating out the images flooding through his head. The beatings from his father, the tormenting by his classmates and the satisfaction he felt from hitting people.

The last guy he'd pounded had been rewarding. With the guy pinned down, his anger had built. His fist slammed downward over and over, turning the face below into a bloody mess. His victim's expression had slowly changed. Danny saw the moment when the fear broke through, and then the pain registered.

That was taking control of things. Shit. He should have let go a long time ago. He turned to look off into the dark night. A big grin flashed across his face. Better late than never.

*****

Texas

Maria didn't dare step any closer to the lantern. They seemed happy with what they saw of her and she didn't want them seeing the fear that had to be pasted all over her face. She could feel her bottom lip vibrating as she fought back the tears. This looked bad. She was in real trouble.

The leader was a big bastard, just barely visible on the other side of the light. She couldn't be sure how much control he had over the others. She assumed she'd be on her back already without him.

She watched as he finally stepped forward. Reaching down for the backpacks, he threw them towards the other guys.

"Empty them out." He didn't take his eyes off her. She turned to look away.

Trying to think on her feet only reinforced the realization she was trapped. *Jesus, Raul where are you?*

The big guy slid one of the lanterns towards the other men in the corner. Now there was just the one small point of light near her feet. She watched out of the corner of her eye as he stepped closer.

"Look at me."

The voice was firm and clear. She turned her head to look at him. Carefully she kept her face neutral, staring at his nose instead of his eyes. Sensing the trembling just under the surface, she fought to keep herself steady.

"That's better. Where you from?"

He was close now. She could smell him. Her stomach revolted and she fought that urge as well. "New York."

He nodded. She didn't know why, but he seemed to like her answer. He picked up the lantern and moved in her direction. She backed up, trying to keep a distance between them.

"That's it sweetie, into the corner, just you and me."

She knew what was coming. She needed to keep her shit together and survive this.

That's what this was about now wasn't it?

Disgusted, she moved again, keeping step with his advance, until she backed into the wall.

He had set the lantern down and was closing the last gap between them when one of his men called out.

"Hey boss, check out these clothes."

He was so close she saw the flash of annoyance at the distraction. He hesitated slightly, before turning back to see what they were talking about. One of the men was holding up a dress in one hand and some high heels in the other.

"Look at this stuff. This is some sexy shit boss."

Maria felt her heart sink, Raul had only brought them along to please her. She had to stop thinking about him, he wasn't there to help and she needed to focus on what was happening right now.

The leader walked away to check out the find. She couldn't hear much, just a few words, "see her in it," and, "dancing." She didn't like the sound of any of it. Somewhere though a small voice said that if she was dancing she wasn't being raped.

He came back carrying the dress and heels, and she said a quick prayer of thanks. Someone was looking out for her.

"Put these on." The guy held out the dress and shoes. "Hurry up."

Maria reached out. This wasn't going to be her favorite dress any more. She held back the tears as she moved as far as she could into the corner. Being humiliated in front of strangers was hard, but it could be worse. She was afraid it probably would get a whole lot worse before it was done.

As she slipped out of the track pants and hoodie she could hear the buzz of excitement rising. The leader's voice stood out, "Do we have anything to drink?"

"I got a bottle of whiskey out of this pack." One of them held it up.

As she bent over to put on the shoes the first catcalls came, obviously they could see what she was doing. Done with the changeover she stalled, hanging in the corner, still trying to hide.

"Okay honey." She heard him again, "Why don't you give us a dance."

This was her chance and she knew it. She had to capitalize on this opportunity, get them watching and keep them focused on the distraction. She would delay as long as she could.

Maria danced in the clubs regularly. So what would be so different here? She knew men watched her in New York all the time. Now she needed to walk a fine line, distracting but not enticing.

Slowly she took a breath and tussled her hair, then reluctantly stepped closer to the lantern and tried to visualize strobe lights and a dance floor. The chorus of catcalls and hoots drowned out her mental image and she was reminded this was no club.

She had to make herself forget she was the entertainment, and try to take charge of the situation, but he wasn't making it easy.

"Gentlemen welcome to the show," he grabbed her arm and spun her to face the pack of toughs. "Tonight just for your pleasure we have the lovely Maria. She's come all the way from New York to treat you guys tonight."

The men laughed and called out as he picked up her lantern, dragging her and it to the center of the boxcar.

"No music sexy, but you go ahead anyways." He moved to the end of the line of men and leaned back against a pallet of boxes.

Maria let herself shake and tremble for a second. *Get it out now girl.*

She took another deep breath and strutted forward. Keeping her eyes mostly closed, she accentuating her motions, taking small steps. Slowly she made a small circle showing her ass and long legs, making sure to keep the lantern between them and her.

Carefully, she started to move to the music in her head, forcing herself to curve and bend in a more exaggerated way than normal. With her back to the men, she slowly opened her legs and bent over. Swinging her long hair around, she made a complete circle before straightening up.

She could hear them enjoying the show as she leaned her head back, her arms hanging down and her breasts pointed to the sky. Maria kept moving and running her hands over herself, wondering, how much was enough to keep them sitting still?

She wasn't sure how much time had passed, but quick glimpses told her the bottle was getting low, and she was worried about that. She was afraid that her only defense was to keep turning up the heat.

She moved slightly out of the light and then danced back in, her hands playing with the hem of her skirt. How far did she need to go? Every time they became restless she had to up the ante to keep their attention. How far did she dare to go?

She stopped dead, hip shot out to the side with one hand still holding her dress up to reveal some silk. She held the pose for a moment and slowly reached up to pull one of the straps off her shoulder. It fell down against her arm and the dress fell open a little to show a bit of breast.

The sudden scuffle of feet jarred her back to reality and she looked at the men. The leader had pushed off the skid. The others had gone quiet and she realized the show was over. Maria instinctively started to back away.

How long had it been? One hour? Two? She could only hope. She'd done everything she could to delay as long as possible. Again, she backed up until she hit the back wall of the rail car. He left the lantern in the middle of the car and moved quickly towards her. At least that left her end of the car in darkness.

She looked up at the big man as he stood right in front of her, pressing his body against her, using his hips to pin her against the wall. What could she do now?

*****

Texas

Raul yelled into the cell phone as he ran, aiming to intercept the gangsters that jumped off the train. "You stop that damned train Miguel. No excuses. Then you meet me at the freight yard in El Paso."

His feet pounded alongside the rails as he clicked off. The two guys who jumped off the train would think he was running scared. He stopped at the building closest to the track, they were in for a surprise.

There was a gap of fifteen feet between the track and cement foundation of the old loading dock. The bastards had to be close. Ducking around the corner, he looked around, searching for some kind of weapon. The knife in his pocket was only useful when he was in close.

The sound of running feet caught his attention. Raul braced against the corner of the building. Concentrating, he waited until the last second, until he judged the first guy was just about to clear the corner, then he swung the two-by-four like A-Rod swinging for the fences.

He wasn't taking the chance that his pursuer would deflect or stop the blow. Staying low, he aimed for the knees. The guy had just placed his foot, shifting his weight onto it as the lumber connected. The knee folded backwards and the guy screamed. His victim's momentum carried him forward as the hit spun him sideways and he fell to the ground.

Raul knew the second one would be a little better prepared, but he took his club all the way back anyways and swung low to start. As his attacker stuck his hands down anticipating the knee shot, the club changed direction and sliced upwards into an uppercut. With his hands down near his knees, Raul's attacker was leaning forward slightly and took the blow square to the neck.

The body lifted up off the ground as a loud crack rang out. The guy's head fell forward for a second, almost in slow motion, before snapping back to follow the body over backwards. He knew right away he'd hit the guy too hard. He hadn't planned to kill them, but it was too late for this one.

He scrambled around to look at the first guy who was still writhing in pain, his hands holding his leg gingerly to minimize the agony. It wouldn't help much, Raul could see where the jagged bone had torn through the grimy blue jeans, sticking bloody and white out the side of the leg. The guy was immersed in his own world of hurt until Raul slammed the lumber down on the other leg, connecting with the soft spot just above the knee.

Well, there was nothing fake about that scream. The guy had a hand on each leg as he looked up in terror, "Please man, don't hit me. Not again. Please."

"Who the fuck was that big guy with the jean jacket on the train." Raul didn't wait for answer, he drove the end of the wood down into the fingers clamped around the broken leg. This scream was followed by tears. The guy's hand was crooked; at least two fingers broken.

"Sam Dorson. He's the boss, his tattoo is number two."

"Where's he going?" Raul just raised the big stick in the air.

"Phoenix man, Phoenix." The guy's head swung down and hung against his chest like he was close to passing out.

This guy wasn't his target and hadn't done anything to Maria. It's the only reason he was going to keep breathing. Raul looked at the dead guy and back. "I'm going to get you on your feet and you're going to disappear. You understand?"

"Yeah." The guy was gasping.

Raul watched the guy hobble down the track before turning to deal with the body of his buddy. He couldn't leave him around for someone to find easily. Dragging the body along the side of the building, he found a pile of plastic to throw over it.

It was everything he could do to not start running after the train.

Shit, shit, shit.

He had to let his boys take it from here. If he was ever going to see her again that part of things was out of his hands. Fucking trains, why couldn't there be another train right away he could jump on?

Raul turned back down the track away from the fight scene and found another building with a loading dock to wait. Climbing up, he sat on the ledge. The anger boiling inside was threatening to explode. He really hated not being able to do something, anything. He didn't care what happened to him

"Fuck, I'm so sorry Maria."

*****

Texas

Sam leaned in, feeling the softness of her body against his. Jesus, was she hot. He hadn't believed it when she'd started dancing like that. She knew what was coming and she still put on a show. The way she'd looked at him made him so hard it was everything he could do to sit back and watch without jumping up and dragging her out of there.

Her body was out of this world. Shit, he hadn't had something that good in years. This one had the right stuff, and she knew it.

"Okay bitch, we're going to have a good time. Right?" He looked down at her. He liked the feeling of her pinned against the wall, his legs on either side of her hips, his dick digging into her belly. He leaned his head down near hers, "Answer me."

She turned her eyes upwards, "Yes."

He laughed loudly as his hands slid firmly up her sides, reaching to grasp her tits. He could feel the stiff resistance in every part of her body. This wasn't the same broad who was dancing in the middle of the boxcar a minute ago.

"Listen bitch, you perform or else I'll give them a shot at you." He stared down at her as she thought it through. He didn't know what she was thinking, but he could tell when she changed her attitude. More impressive to him, he could feel it.

She pushed off the wall and awkwardly leaned her tense body against his.

"That's more like it. Now turn around." She slowly rotated to face the wall. Sam loved the view, he liked his women bent over. "Hands on the wall."

He reached out and grabbed her ass, slapping it and squeezing its firmness. *Fucking beautiful.* Grabbing her dress, he yanked it halfway up her back, with his other hand he grabbed the silky panties and jerked them down around her knees.

Standing back, he admired his prize while he undid his belt buckle and lowered his fly. Usually he had to smack them around a little to really get ready, but this one already had him hard as he stepped between her legs.

What a piece.

He stood there for a while and let the train do the work. As the erratic shaking moved him back and forth he closed his eyes, holding her with one hand around her waist and the other fisted in her hair.

Sam finished and held himself there until he was soft. His heart slowed and his breathing eased.

Now that was everything he wanted, all in one package.

"That was special honey," He slapped her ass once more and stumbled back. The woman seemed to slump for a brief moment before standing up and leaning into the wall.

After that he needed air. Kicking the door jam away, he slid the boxcar door open a foot, letting the rushing wind dry the sweat on his face. Sam was surprised it was already dark, but then they had been on the train for a while. He idly scratched his armpit. He had to make a call about the broad. He could keep her for himself and have a few more goes at her, which is what he usually did. He also knew the guys were eager to get in on this one.

Sam stepped out on the ledge of the moving train, his fingers gripped the upper groove and his toes sought out the thin lower ledge while he shuffled along the outside to the end of the boxcar. Gripping the steel handrail and the corner frame, he swung around the end to stand between the cars. Fishing out a cigarette, he lit up.

He knew the crew wouldn't touch her without his say-so, and he had time to decide if he wanted her again. He pulled at the smoke and smiled, he already knew the answer.

She would be hunkered down inside there, terrified that his crew would be let loose. She should be. Sam was thinking about how much she'd been into it. He wondered how appreciative she'd be when he offered to do her again and keep those other assholes at bay.

He sure had it made. Sam was smiling as he flicked the cigarette butt out into the night. Then he noticed lights in the distance. A bunch of headlights? He felt the train buck as the brakes came on.

Not wasting time, he quickly moved along the outside of the cars towards the back of the train. He needed separation from the others. What was going on? Cops? That had never happened before.

Sam kept moving until he was near the end of the train. He thought about it and decided being up on top of a car would be safer when they stopped.

All he could see at the head end of the train was a bunch of lights blocking the line, and that scared the shit out of him.

*****

Salt Lake City, Utah

David Perez stalked between train cars, lurking in the dark where no one looked. He had gotten good at it. For ten years now he'd been riding the rails and hiding.

His first few years had been spent getting lost and trying to figure himself out. As he watched his mother sink deeper and deeper into depression, he'd become angrier and filled with revenge. When his mother crashed, he was left alone and decided he wanted to see the country.

It took two years before he ran into one of them again. That's when he bought a small brown book and started taking notes. He'd followed that first one for almost a year, keeping his distance, hiding and watching.

Eventually that one led him to the rest, and he took turns following each of them. If anyone knew the Raildogs, it was David. He knew the sections they worked, the trouble they caused, and he knew the bosses intimately.

Once he thought he had enough information and knew their schedules like clockwork, he took a few of the higher numbered ones out, ones he knew were way down the ladder. Quiet conversations away from the tracks in remote fields, or abandoned buildings, rounded out his knowledge.

Then David was left to think. What should he do? He spent another year mulling things over and testing some theories. It was a timing thing. Getting the logistics all sorted out had kept him awake many long nights.

He checked along the northbound lines and didn't see anything. He was working his way around the Salt Lake yard checking north lanes, then west, then south and finally east. When the circle was completed he'd start another. He wasn't missing the big boss. Everything was coming down to right now. This was it.

He alternated between incoming and outgoing lines. He didn't know where the guy was, just that this was his home base. He looked up, the sun was dropping, night would start taking hold soon. David needed to find him, it would be harder after dark.

The biggest problem he faced was getting around the country in a hurry. Once he summoned up the courage to ride on top of the passenger trains, he'd found his answer.

The gang stuck to the freight cars and that strategy had its limitations. When David decided to start this, he knew the whole campaign had to be completed quickly. None of his targets could get any warning.

He wanted to catch the passenger express leaving later for Phoenix. What he needed now was for this asshole to show up. He looked down, hopefully his homemade tattoo would do the job.

The first of the month was the best opportunity, and it had made finding the first targets easy. Now he had to hope the other two were still out there. A few more days and their routines became less structured. David could only count on them being in specific places at the beginning of the month, things became less certain as the days passed.

He watched as the westbound freight rolled towards the yard. Staying near a row of old buildings, he relied on the line of scrub brush to conceal his movements. He knew anyone riding the rails would get off before the train stopped, and sure enough someone jumped as the train passed the perimeter fence.

His heart was beating louder. Funny though, instead of fear, it was excitement that David felt. He forced a deep breath that kept him calm, and watched the guy approach. A distant glow from an overhead light was enough. He had his man.

He pushed out from the building and walked towards the newcomer. "Hey there. You number one?"

*****

Salt Lake City, Utah

Cliff stopped dead in his tracks. He looked the intruder up and down without recognition. Quickly, he glanced around suspiciously, when no one came rushing his way, he turned back to the stranger.

"What are you talking about?" Cliff squinted, snarling slightly. He was annoyed he'd been caught off guard.

"Hey, Sam sent me." The stranger moved his arm so the tattoo was visible, one hundred and one. It was ugly, but got the job done. "Shit is hitting the fan and he wanted to get you a message. He said no phones."

Cliff nodded. This one didn't need to know he'd thrown away the phone. He pulled out his little black book and checked the number. It wasn't in the book. The last number he had was ninety-nine. Cliff looked at the guy again, "Who gave you the tattoo, Sam?"

"Yes sir. I'm new, but he said it was important to find you, and he told me where to look."

The guy was huge, probably why Sam liked him. So Sam knew what was happening, which meant he knew about the others.

"He knows about Albert and the Rackmans?"

The guy nodded slowly, "Fucking crazy if you ask me."

Cliff relaxed a little and closed the ten-foot gap between them. "What's the message?"

The guy looked covertly around the yard, "Let's get out of the open. Someone's going to see us."

Turning quickly he headed for the train that had finally come to a stop. Cliff watched the guy climb up into the car, motioning for him to follow.

Made sense, they hid in the boxcars all the time. Something about the way the guy effortlessly climbed up into the car eroded the last of Cliffy's concerns. He was satisfied that this guy was comfortable around trains and must be a Raildog.

Cliff was reaching up to grip the ledge of the boxcar when the guy's hand came out of nowhere to assist. He grabbed ahold and felt himself pulled up into the train.

The sudden explosion of power that swung him around in a circle and slammed him into the interior wall wasn't expected. Cliff realized his mistake as his shoulder took the brunt of the impact. He should never have accepted the tattoo at face value.

He was the one that gave them out, they always called for the next number in line. *Idiot.*

The next thing he knew he was fighting for control. He slammed against the wall again. His opponent was strong as hell and was keeping him off balance. Cliff thought he had an opening, and let loose a looping right hook. Before it connected, he met an elbow and everything went black.

Breathing shallowly, Cliff examined the ceiling of the boxcar. The wooden floor bit into his shoulder blades. Confused and disorientated, he tried to move. Nothing happened.

Fuck no. Not like this.

He cursed. Hadn't he been doing the right thing? He had been trying to get away, to get off the tracks and not look back. How could this be happening?

Blinking, he tried to focus. Concentrating, he tried to move, and realized he had to have been drugged. His muscles were dead and nothing was responding. Only his eyes were moving, but that wasn't much help.

The lighting changed inside the car and Cliff heard the footsteps of someone moving around. Sliding his eyes toward the movement, he tracked the stranger as he came close.

"I see you're back with the living." The guy seemed to be enjoying some kind of joke. "At least for a while."

Cliff realized the joke was on him. As he tried to speak all that came out was a slurred babble. He couldn't even get his words straight.

"Don't bother," the stranger laughed. "When it wears off you'll have plenty of time to talk."

Kneeling down beside Cliff, the guy reached into a gym bag and started to take out rolls of material that looked like cotton bandage wraps. Something you would see at a hospital.

Cliff shook violently. He wasn't sure why.

A large bottle full of amber liquid came out of the bag next. Cliff strained to see what was happening. The guy was carefully soaking the rolls of material in the liquid. Cliff found he was beside himself in fear even though he didn't know what was coming. Then the voice was speaking to him in a deep and soothing baritone, and he began to tremble.

"I should explain what's happening here," a roll of soaked material was waved in front of his eyes. "This wrapping is being soaked in linseed oil. Nothing major."

When the guy laid the soaked material on his leg Cliff was shocked. Was he naked? He could feel the cold wet cloth against his skin. He struggled to look down at what was happening to him.

Fuck no. What's going on?

Cliff tried harder than ever to move. Still nothing happened. Forcing himself to look he realized the guy was using the material to wrap his feet and legs together.

"This is how they wrapped the pharaohs in Egypt," the stranger explained. "I'm not sure I'm following the exact procedures, but I think it's close enough."

Was that a good thing? He didn't think so. With his legs wrapped together tightly the guy kept rolling him, tilting his body left and right to keep the wrapping process going. Tears started seeping from under his eyelids, running down the sides of his face, as the guy trapped his arms against his waist and continued to wrap.

"I suppose you'd like to know why this is happening?" The guy didn't even look at Cliff as he continued his task.

Actually, he did want to know. He had to know why he was loosing everything. Why was he being tortured? That's what was happening here, right? He wasn't feeling any pain right now, but had a pretty good idea that this wouldn't end well.

"You need to think back to ten years ago." The voice had picked up an edge of anger.

Ten years ago? Shit, he'd done so much stuff in that time he wasn't sure he could even get back that far.

"You better remember it." A train pulling out of the yard drowned out part of the words, "…You five were all there."

Through rubbery lips Cliff tried blurting out a random catalogue of things he'd done to people over the years, in hopes of hitting the right one. He couldn't remember names or faces, but he babbled a list of beatings and robberies that he could remember. He must not be hitting the right one, because the guy kept wrapping away.

The wrapping had reached his neck and the guy started pulling the bandage around his head, covering his forehead, and over his cheeks. Terrified, Cliff waited for the moment the gauze blocked his eyes, but the man left his face uncovered.

Gradually, he felt his body starting to respond, he struggled to flex his legs. He thought they moved, but constricted inside the wrapping he was still being held tightly in place.

"While you try and remember," the stranger rocked back on his heels. "I'll explain a bit more. This wrapping will begin to warm up a bit as the linseed oil reacts with the air."

The stranger's face hovered above him. "Have you ever heard of human combustion?"

Cliff really started to freak out now. His whole world was reduced to moving his eyes. He kept trying to speak, and as the drug wore off he was getting closer to forming real words.

"Wheee, whhhy?"

"You needed to remember a young woman and her son from Chicago, but it doesn't matter now." There was finality in the voice. Like the excitement was over.

He racked his brain to remember. A woman and her son from Chicago, ten years ago. Cliffy's foggy mind slid back.

When he hit on it, it made him cringe. As Cliff replayed it in his mind he actually closed his eyes. *That fucking Sam.* If this is what it was about, then Cliff was a dead man. He'd known it back then, he'd known it wasn't right. He'd been sure that it would come back to haunt them. So many years later he'd almost managed to forget about it.

He opened his eyes and tried to beg for his life. "Sssam." He mumbled, "Not mmme."

His tormenter came in fast, shoving his face close, anger burning through his voice. "Not true," he accused. "You were the leader. You could have stopped it."

"Sssorry." Cliff knew the guy was right.

"So am I. You could have saved us all a lot of shit." The guy was packing up his stuff. "You should feel the heat in an hour or so. Then you'll start to cook. Then it could get up to six hundred degrees inside the wrapping. So, have a good day asshole."

Cliff went to speak and the guy finished wrapping his face, leaving a breathing hole over his nose. His world went black, reduced to the faint sounds he could hear as the guy jumped down to the gravel and the overpowering smell of the linseed oil in his nostrils.

Cliff lay there. Why had he ever joined up with Sam? The guy was always bringing the wrong kind of trouble. Why had he even left his house to come and do this again?

Greed. Simple greed was the answer, and he was sure going to pay for it.

What was coming next? Cliff struggled against the wrappings, he had more muscle control now, but it wasn't enough. The wrappings were too tight and he couldn't move. Time slipped by and sure enough, he felt his skin getting warm, then hot. He told himself it was his imagination, but soon enough he felt like he was in a sauna.

Oh god. That was where he had heard about it before. Oil soaked rags. How many buildings had burned down because oil soaked rags had spontaneously burst into flames? *Shit, shit, shit.*

As the temperature began to rise, he became more desperate. His mind was screaming at him to do something. Then he noticed a different smell in the train car.

It took a few minutes before he realized it was his own skin starting to cook. Then he lost it. His brain and body became two separate entities. He thrashed desperately, moving by inches, working every muscle as he screamed out in pain.

He was near the door as the wrapping started to smoke. Cliff didn't know where he was anymore as he felt himself burning up. He just wanted it to be over. He could feel his skin melting, his brain kept screaming out again and again.

CHAPTER 14

Reno, Nevada

The clock said two in the morning. Sarah was wide awake. The lights were still blazing bright in her room. She didn't think she'd slept at all. Every nerve was alive.

She couldn't hold back the smiles. The package had come with the mail delivery that afternoon. Thank God someone on the staff hadn't stolen it. The only mail she ever received came from David, so when she first saw the package she assumed it was from him. She hadn't been prepared for the sight she found.

Looking down again, she opened up the package on her lap for the fiftieth time since it arrived. It was breathtaking. The two flowers were identical to the first one David had handed her on his last visit.

She knew their significance the second she opened the box. Was it relief, or was it a new lease on life that had her feeling giddy and lightheaded? She reached in one more time and pulled out the note. Carefully she unfolded the small piece of paper. She stared at David's blocky handwriting.

Two more flowers Mom. Would you like to come and pick one yourself? I'm coming to visit soon.

Sarah's heart raced. She looked away, not because she wanted to, but because she needed to calm down. Finally, he was getting her out of there. It came with the knowledge that she was going to have a new life. Carefully she buried the strands of anger that seeped in when she thought of picking her own flower.

No, there would be no sleeping tonight. She needed to make plans and get herself ready. What folks around here might think about her leaving was another subject.

*****

New Orleans, Louisiana

It was damn hot in the south. *Jesus.* Bart had been carrying the leather jacket for days and it was getting heavier with every degree the temperature rose. He stayed low, out of sight going through towns, but when he could he hung off the side of the train catching as much of a breeze as possible.

He didn't want to admit it, but he'd been worried after Danny left. He'd gotten used to the extra protection having another person around provided. In the end, he reverted back to being on his own. He'd been there before.

The problem was figuring out which trains to take. Before he had relied on Danny's research. Even though he was always watching for them, he couldn't know that he was outside the Raildog's box now, and well away from their influence.

Bart was proud on some level. He was almost in New Orleans, a place he'd always wanted to go. There was something about the lure of the craziness and partying that he knew went on there.

He tucked back in as the train rolled into the city and stayed hidden until it came to a stop. After an hour he was getting real fidgety because of the heat and couldn't sit still any longer. A slow freighter rolled past, taking a deep breath, he finally stuck his head out and looked both ways.

Something big on the freighter didn't look normal, and Bart stared as it came towards him. Going past was a large concrete cylinder that looked like ... a submarine? Instinctively he looked up where the periscope should be, and noticed a guy resting his arms on the open turret, casually enjoying the landscape going by.

Bart didn't know why, but he yelled out, "Hey you!"

The stranger turned towards the source of the sound and waved as the freight car was disappearing from view. "What's up!"

He couldn't believe he'd just seen that. Sitting there with his legs dangling over the side, Bart began to wonder if he was on a two-way or one-way trip. There wasn't much to go back to, but he didn't know what was ahead.

A noise caught his attention and Bart started to jump back inside the boxcar. Then he saw the two women and stopped. No reason to hide from them. They had gotten close without even noticing he was there.

When he saw the women's concern, he spoke up. "Hey, I'm by myself," he said. "I'm cool. Just travelling."

The two girls looked him over like they were judging him. He must have passed some kind of test.

"Hi, I'm Jackie," the blond pointed at her friend. "This is Beth."

"Hey there. Where are you guys going?" Bart's mood was lifting. "I'm heading to the Keys."

"That's where I'm from," Jackie said, "We came up to N'Oleans for a few days of partying. We're heading home now."

"Well maybe you can tell me which trains to take. It's my first time down here."

"You got a funny accent. Where you from?" Beth asked.

"Billings, Montana." Bart laughed, "The middle of nowhere."

"We got ourselves a cowboy." For some reason that made them giggle.

And as if on cue, the train jerked once and then twice, before rolling forward.

"No, I don't know much about cows."

"Well we'll find out what you do know soon enough."

*****

Salt Lake City, Utah

David treated passenger trains differently than the freights. He didn't wait for them to start moving and then jump on. That wasn't a great strategy when the passengers looking out the windows could see what you were doing.

The answer was getting on the train ahead of time, lying quietly behind a ventilation unit on top of a restaurant or bar car, until the train was moving. As soon as possible he'd get down between cars. Everything had gone off without a hitch tonight and David wanted that. He needed it. He needed everything to go smoothly for the next few days.

His mother would be proud. She'd tried to do the right thing for him and it had gone to hell. But that wasn't her fault. Now he would make part of it right. She hadn't deserved what happened, but at least she'd get some closure.

The passenger train pulled out of Salt Lake heading south. Once they were up to speed he knew he'd be in Phoenix in great time.

As always, he carefully examined the other trains they passed. He focused on the ends of the storage and grain cars, looking into any open doors on the boxcars. A freight was moving into the yard, pulling a string of mostly empty boxcars. *Except that one.*

David watched the man standing in the open doorway. Other riders usually never noticed him hidden like this so he stayed where he was behind the unit and stared. As the two trains passed by each other David realized the guy was looking his way.

This was no drifter, he looked too well dressed for that. He wasn't drunk, or a druggy either, the rider seemed focused, staring as intently as he was. Something about him didn't sit right and David kept watching as the train moved on, turning his head to continue looking over his shoulder.

Then the guy was gone out of view, lost to the night. The passenger train was picking up speed as David slid back to climb down between cars. He was already thinking ahead. The plan had worked in Salt Lake, he was confident it would work in Phoenix too.

*****

Texas

When she was left to herself Maria turned and sat down on the floor beside the pallet. The sudden slowing of the train didn't mean anything special at first. Then she wondered if they were pulling into a station where she might get help.

When the train slowed down enough that it seemed like it was going to stop she knew she had to act. Slowly – carefully – she reached for the pile of abandoned clothes. Pulling the track pants up her legs, she tucked the dress into the waistband. The hoodie slid over her head and she sat back down. She was toeing off her shoes to put on the hiking boots when the train stopped completely.

She heard the men talking, and shivered.

"Where's Sam? Do we get to do this bitch or what?"

Maria tried to be as small as she could, slinking back into the corner.

The voices were getting louder. "Why is the train stopped anyways?"

The door slid open slightly and Maria got a good look at the man. Scruffy and dirty, he looked like a bum. The guy leaned out and called backwards, "Hey Sam, what's up?"

When the guy didn't hear a response, he turned to look forward. Jumping back from the opening, he turned to the others. "We got company, couple guys coming this way."

The conversation changed suddenly to 'where the hell was Sam', before voices started urging each other to roll the newcomers.

"Raildogs rule!" the scruffy one yelled.

"Raildogs rule," the others shouted back.

Three of the men jumped through the open door, landing on the run, sprinting down the rail to deal with the strangers. That left one to stay and watch over her.

Maria didn't move – she hardly breathed. The Raildog came closer and closer, until he was standing over her, looking down. As the yelling outside intensified, she realized she was hearing Spanish.

She heard a voice yell out in English, "Rick, help us." Then the guy beside her ran to the door. She couldn't figure out why he didn't jump down like the others. Quickly she hustled around to hide behind the stacked pallet.

To her amazement the next sound she heard was, "Maria, ¿estás aquí??"

She hesitated for a moment, still fearful, then relief surged as she screamed out at the top of her lungs, "Estoy aquí! I'm here!"

Ten faces crowded the door. "You okay? Raul sent us to stop the train."

Her legs wobbled slightly as she sat down with a thud. She couldn't stop the sudden stream of tears that rolled down her cheeks. She shook as she realized she finally was safe. *Thank you Raul.*

Maria was still trembling and wobbly as one of the men jumped up into the car and grabbed the remaining Raildog. The guy didn't resist as he was thrown from the car into the waiting hands of the Mexicans.

Then someone was beside her, "Come on, Raul is waiting for us."

Maria let them lift her up, she didn't care. The tears continued to stream down.

*****

Salt Lake City, Utah

The freight train pulled into Salt Lake with Bill standing at the door, alarmed and alert. Red and blue lights on the streets seemed to be heading towards the yards. *Were they coming this way?*

As the train entered the yard and he lost sight of the flashing lights as a southbound passenger train blocked his view.

Instinctively he ran his eyes along the tops of the cars, there weren't a lot of other places to hide on those things.

Something caught his attention and he waited for the passenger train to get closer. The odd shaped dark object turned into a guy lying down on top of a car. *Fuck, another one.* Bill stared at the rider. Locked onto each other, they held their gaze, as the trains rolled past.

The guy seemed to be dressed in black. Just like the previous rider, there was something about this one that bothered him. He sure didn't look like a beginner on the rails.

Bill watched until the rider was out of view. Then he remembered the lights and began looking ahead, wondering where the train was stopping. Unlike the illegal riders, he didn't have to hide from anyone.

When the train finally did stop, he climbed down and started looking for someone. Crossing some tracks and walking towards an overpass, he ran into a yard worker. "Hey, did some cop cars come in here?

The guy jumped before turning, a sure sign he'd been startled. "Who the hell are you?"

"Hey, easy buddy," Bill pulled out his wallet waving his I.D. "I'm a cop."

"The cars went along the upper road, over the bridge, where the east and west tracks are." The worker didn't look like he wanted to answer to anyone, and turned his back, insinuating Bill should go about his business.

Bill was already jogging off in that direction and didn't see the act of dismissal. He wouldn't have cared anyways. He had other things on his mind. *Why was he so sure this was another one?*

When he climbed up the steep slope to the road he could see the cruisers parked together on the service road. At the sight of the meat wagon, he took off running towards the lights.

An officer heard him coming and turned at the noise of his boots pounding on the gravel. The uniform stepped out to intercept him, his hand up. "Stop right there."

Bill noticed the other hand resting on the sidearm and dropped his pace down to a walk. "It's okay, I'm a cop." He reached towards the front pocket of his jeans to pull out his I.D. again and the cop reacted.

"Freeze, don't move."

Bill froze like a statue, held still by the business end of the handgun.

"I'm getting my I.D. out," Bill waited.

"Go ahead," the cop nodded, "slowly."

He carefully slid the small wallet out and opened it towards the officer.

The man stepped forward to get a closer look. "Where you from?"

"Colton, California. I'm working a case. Bill Dewton."

"And you ended up here in our freight yard?" The cop was curious.

"I'm following a trail of bodies and they all come from rail yards. You got one?" Bill pushed the matter.

The cop hesitated, then he nodded towards the tight knot of cops near the freight train "You won't believe it, see for yourself."

Since the guy didn't seem inclined to explain any further, Bill followed the cop towards the others. He was introduced to the group as they shuffled aside to make room for him to see what was causing the commotion.

He was perplexed by the sight. He knew exactly what it was, a mummy. But what the hell was it doing here? The edges of the wrappings were burnt and the whole thing bore the scorch marks of having been on fire. No one spoke and he knew the drill, but these being cops, he was sure there were punch lines waiting to come.

"Okay, what the hell is this?" No smart-ass stepped forward with a wise crack. Unusually, everyone remained quiet. It seemed they were on edge.

Finally someone answered. "The guy was mummified. Are these things supposed to burn up? It's like something went wrong."

"The poor bastard definitely started to cook."

Bill shuddered. The guy had been slow roasted, mother-of-lord. "Where was he?"

"A yard worker found him. Saw a bundle of rags along the track smoking. By the time he got here it was on fire." The cop stalled a second. "The worker said he rolled the bundle around in the gravel and sand on the edge of the tracks to stop it from burning up. That's when we got the call."

"Can you make out anything on the guy?" Bill had to know as much as he could.

"Look yourself. Face wasn't too bad but it did melt a little. The rest of the guy is a mess. I figure we'll have to wait for the coroner to open the wrapping." The cop was being pretty straightforward. "But the yard worker was looking around for more bodies when he found some burnt rags and this book in a boxcar."

"Can I see it?" Bill reached forward.

"Sure, you seem to know more about these guys than we do."

Bill stepped forward into the floodlight. Leaning down, he looked at the face, turning his head sideways to get a straight-on look. *Shit.* He'd seen this guy before. *Where?* He flashed through the images from the week, and it hit him. This was the guy he'd seen on that other freight train as they passed each other in Spokane.

He'd had a bad feeling about the guy back then, and now here he was, killed in some bizarre fashion. He was sure this had to be another high-ranking Raildog.

He'd give anything to see the inside of the victim's wrist but knew that wasn't happening. This body was going to a lab. Period. For some reason he thought of the rider he'd just seen heading out of town on the passenger train. He shook his head to clear it. He didn't need distractions.

He didn't want to wait for autopsy results either. If he missed catching the leader here, he was down to whoever the number two Raildog was, and that meant Phoenix. He thought about the intense stare of the rider that was dressed all in black. "Can someone check out my hit criteria in the system and call me about this guy's results?"

Bill left his cell number before heading back towards the southbound tracks. He quickly checked the small black book into his inside coat pocket, hopefully he'd be long gone before they discovered he hadn't returned it.

"Where you going?" One of the officers yelled at his back.

"Phoenix." There was only one left.

*****

Texas

Sam Dorson struggled to the top of the stacked containers at the rear of the train. He wanted to get up as high as possible where he would be able to see well and to hide even better. Once on top, he inched over to look down the side.

Two groups of men were walking down the train, searching inside the cars. There were too many of them to be cops. Someone yelled from the other side and Sam inched over that way.

Damn it. He watched three Raildogs jump out of the car where he'd left the woman and start towards the other men. As the group spread out it became apparent his guys were out-numbered. Sam didn't move a muscle.

The three Raildogs realized their mistake too late and were quickly surrounded. He tried to look away when he saw the clubs and bats, but couldn't stop himself watching as his crew was beaten to a pulp.

The newcomers surrounded the door to the boxcar where he had stashed the woman and one of them climbed in. The last of his men was thrown out into the crowd, he didn't fair any better than the first three.

Sam kept watching, he wanted to see what happened to the woman. She'd been something else. He was surprised when she was helped off the train, the newcomers giving her room as she got down.

It hit him that they were a little late to the rescue. Then he couldn't believe his luck. He'd known there was something about her, obviously something special if this many people came looking. How did they know where to look?

Then Sam realized the woman's boyfriend must have had a hand in this; which made him wonder about his other men who had jumped off the train to deal with him earlier. Shit, how many men did he have left?

He smiled to himself, he'd had her while he could. *Yes sir, he did.*

When the men fanned out to check the last boxcars, walking around the end of the train, Sam rolled to the center of the container and lay on his back staring at the sky. He didn't move at all. He hardly breathed. As the group headed back to the front of the train, he dropped his head back down against the cold steel in relief.

Once the train started to move again Sam realized they had been stopped at one of hundreds of road crossings that littered the rail line.

As the train picked up speed, rumbling through the intersection, he could see a pair of dump trucks alongside the road. A number of pickup trucks were already leaving.

Sam was shaken. These guys had the balls to stop a train. They must have put out lights that the engineer saw, with the trucks on the rail the train had no choice but to stop. *Balls, that's for sure.*

CHAPTER 15

Phoenix, Arizona

David arrived in Phoenix and headed right for the east-west lines. He knew the number two Raildog didn't venture far from his section, and spent more time on the rails than the other bosses.

Phoenix or Houston? One end, or the other? Where was he? David knew the run always came west to start the month and he wondered if he had missed his target.

Knowing where they hung out and where they jumped off the trains was helpful, and David set himself up where he could watch for a while. When midnight came and went he was confused. Pulling out his little book, he rechecked his data. The train was late. *What the hell?*

He didn't want any surprises at this point. Everything was too close to a conclusion. Shifting around in his hiding spot, he was getting uncomfortable and pissed off. He didn't need this aggravation. His tight schedule didn't need any last second changes.

An hour later David was still vigilant. Trains came and went, but he still wasn't seeing the one he was watching for, then he heard one slowing as it approached the station.

There it was, late, but finally here. This one came all the way from Houston. It had potential. Scrambling down from his vantage point, he worked his way closer to the track. He used the shadows to move towards the old building knowing where the gang usually hung out.

David had already identified where the outgoing eastbounders were parked and he'd set his trap well. Now he just needed a body. When the train was almost stopped he realized that anyone on board should have jumped by now. He was almost ready to give up, then he saw a flicker of movement.

A figure dropped down out of a car and landed crouched beside the track, pausing to look both ways before straightening and starting to walk. It was obvious the guy was alert, he was swiveling his head to look around, checking over his shoulder. Did he have some warning? David didn't think so, but he had to expect anything.

When the guy turned away from the train, angling across the tracks towards the old building, he knew it was time. He wouldn't be able to make a positive I.D. until the man was closer and he was able to get a better look.

A quick breath for calming; a flex of the shoulder muscles to get the juices going; and David stepped out of the shadows.

"Hey man."

The figure stopped short and stared. He was clearly caught off guard. David watched the assessment going on and knew the guy was calculating distances. *Jesus, he was a big bastard.*

"Who are you? You looking for trouble?" The big guy seemed drained, tired.

"No way man. Cliff sent me. We got problems." David pulled up his sleeve slightly and rolled his wrist over to reveal the tattoo. He was sure he had the number two man standing in front of him.

"You're a Raildog?" The man seemed to relax, "Shit. I though I was going to have to kick your ass."

"No, I don't want that. I'm here to get you."

"What you mean, get me?"

"There's a big meeting. Bobby went up to pick up Cliff and then over to get Doug. They're heading to Houston and we're supposed to meet them there." David tried to make it simple.

"Why the meeting? Why didn't someone just call me about it?" The guy didn't sound convinced.

"I can't help much there. I'm new, but he said no phones and all the bosses." David kept a straight face. He didn't want to give anything away.

The guy looked down, tilted his head so he could get another look at David's wrist and then shrugged. "So we're supposed to get right back on a train east?"

"Yes sir, there are a few of us already on the train waiting for you. It should head out in an hour or so." David started to walk towards the eastbound lines. He looked back at the number two, "This way sir."

*****

Phoenix, Arizona

Sam rode further into the station than usual. He was on high alert. He still had a vision of the Mexican gang walking along the tracks as he hid on top of the container car.

From his vantage point he'd seen the crumpled and twisted bodies of his crew that had been dragged into the ditch. As the train started moving he'd just stared at the four forms on the way past.

So he was worried about more attackers and wasn't taking chances. As the train rolled to a stop he stuck his head out and looked both ways. He jumped down and looked both ways again, before starting towards the hangout. He needed to see if anyone was there.

The guy speaking to him from the dark had jump-started his adrenaline, his eyes darted back and forth but didn't see anyone else. When he got talking and realized it was a Raildog, he was surprised how much his nerves relaxed.

The guy's story about a meeting was a little strange, but the fact there were other Raildogs around was reassuring. Extra men around would be good.

"You coming?"

The guy was leading him towards the eastbound lines. Sam didn't know the tattoos went over one hundred, but the guy said he was with Cliffy and he was the one running the numbers. He had no idea how many members there were these days. "Yeah, yeah, I'm coming."

A little relieved, Sam walked along behind the guy, stepping over the rail lines. The guy kept looking back as he went and eventually he slowed down until he was beside him as they walked, "Glad to meet another boss. Never been down this way before. Names Dan."

Sam looked up. Something about what the guy had just said didn't make sense, but he couldn't figure out what it was. He was trying to place it, "Welcome to the Raildogs Dan."

Sam didn't notice he was now ahead of the guy as he looked up at the doors of the boxcars expecting to see the other Raildogs. Suddenly it hit him like a brick. The guy had said that the train east would be leaving in a few hours. How did he know that if he'd never been in the area before?

Examining the boxcars, he didn't hear a single voice and he sure didn't see anybody. He was getting a bad feeling and turned to question the fucker behind him. That's as far as he got. The metal bar hit him hard in the front of the head. Falling backwards he saw the bar in the guy's hands and thought to himself, I've seen that thing, it was leaning against the train a few cars back.

Shit, I'm in trouble. And then the world went black.

*****

El Paso, Texas

"Thank you," Maria whispered. The miles flew by as the pick-up truck raced down the highway. Being squashed between two strange men was both disconcerting and in some strange way, comforting. Occasionally her rescuers talked over top of her head, exchanging words in Spanish, raising their voices above the music pouring from the cross-border station on the radio. Slowly, she relaxed back into the solid warmth of the shoulders pinning her to the seat.

"It's okay Maria. We'll get you to Raul." The driver was apologetic. It was taking longer than he would have liked, but they stayed off the interstate highways whenever they could. The hundreds of back roads along the border, through the lower states were endless. The gang knew them all like the backs of their hands.

She hadn't had time yet to replay the events in her head, but the images were starting to slip into her consciousness. She shivered and pulled her hoodie tight.

Why couldn't they have stopped the train earlier? Sharply she pulled herself up, she realized that wasn't the way to look at it. Thank God they stopped things when they did. She had to be grateful. The next thing on her mind was Raul. What would he think of her now? She felt like garbage, as dirty as she could get. Silently she fought back the tears.

"How long before we're there?"

"Soon, Maria. Soon." The driver grabbed his phone off the dash and thumbed a number. "¡Hola, Raul?"

Maria couldn't hear the voice on the other end but listened to the driver, "Yes, we have her. No problem man, anything for you."

The conversation went back and forth, "Okay, we'll watch for you on the west side of the yard. Another hour at most."

"See Maria, we are close now." The driver was still trying to reassure her.

She struggled with mixed emotions. She was away from those bastards, but she still had to face Raul. And he still needed to find out what happened.

Her small fists clenched tightly on her lap as she stared straight ahead out the window.

*****

El Paso, Texas

Raul sat with his back against the old warehouse, waiting for his friends to bring him his Maria. He'd almost lost her, and that would have haunted him for years. He couldn't believe this shit had happened so close to home.

He was glad he was able to call on them to help. Raul'd set up some of the gangs on this side of the border, and had worked with others before accepting the job in New York. Connections had paid off big this time. He wished he could have been there when they found her just to get his own piece of the big guy in the jean jacket. He stood up on the dock so the three pick-up trucks rumbling across the open field could see him.

Sure enough, the trucks caught him in their lights and headed off to find an entrance. Soon they were driving along the tracks and stopping as near as they could. Ten or more guys jumped out of the trucks and started walking his way. Raul watched intently for Maria.

He recognized a few of the men, and became distracted with greetings, "Hey Raul, long time no see."

"You too Hector." It was good to see a bunch of his own. Raul hugged the old friend. "Where is she?"

"Right here." Hector turned and realized they were boxed in with gangsters. "Let her through you fools."

He watched the men spread apart and there she was, standing at the back of the group. He could see from her eyes something had happened. She looked like she was trembling, almost afraid.

Stepping forward, he wrapped his arms around her. Holding her was all he needed right now. He felt her relax in his arms, the stiffness of her spine letting go as she leaned into him. He didn't understand her hesitance, the fear in her eyes.

He needed some space. "We'll be right back."

The parked train offered a wall. He squeezed through to the other side, pulling her along behind. Away from spectators, it was just the two of them now, he turned to face her and tried to look into her eyes.

"Are you alright?"

"Yeah, I'm okay."

He saw something there in the moment before she looked away. She was holding something back. Reaching out, he grabbed her around the waist and pulled her close. Hugging her tightly, he tried to settle her down.

Raul pushed her hood back and put his head down into the soft corner where her neck and shoulder joined, kissing her there. As he pulled away he noticed the dress under the hoodie and froze. *What was this?* When did she put it on? He had a number of bad thoughts all at once as he leaned back to look her in the face.

There it was again. The fear in her eyes. She was watching him closely and he realized she knew that he knew. She was waiting to see how he reacted. This was important to her. And it was important for them.

This time he pulled her gently close, cradling her against his chest. She tried to speak, but he just said, "Shh," resting his chin on her head.

She started to shake again and began to cry. He heard the words, "Thank you, Raul."

His own eyes blurred, "I love you, Maria."

The sound of an approaching train jarred him back to the present. He watched the train slow down as it pulled alongside them. Before it was completely stopped, three strangers jumped off and headed straight towards them.

He was already angry enough to deal with these guys himself. He wanted to hurt someone. But with Maria there, the decision was easy. He stepped back through the gap between railcars and called out in Spanish. "Take care of these bastards on the other side of the train."

Raul walked Maria towards the pick-up trucks as his friends climbed under and around the boxcar, sprinting towards the newcomers.

*****

El Paso, Texas

Danny and his new companions stood at the boxcar door as the train rolled into El Paso. His confidence and the belief he belonged in the gang had grown steadily along the way.

In his mind he practiced what he would say to the Raildog's leader when they got a chance to talk. He couldn't wait to become an official member. Then he knew he was going to have some fun. This was his time to kick ass and take whatever he wanted.

"People on the tracks." A yell from his fellow Raildog broke through Danny's thoughts.

"Right on. It's a couple man. We can get some ass." The gangster was excited.

Danny took a second to figure out what the guy meant. Then he understood. Shit, these guys took women whenever they felt like it too.

"Let's go." The two Raildogs jumped off the train. Danny landed behind and took off running right past them, towards the couple.

He saw the guy step through between the cars, they were starting to get away and Danny ran harder. This dude wasn't going to escape. His shoes pounded on the gravel, his lungs bellowing as he gave it everything he had. Danny was almost on him when someone else stepped out to confront him from the same spot.

He hit the new guy hard, slamming him against the side of the train car. Danny bounced off the guy and shuffled a couple steps to catch his balance. The second one through the gap caught him off guard. As he took a half step back the guy landed against the side of his legs and knocked him down to the ground, partially pinning him.

Conscious of the voices yelling, Danny realized more men were coming through between the train cars. He scrambled backwards to get out from underneath his attacker and back to his feet as he searched to see where the Raildogs were.

What the fuck? His two guys were running the other way. They must have turned around and left him there.

Fuck, that's not right. I helped you guys.

A punch to the side of the head knocked him to his knees, and he was forced to return to the fight.

A knee to the head knocked him over sideways. Letting his momentum carry him, he rolled and stood up. *Shit.* It looked like ten or more people. Who were they? Mexicans? One stepped close enough, and Danny swung hard. He caught the guy in the neck and the body folded sideways.

One of his opponents laughed and said something in sharp Spanish.

The men surged forward, swinging fists, feet, bats, and clubs. Danny starting swinging in self defense. He may have connected with one or two, but it didn't matter.

He took a bat to the side of the head and stood there stunned and rocking on his heels, a club connected with his ribs and he crumpled to the ground. No fight left in him now, Danny tried to curl inward to protect himself from the blows, but his attackers kept reaching down and pulling his legs out straight, holding his arms out to the side. He was hit again and again.

He didn't feel the blows anymore, just drifting away. He thought about the playground back home, taking walks and bike rides by himself. Why hadn't that been good enough? Why had he wanted this? He pictured Bart and realized it was the leather jacket. It reminded him of thugs and bikers. Tough guys.

He knew that's what had drawn him to Bart in the first place. Now he was thinking that he should have never talked to the guy. He was wishing he was back home. He managed to turn his head and look up. The last thing he saw was the heel of a boot.

*****

Phoenix, Arizona

Sam woke up in the dark. Confusion set in, then the pain pulled him from unconsciousness as he realized he was hanging from his arms. Movement near his feet jolted him fully awake as the rats scurried away.

He kept blinking his eyes to adjust to the darkness. He looked up at the chains and the I-beam they were tied to. *What the hell was going on?* It took a second but then Sam remembered the guy at the station who said he was a Raildog.

As his head cleared it started to hurt and he remembered seeing something coming at his face. Twisting and opening his mouth wide he could tell his face was bruised and swollen. *Jesus Christ.*

The small irritation on his ankle didn't register right away, but once he realized it was there it became alarming. He couldn't tell, but he had a feeling the rats had been biting at him while he was passed out. That had him eyeing the floor.

When he finally saw the first one it freaked him right out. The rat seemed to be watching him with his beady little eyes. He just knew it was waiting for a chance to take another piece of him. He wondered how many more there were, and kicked his foot out, in practice for the real thing.

He had no idea where he was. Was he still near the tracks? One of the buildings his crew knew? Hopefully, they would find him before the other asshole came back.

Was the guy coming back? Was he being left here to rot? Would anyone find him? He wondered how long he could stay awake. Falling asleep was just what the rats were waiting for.

CHAPTER 16

Reno, Nevada

Sarah sat on the edge of her chair staring out over the darkened lawn. The streetlights lit the pathways through the grounds, but she wasn't focusing on the view. She'd been packed and ready to leave for two days. Her patience was near its end. She balanced between going over the deep end and grinning foolishly in anticipation.

Her single bag was ready to go. As she looked at the small blue backpack, it seemed to sum up her life. A few belongings, a coat, two pairs of shoes, a book and a couple items she had plans for. And then there was the mental baggage that sat squarely on her shoulders.

She had collected everything she needed over the past forty-eight hours. Some of it was coming with her, but some of it was staying. A couple things wouldn't come into play until after she left. David didn't need to know about everything.

Sarah had talked the cleaning bitch into giving it to her some of the toxic solvent. "Well if you're not going to clean anything around here at least let me have the bottle."

The old hag had dropped the bottle off her cart onto the bathroom sink. Probably the first time it had moved that day.

The first surprise was for the staffer who took her food whenever he felt like it She'd pocketed a syringe during her last visit to the building's medical wing. She had carefully concealed the puddings that hadn't been stolen over the last couple days while he was on a different shift and carefully injected through the outer seal.

The pudding would cut the smell and if she was lucky the idiot wouldn't notice while he gorged himself. He wouldn't die, but he was going to have a hell of a few days – weeks maybe. A smile played out across her face.

The items that Sarah stole from the other residents over the same period were all in a box that she'd hidden behind the yellow azaleas on her walk that afternoon.

In the bottom of her purse was the anonymous letter she'd written to the home's management, explaining that the cleaning lady had been observed hiding stolen things in a box on the grounds.

These were small victories, but they raised her spirits just the same. When she saw a figure crossing the yard she pressed her face right up against the window. Sure it was David, she could hardly contain herself.

This was it. It was happening. Finally she was going to get her life back.

Sarah gathered up her stuff up. The box of flowers was buried deep in her bag. Anything she didn't plan to take was left in place.

She stood motionless in the middle of the room facing the door.

I'm ready David.

*****

Reno, Nevada

David pushed through the front doors and strode past the front desk.

The night desk clerk yelled as he went past, "Hey buddy, it's too late for visits."

He kept walking. "I'm not visiting. I'm here to get my Mother."

"Hey, you can't do that, there's rules around here." The desk clerk came around in front of the counter.

David stopped and turned, "You call the boss, call whoever you have to." He pointed a finger at the clerk. "This has already been arranged. I take her when I want, or when she wants."

He didn't wait for an answer, turning to continue towards his mother's room.

"Oh, I'm calling right now. Don't you worry."

David held up one finger as he strode down the corridor.

He didn't get a chance to knock, she was waiting with the door open. "Hello son." Her face beamed with pleasure.

"Hi mom, you ready to go?" He stood there waiting.

"Yes, I am." She pointed to the single bag. "This is all I'm bringing."

It hit him that it wasn't much to show for a lifetime. He picked the bag up gently, like she must have something of value hidden in there. He hoped she did. How was she going to make it through the rest of her life starting out with only a shoulder bag? He knew the answer, it was simple really, he'd help her.

"Let's go then." He led the way, approaching the lobby. Looking back, Sarah was right on his heels. The clerk was waiting for them in the middle of the lobby, with the phone's extension cord stretched over the desk.

"The manager wants to speak with you." The clerk looked full of steam.

David took the phone and his side of the conversation went swiftly, "Yes, she wants to."

"This is your notice period. It's already paid up."

"No. That's why I kept it month to month. So we could check out like this when we wanted."

"Look it worked for you for ten years, now it's going to work for me. Thank you for your service, we appreciate it."

David handed the phone back to the clerk and marched out the door, his bag on the one shoulder, his mother's on the other, and Sarah in tow.

She didn't say a word until they were off the property, still fearful something might go wrong. "Where we going David?"

"I'm taking you somewhere Mom. Trust me." David nodded like he meant she would approve.

As they got closer to the rail yard he sensed that Sarah had stopped behind him. "What's wrong?"

"Why are you bringing me here?" Her face was closed. Tight.

"You're going to have to trust me on this Mom," David stalled. "Everything is set up. I just want to take you there. It'll be worth it."

He reached out and grabbed her hand. She squeezed back firmly. He could tell she was scared and he realized he hadn't considered what her feelings would be about getting on another train. The last time hadn't gone so well.

They ducked through the bushes and tucked through a hole in the fence. Once inside the rail yard David knew exactly where he had to be. The southbound lines where off to his right.

The closer he got her to the train the harder she squeezed his hand. He could feel the trembling vibrating through her and he wondered if she would make it.

He had to get her to Phoenix, and there really was no other way, "Come on Mom," He pulled a plastic wrapped flower out of his pocket. "Here's number four Mom, I'm taking you to the last one.

She didn't respond.

"I made sure to keep him for you."

When her eyes met his he realized she understood what he meant and it seemed to energize her. She was preparing herself, her anger taking over, he saw her upper lip tighten.

"Okay David. Let's go."

*****

Pensacola, Florida

If he ever had any doubt about taking this trip, it was all gone now. Bart had been riding with the two women for hours and was having a blast.

The two girls were fun and kept kidding and joking during the trip. The one kept looking at him and he wasn't sure what to do except stare right back. They all stood up as the train came into Pensacola. He was finally in Florida.

He was curious when the two women started to hug and say their goodbyes. He quickly realized one of them was getting off.

"This is my stop." Beth gave him a quick wave. "Good to meet you Bart."

"You too Beth. Maybe we'll see each other again."

He caught the look between the women and then Beth said, "That might happen yet. You guys take care."

She jumped down from the slow moving train and stood waving at them. A slight curve in the track meant they lost sight of her fairly quickly and it hit him that they were now alone. Turning, he was surprised that Jackie was standing beside him.

"So cowboy, what are we going to do now?

"What do you mean?" *God, that sounded stupid.* But she came even closer until she leaned the entire length of her body against him. He felt her push against him and he moved back slightly.

"You know what I mean." She kept moving him back until they were away from the door. He felt the wall against his back and she smiled. The look on her face was mischievous as she rubbed her hips against his. Bart felt himself bulge up in the pants. So did Jackie.

"That's more like it cowboy. Now take off your clothes." She stood back and started to peel off her jeans. He watched without comprehension. Looking up, Jackie noticed he was still dressed, "What? You want me to lay down on that?" She pointed at the rough wooden floor.

No. No, he didn't want that, he fumbled to unlace and kick off the Doc Martens then went to work on the pants. Jackie took his clothes and laid them out on the floor while Bart stood there naked. He realized he was grinning and he had an image of Danny flash through his head. *Hope you're having fun buddy. Cause I sure am.*

"Are you coming down here?" The sexy voice reclaimed his attention.

He sank down to the floor of the boxcar. "Yes I am."

*****

Caborca, Mexico

The party was in full swing. Thirty or more gangsters and their women were spread out around the large back yard. The pool was open, two bars were set up and no one waited in line.

The music was loud, but there were no neighbors nearby to complain. In just a bikini, Maria was holding a wine glass, dancing to the music in a world of her own. Groups of people in fancy clothes drifted past, outside her bubble.

She knew a lot of men watched her. She didn't mind, these were Raul's friends and she was safe here. They'd crossed the border south of Tucson. One vehicle drove them across, and then someone else had picked them up and brought them to the villa.

There was talk of going out the next day in the large sailboat on the Pacific an hour away, and something else was planned for the day after that. This was the life he had said he would give her, and she'd believed him. Now she was wondering where he was.

Walking around the party, easing between the clusters of dancers and drinkers, she couldn't find him. Finally, she did run into someone she recognized. "Hector, have you seen Raul?"

"Out in the garage." The gangster aimed his thumb back over his shoulder and headed off towards a short little blonde in a tiny mini skirt.

Maria wondered why he wasn't partying with the rest of them. She found him with the big garage door open, Raul was doing something with a barrel.

She stood there perplexed, "What are you doing? There's a party going on."

She saw him jump. He'd been so focused he hadn't noticed her. He didn't answer, but waved her over instead. Standing beside him, she looked into the barrel.

It took a second to register that she was looking at her dress and high heels. Raul tipped the can and poured gasoline in on top of the clothes. Maria started shaking, it was like she was there all over again.

When Raul lit a match, she looked up at him. He stared back at her while he dropped the match. The barrel flared up, flames shooting out the top for a few moments before settling into a steady burn that quickly reduced the dress to ashes. All she could do was watch.

"It's over Maria. I just wanted to get rid of them for you."

She fought a bunch of emotions that he seemed to understand. He hadn't wanted her to see the clothes again. Relieved, she leaned against him.

"Did I tell you how hot you look today? And what about this party?"

Maria looked up and saw the energy in his eyes. He was with his boys now, and he was happy about it. She grabbed him by the hand and led him back to the party shaking her ass a little more than usual on the way. It didn't matter what happened in the past, it mattered what you did with the future, and they were home now.

*****

Phoenix, Arizona

David urged his mother along the side of the tracks. It was still dark out, but at four a.m. it wouldn't stay that way for long. They walked about a half-mile along the eastbound lines before he stopped to take a break and look around. An old fence surrounded a field with a building set off from the track.

"I still don't understand David." She really didn't. Why were they walking in the middle of nowhere?

"Jesus mom, you're hard to surprise. Just take a break."

That made her bite her lip before asking anything else. David forced them to hang out there a few minutes more while he checked back and forth, ensuring no one was following them.

"You okay to go?"

"Lead the way." She seemed excited now at the prospect of a surprise.

David grabbed her hand and started down into the ditch. He took his time, waiting for his mother to come along without being pulled off her feet. As they approached the fence it became clear that there was a large tear where the chain link was peeled back and bent away from the post. He leaned down and turned sideways to push through the fence, then he pulled his mother through.

The little winding path leading towards the building was beaten down from years of use. David heard a train coming and looked back over his shoulder as he hurried his step. A freight train was heading out of Phoenix going east. Shit.

David didn't expect anyone to see what they were up to, but he stopped dead anyways, they were less likely to be seen if they weren't moving. His mother ran into him. "Just a second Mom."

The train was moving fairly quickly now. It looked like a bunch of storage containers. David watched them stream by, nothing to bother him, then he saw the boxcars tagged on the end, only a few – but still.

His eyes were trained on the doors, they seemed empty, then the last one wasn't. David saw a guy staring out of the car as it approached. The guy wasn't looking their way.

Shit. *Again?*

It looked like the same guy he'd seen in Salt Lake a day or two before. That was too much of a coincidence. Just when he thought the guy would go past without noticing them, his head turned.

How the guy picked them out in the morning darkness standing in a field was beyond him, but when the guy's eyes found him, David turned to show his back and he started forward with his mother in tow.

He had only one thought now – they had to hurry.

*****

Phoenix, Arizona

Bill wasted little time when the train got into Phoenix. He'd found someone to point him to the eastbound lines and he'd hustled over there. The guy had told him to stay on the outside track. It would have a train heading out sometime that morning.

It was a good thing he hustled, because the guy was wrong. There was a train on the outside line but it was starting to chug and jerk just as he got there. Decision time. Every time he thought about it, he came to the same conclusion. Sit and wait, or go out and search.

Sitting was out of the question because he was always too late. He needed to get lucky and get one of them. Any one of them would work. He needed the name of the boss who was still alive, and only someone in the gang would be able to provide it.

Bill jumped onto the end of the train as it rolled away. He couldn't afford to wait for the next one. Leaning against the door of the car as it sped up, he realized he was becoming used to the trains. His legs weren't spread out like a deer on ice, and he no longer held on to the side of the car for balance.

He couldn't help but see why people did it. He could see the sense of freedom and the adventure, if you could avoid the assholes. He'd seen more countryside in the last week than he had in the last ten years. Jobs did that to you.

Daybreak wasn't far away and he strained to look out over the fields as the train left Phoenix. He was staring out at nothing when a building caught his attention.

His eyes traced a footpath leading back towards the tracks. Then he noticed a couple people standing in the middle of the field between the building and the trains. As he rolled passed them, the guy turned and started to walk. It looked like he was pulling a woman behind him.

Right away Bill felt something was wrong. He looked down at the passing ground and knew the train was moving too fast to jump. With a second to think about it, he knew he shouldn't jump anyway. Some guy and woman out in a field weren't what he was searching for. He wanted a Raildog.

Still, he had a feeling, something else about those two was nagging him, but he couldn't place it. It wasn't the woman, but something about the guy was picking at the edge of his brain, and he hated that.

*****

Phoenix, Arizona

Sam woke with a jolt and kicked out with both feet. The rats scampered away and resettled a few yards distant. They were getting brave now. He kept nodding off and they seemed to have figured out that he was helpless.

He didn't scream or swear. He'd done that already. In fact Sam had literally had a fit and almost had a full breakdown. He cursed as loud as he could and swore to Jesus until he was shaking and dripping with sweat.

Then his will to live had taken over. He knew it was life or death. If he didn't stay awake they were going to eat him alive. His brain refused to accept that.

He was hungry, thirsty, and couldn't feel his arms anymore. Funny, how that worked in his favor. It allowed him to snap both feet out at the same time and drop against the chains. He didn't feel a thing.

Taking another shot at the rats, he did just that, and snapped his feet out at the same time. His feet swung through the air just a foot from the rodents, but they didn't move. He had to stop wasting energy, everything was about staying alive now.

This sure as hell wasn't the way he'd planned on going. Fuck, what a mess. He would give anything to be back on the train with a couple young babes to play with. Sam thought about the one he'd had earlier. Now she was something to think about.

He envisioned her dancing there in the middle of the car with the lantern light casting on her long legs. Then he felt her pushing back against him as he gave it to her from behind. Sam was smiling for the first time since he woke up.

Was that a train? Sam cocked his head, sure it was. Why hadn't he noticed that before? Christ, how long had he been out? He'd give anything for some light in the place, but as he thought it over, maybe not.

He knew the rats had bitten both his ankles, and he wasn't sure if he wanted to see what that looked like. Somewhere inside his head there was a struggle going on, he was trying to keep it together. He knew he had to.

"Don't lose it man," He kept talking to himself, "Jesus Christ, keep it together."

CHAPTER 17

Phoenix, Arizona

This was a scene he'd waited a long time to see. David sat on a bench at the side of the room and waited quietly. He would be a fly on the wall during this bit of theater. He lit a small fire in a rusted out old barrel to bring life to the scene and turned her loose.

He'd watched her fascination with the man strung up by his wrists. She'd seen the rats scurry out of the way as the fire got bigger. Walking around him, she'd studied him carefully and seemed to be placing him somewhere in her memories, confirming he was the one.

David had followed her rapid-fire instructions, "Find a chair, tie him up and gag the bastard." He'd foraged around in the old building and come back with a pair of chairs and some rope.

He knew that she wasn't going to be particularly nice to the guy, but what could he do? The guy did have it coming. Shrugging his shoulders, he couldn't complain at all, violence was just a means to an end. That's why they were here. So he sat and watched.

His mother perched on the edge of a chair facing the Raildog across from her who was roped tightly to the other one. A block of cement behind him acted like a spacer between his body and the back of the chair, forcing his ass forward onto the edge until he was almost falling off, while his shoulders were still tied to the back of the chair.

David had knocked the guy out with a crack to the head with a piece of wood to get him tied to the chair, and now Sarah was waiting for him to wake up. He knew this was the end of something. Hopefully it was also the beginning of something else.

Was it a new life? Maybe. David didn't know much except the rails, but he'd only spent the time there because she'd asked him to find them. She'd been disappointed when years had gone by without any progress, but did she understand how hard it had been?

Fifteen wasn't the age to be out on your own. He hadn't known shit. Since his mother had planned to use the rails in her bid for safety he'd done the same. Considering what had happened to them, he had made sure he hid well and stayed alert, but still he could remember eating out of garbage cans and stealing what he could, just to stay alive.

David watched her light another cigarette. He hadn't let her smoke on the trip, to avoid someone seeing the lit tip, so she'd been chain smoking ever since they entered the building.

She crossed one leg over the other and leaned forward with one arm across her lap. Her palm held the other elbow as her arm bent upwards, keeping the cigarette near her mouth. She swung the hand around to smoke on the stick – long slow draws that hung around her mouth before drifting upwards. Then she'd released the smoke from her lungs and blown it into the Raildog's face.

She had patience, he'd give her that. After waiting ten years some people would have torn into someone they wanted that bad in the first minute. They wouldn't be able to contain their rage once it had a target. But Sarah was sitting it out, probably planning it out.

One thing was sure, it was going to be a show. The small container that Sarah had taken out of her shoulder bag was sitting there on the floor beside her. Everything inside him said this show was going to get ugly.

David kept going back to what he was going to do when this journey was finished, what was next? Was it time for a new life? A real one? One with his mother at his side making up for all the lost years?

The sudden stirring of the man in the chair was like the lights going dim in a theatre. The show was about to begin.

He focused on the Raildog who didn't seem to wake up very happy. He kept trying to kick out with his legs. Little streams of blood running down the guy's boots said the rats had probably been at him.

He watched closely as the guy realized he had company and then started to take in his new situation. David had been a bit hesitant at his mother's last instruction, but had carried it out. Now he couldn't wait until the guy looked down at his crotch.

*****

Phoenix, Arizona

By habit, Sam instinctively tried to kick out with his feet. Nothing happened and he felt the fear grab him tight. His first thought was that the rats had gotten him.

Then as the light of the room really brought him around, he saw the woman sitting in front of him. *What the hell?* Groggily, Sam remembered the two people who entered the building earlier. He thought they were coming to help until he saw the tall bastard in black clothes who had put him here. Suddenly, seeing them wasn't such a good thing.

He could see the pretend Raildog sitting against the wall, watching. It was like he was settled in for the long haul, which brought Sam's eyes back to the woman camped on a chair right in front of him.

She was staring at him hard; riveted on him. He found it difficult to look back, there was such a glare in her eyes. She sucked on her cigarette while she stared right through him.

Who the fuck are you bitch? He wanted to speak, even though he was tied up, but something about her was frightening,

She kept glancing downwards and Sam let his eyes follow hers. The sight jolted him in his seat. *What the fuck?* His ass was pushed forward on the seat, which explained the pain in his lower back, and a big circle of his jeans and underwear were cut away.

His junk was hanging out in the open. He'd always been proud of what he had, but suddenly wished it didn't take up so much space. He looked back up at the woman.

"So you know what this is about now," she smiled.

Sam looked down again quickly, he didn't like where this was going. In his head he'd known that some day he might pay for all the fun he'd had, but he'd assumed a jail cell was the worst he would face. Now he felt his penis shriveling as real fear started to grip him.

The woman dropped the cigarette on the floor and carefully ground it flat with the sole of her shoe. Quietly, she moved her chair closer. She was within inches and Sam felt helpless. He wasn't sure what to expect next.

When the woman reached between his legs and ran her hand up and down, he became confused. Was she trying to excite him? He looked around the room, the only one there was the guy against the wall, still watching.

Don't tell me these two are here for some kind of kink. That thought alone was like a trigger, and he felt himself start to harden at the brush of her hand.

"Ah, there he is. Wow, you're a big boy." Her face lit up with excitement, and Sam thought maybe, just maybe, all they wanted was sex.

He desperately tried to regain some control over the situation. Sam pushed forward as much as the ropes would allow and tried to rotate his stiffened member. He wanted her to know it was available for whatever she had in mind.

Suddenly he screamed. The woman grabbed his balls and squeezed like her life was on the line. He was sure she broke them. Every nerve in his body was firing as he pulled and twisted against the ropes.

"Look at me." She ordered him, gripping even tighter. "Look. At. Me."

With considerable difficulty he turned his eyes back towards her while she kept on squeezing.

"You don't want to get the wrong idea dickhead." Her eyes narrowed as she whispered, "These little things have got you in a pile of shit." She gave the balls one more squeeze before letting go.

Sam thought he was going to pass out. His head dropped back in relief. Looking up, the flames from the fire made shadows that danced on the ceiling and in the corners. *He'd give anything to be on a train right now.*

Was this about something he'd done? Shit, he'd done a lot. Especially to women. He looked at the woman, but couldn't place her. Who was she?

The clatter of hard objects against the concrete got his attention, and against his will he looked down into her world again. The sight made him squirm.

She was taking what looked like tools out of a small black bag and placing them in on the floor. This fucking nightmare kept taking turns that Sam couldn't keep up with. His eyes came up from the floor to meet the woman who was waiting for his reaction.

"I got your attention now, don't I? We're going to take a walk down memory lane, just the two of us. Okay?"

The bitch was crazy. He looked at her sitting there all lady-like with her head cocked to the side, yet her eyes seemed to bulge out of her head. She looked ready to explode.

Sam didn't realize his lips were moving, but his ears heard the long drawn out, "Nooo…".

Then the high-pitched squeal of the woman's laugh echoed through the old building.

*****

Phoenix, Arizona

Sarah never felt so alive. She leaned her head back and laughed. The strange sound of her own voice motivated her. It sounded primal, and predatory. She couldn't slow herself down enough. This was something she wanted to enjoy, but to accomplish her goal she needed to reel in her anger.

For ten fucking years she'd dreamed of this moment. David could have killed him and just told her it was done. That would have been enough. But this, this, was beyond redemption, this was destiny.

She reached out again because he was getting soft, and that wouldn't do. He had to marry his hard-on to the coming pain, that's what she wanted. She loved the confusion written all over his face.

Looking at the thing made images rush through her brain. She knew this pink chunk of flesh personally. She had experienced it before, and not another since. If the guy only knew the fixation she had. But time would be his educator. She stroked it again and felt the first pulses of blood rushing, throbbing under her fingers.

Lighting another smoke, she alternated between taking a drag, and slapping or stroking his package. "I want you to remember ten years back." Smack. "A mother and a teenager." Smack. "Your life is depending on that memory."

The guy looked left and right. Sarah bet the fucker had a lot of women to sort through. She knew it was going to take awhile, too bad for him, she reached down for a wooden spoon.

Smack.

"Christ," the guy's eyes were like saucers as she tapped his balls from below.

"You need to remember faster big boy." And then she delivered a fast snapping shot to the same spot.

"The woman was from Chicago, she had her son with her. There were five of you there. The other men just robbed us. You on the other hand…" She trailed off, "You bastard."

Sarah's control slipped slightly and she slapped the penis hard with the spoon, then a second time that caused a slice in the skin. She liked seeing his pain. The shock in his eyes each time the blow struck made her heart pound.

"I've been trying to decide what to do with you ever since I knew I would get this chance. When I got here and saw the rats, it was revolting at first. But seeing the way you reacted to them, gave me an idea." She could tell that had struck home. He'd already built a cage of his own fear and all she did was climb in there with him.

She could see that the waiting was killing him. The apprehension must be building. She could relate. He'd done the same thing to her.

She remembered the disgust. The taste that took months to get out of her mouth. The endless abuse, repeated over and over. He'd been like a machine, stopping only for food and to have a piss. Those two days had been a living hell.

She had led a pretty sheltered life up to that point, and the things he'd done hadn't even entered her head. She didn't know they were possible. She felt herself starting to tremble and couldn't allow that. Taking a deep breath, she reached down to the floor again.

She opened up a couple small containers of honey, the type the hotel gives you for your toast in the morning. The care home had stacks of them in the kitchens. The honey coated the wooden spoon. She spread it on, under and around the man's package. It got stickier as it dried and the spoon began to pull at the hairs.

Sarah hoped he would make the connection to his actions in the past, she watched for the moment of recognition. But no, there was no flicker of awareness yet.

She grabbed her stuff and dragged the chair away. Now he was alone in the middle of the room. He looked questioningly at her.

Sarah walked around until she found a nice long hollow metal bar about three feet long. Stalking back to the Raildog she let her caged anger go, swinging the bar between his legs. After a few random shots to get her range and aim right, she started to really wallop his inner thighs, penis, and testicles. Her vision narrowed until the only thing she could see were her own hands gripping the cold steel.

The rasping of her own breathing wasn't enough to drown out the Raildog's screams, and with each blow, as she became more and more furious, the screams all rolled together in one long wail.

Sarah finally stopped swinging, exhausted and panting, her initial rage beginning to subside. The muscles in her arms burned. She reached up to swat hair out of her view. There was the look of a madwoman swimming in the glare of her eyes. She licked her lips in satisfaction. Some things were worth the effort.

Standing back to admire her handy-work, she watched the blood and honey slowly drip to the floor. She could leave it at that, the puddle slowly spreading. Knowing what was coming was enough. She only had one thing left to do, and that was set the fucker up. She didn't want the end to be a surprise, she wanted him thinking about it.

"Seen those rats chewed on you a bit. Good thing you were standing and able to kick them away." She smiled, "Not sure what you're going to do now to keep 'em off, but you're a stud, you'll think of something."

The look of horror on his face was priceless. She ought to stay for the show, but she had enough images in her head of the bastard and didn't need to add any new ones. As she led David towards the door she hoped the rats took their time.

"That's for me, you fucker, and all the others."

*****

Tucson, Arizona

Bill Dewton had finally gotten mad at himself. An hour after leaving Phoenix it hit him. The guy out in the field was dressed in black from head to toe. That was why it had been so hard to see him.

It had to be the same guy he'd seen on the passenger train leaving Salt Lake. Where they had found the mummy. Bill replayed the scene in his head. The guy had been just as suspicious looking the second time round.

When Bill caught sight of him, the guy had been watching him back. That meant the guy had noticed him first. As soon as he realized Bill had seen him, he'd turned his back and started moving. It was like he knew a moving person was harder to recognize. *Fuck.*

He should have jumped off the train right then. He'd had the thought. A few bruises would be better than the pissed off attitude he was giving himself right now. The soonest he could turn back was Tucson, so where the hell was it? It should be close. Christ, he'd been on the train three hours now.

The more he thought about it, the more he didn't like the guy in black. Was he a Raildog? He didn't act like one. But seeing him twice in a twenty-four hour period couldn't be a coincidence.

The burden was weighing heavy on his shoulders. For some reason this wild goose chase kept bringing his daughter back to the top of his mind. His wife thought he hadn't shown enough sorrow and in some ways he had silently agreed. He knew if he did start to really grieve, he'd die in the hole it would create.

Now he was running out of time. The question was, time for what? He wasn't going to find her, so what was he really after?

Finally, Bill was able to see buildings and smoke in the distance, Tucson. He'd switch trains and head right back to Phoenix. Three, maybe four hours tops.

He kept thinking about what he was after. He supposed he knew the answer, it had been the same all along, he was trying not to fall into that hole.

.

CHAPTER 18

The quiet that engulfed the old building after his tormentors left was disturbing. Sam had tried to keep a straight face until they were gone, he wasn't giving the bitch the satisfaction. But as soon as they were gone, it was pure panic.

This wasn't happening. The brutal pain between his legs was unbearable, he could feel his penis wasn't hanging correctly any more, and he had a picture of raw meat in his head. He didn't waste any time, sliding the chair backwards until he slammed into a wall.

He was preparing for the battle he knew was coming. Alternating between sheer panic and intense pain, he kept trying to look down at himself to see how bad the damage was. But tied back against the chair the way he was, he couldn't get the line of sight right.

How was he going to protect himself if he couldn't see it? Sam screamed out as loud as he could in frustration. Earlier he had held onto some chance of getting out of this mess. Now he wouldn't take that bet at any odds. He screamed again, his eyes wide, his mouth stretched open, his lips pulled tight against his teeth.

When he heard scurrying, his eyes darted back and forth across the floor. *No, this can't be.* For some reason there were more of them. Did the others go and get help? Did his screaming bring them in? Or was it whatever the bitch had smeared on him?

Sam hovered on the chair, almost as if he was trying to lift up off the seat. That wasn't working. He tried to stay focused on the main issue, figuring out how to keep the rats at bay. Earlier he had to contend with three mid-sized rodents, now there were six, or seven. They slunk around so much it was hard to be sure.

The big one however, had Sam's attention. It sat right in front of him, ten feet away, no more. He could see its pointed little nose working as it narrowed in on the source of the smell. When the rat moved forward a few feet, he jerked against the ropes and pushed the chair harder against the wall.

"Fuck off! Fuck off!" he screamed. He was hissing, spit running down his chin when he finished. The big rat took a few more steps until he was sitting right in front of Sam.

He felt his pulse pounding. He couldn't break down or give in. *Jesus Sam, fight.* How? The other rats seemed to gain courage from the big one, closing in behind it.

He was going to loose it and could feel it coming. His brain couldn't, or wouldn't, take it. He fought to breathe. The air seemed to hold less and less oxygen with each gulp.

The big rat waddled closer and disappeared from view. The terror was enough to make him squeal like a little girl. He didn't recognize his own voice. The realization that the rat was below him kicked every basic instinct he ever had into gear.

He shuffled sideways, sliding the chair three feet left, making a bunch of noise in the process. The rats backed up slightly and he had the big one in view again, out in the open to his right.

The small victory brought him new energy. "That's it you fuckers, come and get it."

He had a thought. What if he could raise the chair up on one side and smash it down on the rat? Would it work? Since moving the chair had bought him some time, he did it again. This time he moved more forcefully, scrapping and banging the chair up and down.

When the rats backed up a few feet more, he took a chance and tried to lift one side of the chair. With it up on one side, he balanced it there. Okay, he had a weapon. Then the chair almost tipped over the wrong way, and his entire body shook as he fought to get it back on all four feet.

Shit, he didn't want to fall over. That would be the end of him. Sam shivered at the thought of being eye level with them. They'd start on his face. Closing his eyes for a second, he sucked in a big breath. This wasn't right. No one deserved this, did they?

The pain in his balls hurt so much he wanted to cry. Yet his brain was busy going crazy and didn't care. His eyes snapped open when he realized he was drifting. A couple of big rats were moving closer. He tried yelling at them and growling to slow their advance.

The sudden change in the pain tore his attention away from the two rats. Then he realized the other big one wasn't on the right anymore. Hysteria began to overwhelm him. He jerked the chair back to where he started from. The noise flushed the big rat out from under the chair.

"No." Sam squealed, "No."

He couldn't get any other words out. His mind was locked on the rat that had scurried free. "Please no." His eyes saw the blood all over the rat's mouth, but his brain wouldn't let the image in.

The rat had a first taste and now it was motivated. When it moved towards the chair again, two other big ones shuffled forward with it. Sam was no longer thinking, his mind had shut down, and his fear had completely taken over.

He yanked the chair sideways and then jerked at it again. This time he wasn't careful enough, and the chair tipped up on one side. Too freaked out by the rats, he didn't react quickly enough, and the chair toppled over.

Two things happened. First the concrete block fell out from between him and the chair and he was able to sink back to a sitting position, even if he was on his side. Second, his brain had a moment of utter clarity. Was it really better to be able to see what was going on? His brain started laughing at him. No, it wasn't.

The rats scurried from everywhere now that he was on the ground. The big ones crawled between his legs, shaking their heads like lions ripping meat from a carcass. He saw his privates for the first time, and vomit rushed to his mouth.

Sam turned his head sideways to launch the puke and realized his mistake. The additional food brought a pack of little rats. He was killing himself, *fuck*. He'd give anything to be sitting upright again. He almost looked down between the legs one more time, but managed to stop himself. He didn't need to see what he could already feel.

The chair jerked back and forth as the big ones tore and pulled at their meal. Sam heard the screams again, but all that registered was the pack of small rats working their way up the splatter of vomit towards his face.

Then the sound was muffled and his brain finally let go.

*****

Phoenix, Arizona

Retracing their steps back to the freight yard in Phoenix, David stopped to let his mother catch her breath.

They hadn't exchanged any words since leaving the warehouse. He was thinking about the future and figured she was too. They couldn't stick around here. And with everything that happened over the last week he didn't think the rails were necessarily a good place to spend much time.

But they had to take one more ride at least. He figured the west coast. Somewhere away from the box, away from everything.

Somewhere new.

When she used the break to pull out a cigarette and light up, he didn't object. He could tell she was on edge. She must be coming down from the adrenaline high.

"You shouldn't smoke those things." Not the best way to start a conversation.

When she didn't answer, he thought to himself, *okay*. He wouldn't hold it against her, she'd had a crazy night. He could tell she wasn't quite back to normal. But then, after what she'd gone through and where she'd spent the last ten years, neither promoted sanity.

David was determined to help her though it, after all everything she'd done in the first place was to save him and make sure he was safe. He would always feel it was his fault that she was trapped in this nightmare.

"You good to go mom?" The break was long enough.

She gave a solitary nod of her head. She must be somewhere else, he thought as he led her farther into the yard, towards the westbound lines headed for the coast.

If he thought about the violence, it never did anything for him. But recently he'd been thinking about what he'd done to the gang. The payback all made sense from a revenge perspective. But sometimes he wondered about his victim's friends and relatives.

Everyone had someone waiting for them somewhere. Had David made someone out there as angry as he'd been back at the beginning? Did he deserve to have someone come and find him? He realized the answer was yes, and it deflated him.

It would be easy to build up anger against her, everything he'd done had been for her. He'd known what she wanted and that she wouldn't settle for jail time.

David let it wash off his shoulders. He didn't care about the past anymore. There had been a debt to pay and it was done. He didn't have it in him to hurt anyone else. In fact there was a relief it was over.

It was over. He thought about that. He must have known subconsciously, but hadn't understood when he had dropped the brown notebook on the bench in the old building.

David had spent a lot of time recently thinking about relatives and the home life he'd had before they'd skipped out. For some reason, now that he didn't need to go forward he was slipping backwards.

Shaking the thoughts away, he pointed to a place she could sit. All they needed now was a train heading west. All the love he felt for her and the guilt over what had happened because of him came together, and he was just happy she was free. Perhaps some day he would be too.

Maybe he thought, just maybe, there was a life to go back to.

"Mom, I've got this idea."

*****

Phoenix, Arizona

It was almost noon when Bill finally got back into Phoenix. He'd walked the tracks out of the yard and found the spot where he'd last seen the man and woman.

Pushing through the fence, he followed the trail that led to the building. What was it that irritated him until he suddenly felt a need for his gun? Years of experience told him not to ignore the feeling. With his gun held out in front, he moved from the building's doorway to the inside wall. Then he moved sideways, keeping the wall at his back as he circled the open room.

Smoke from a dead fire drifted out of an old barrel. The shadows made it hard to see what it was that was moving over against the far wall. He looked around the room until he was sure he was alone before stepping closer.

Moving slowly, gun still held out at shoulder level, Bill tried to focus on what he was seeing. Rats. *Oh Fuck.* Rats eating a body. He turned away and fought not to empty his stomach.

Pissed off, he emptied the magazine into the squirming mass of filthy rodents.

The rats scrambled away, temporarily disturbed. He took a deep breath and forced himself to take another step closer. It looked like the body was tied to a chair. The best he could tell, the rats had eaten a hole into the stomach through the vic's crotch area. Bill's knees wobbled for a second. "Ouch."

He pulled out a pocketknife and cut the one arm loose from the chair. Using the tip of the knife he peeled back the sleeve of the jean jacket. There was the tattoo; number two. He hadn't heard back on the mummy in Salt Lake yet, but he was sure it was going to be the number one. That meant the gang had effectively had its head cut off. What were the rest of them doing? Where were they?

Bill stood back, he needed to regain some composure. The view wasn't any better from a few feet away. He turned and walked a large circle in the middle of the empty warehouse. He wasn't sure what he wanted to do next. Was this it? Was it over? Was there one guy he was supposed to find? Who was going to admit to doing anything to his daughter? *No one, that's who.*

He was walking past a bench against the wall when he noticed the brown leather-wrapped book. Instinctively, he checked to make sure he still had the black one inside his jacket pocket. The leather book didn't belong. Curious, Bill opened it up, facing it towards the faint light from outside. His forehead wrinkled as he flipped the pages. Slowly, he realized it was important and went back to the beginning to start again, this time turning the pages slowly.

It was the killer's book, no doubt about that. An hour later he had it figured out. The book began seven years ago tracking someone. Over the years others were followed and schedules added. Someone had spent years following and tracking them. Why?

He thought of his daughter, and the answer was obvious. He thought of the patience the person must have had, the anger and the burning desire for revenge required to keep such a long-term project going. Now Bill was sure the guy in black was the killer. Shouldn't he go after this guy? Let the other agencies know about him?

He wasn't sure what to do, this had all started for his daughter's sake.

The guy in black had a woman with him. Considering the mess between this last guy's legs, it wasn't a stretch to think this revenge was sexually oriented. Maybe this guy had taken care of the gang on her behalf, and for anyone else they'd abused.

He'd been one step behind the whole time, but at least he'd seen the damage that had happened and knew if these were the people who harmed his daughter, they'd paid a steep price. He supposed he could give the two books to the cops. Maybe.

The book from the Raildog's boss would definitely be given over. There were a lot of numbers still out there who needed to be taken out of commission. He turned the killer's small brown leather-bound ledger over in his hand. Finally, he made the call and dropped the book into the smoldering ashes at the bottom of the barrel.

Some things just felt right.

*****

Phoenix, Arizona

Sarah didn't hear David's comment. She was trying to sort out her own thoughts. Where was she going? After ten years in the home she wasn't used to making her own decisions. What was she going to do now? Depend on him?

He'd helped her climb onto a westbound train. He said they were going to the coast. That didn't sound too bad. She couldn't help but feel she was going to become a burden on him. Then what?

She wanted her life back, so what should she do next? Ten years ago she'd had plans for them both and he still needed her then. He didn't now. He seemed so sure of himself, and yet he hadn't settled down in any way, or created any kind of life.

It was hard to blame him if he became a drifter. She'd put him out on the road in the first place.

"Mom, I'm talking to you. I said I have an idea."

"Sorry David. I was thinking"

She looked at the little kid in the big body. He seemed especially vulnerable for some reason. Then she focused on the slop he was talking about.

"I was thinking about before. We left home because Dad was beating you and you always said that it was only a matter of time before he started on me too."

Sarah looked at him intently. Where was this going?

"I'm older and able to take care of myself. I thought maybe we should go back home. See grandma and grandpa. Maybe Dad is older, wiser. Maybe he misses us."

Sarah sure hadn't expected that. She looked into his pleading eyes and realized he wanted to be part of a family. *Christ*, what was she going to do now? She looked at him intently, was he old enough to take the truth?

Sarah started to answer, then she paused. On some level she knew this was going to hit him hard. On the other hand, she hoped he would be able to see her side of things. Still she knew it was going to hurt to hear. But it was the truth, so he'd better find a way to deal with it.

"Your father's dead." Immediately she saw the look on his face and regretted saying anything. There was nothing left to do but continue. "I had to kill him."

"What?" His look of disbelief was heartbreaking.

"He caught me with the neighbor and demanded a divorce. I couldn't have that. So I cleaned out the accounts and he disappeared." She seemed to stall, "They're probably still looking for all three of us."

*****

David shook his head. *Had she really said that?* Did that mean he'd lost his chance at a normal life for all the wrong reasons?

He stood in the boxcar's open doorway watching the night fly past. He'd spent years trying to make it up to her for what she had done for him, now it turned out it wasn't even about him. It had always been about her and what she wanted.

The more he thought about it the more pissed off he became.

He looked at her over his shoulder. She'd taken him away from his family, he'd been alone on the rails for years because she couldn't be loyal. Wasn't that what he'd been to her all these years? Loyal.

Now what?

He looked at her sleeping, curled up on the floor. He didn't recognize her any more. Who the hell was she?

The warm tears he felt running down his cheeks weren't for the things that had happened in the past, they were for what was going to happen next. And still it hurt. The train was hurling towards California and what promised to be another beautiful day.

How could he? He struggled with the idea. Why shouldn't he?

He loved her. *No he didn't.* At least not anymore.

His fists clenched and his jaw set tight. Somewhere in his head he turned off. He'd done it before when he was so mad he couldn't stop. It created a clarity of mind, he just couldn't control it.

Somewhere inside his brain, the decision was made.

David reached down and grabbed his mother by the shoulder. He dragged her to the door, towards the landscape rushing past. She woke up as he pulled her across the splintered floor. And she screamed as he flung her out the opening.

For a moment he had her by the arms, hanging beside the train. He wasn't letting go yet, but his grip was the only thing holding her. He watched her flailing to keep her feet from hitting the gravel, her shoes catapulting into the air when they momentarily touched down.

She screamed again. Looking up at him, the fear and confusion were etched in her face, "David no. Please. Please, I love you David."

She didn't understand what he was doing when he started to swing her out away from the train. Didn't understand until her momentum carried her back in, bringing her far too close to the wheels.

"David. Please God." He could hear the panic in her voice. "I love you, don't do this."

He closed his ears. He focused on the swinging motion, out a little farther this time. As his arms came back towards the train, he let go.

His mother's body was carried right into the wheels of the train.

She was swept under the first axle, only for her body to be flipped sideways as the next wheels ripped at her. Blood and guts splattered everywhere, spreading pieces of her along the tracks.

David dropped to his knees in the open doorway. He wanted off the train. This would be his last ride.

The tears streaming down his face hit the wooden floor of the boxcar, the salty water leaving dark spots as it soaked into the dry timber.

"If you'd loved me mom, you would have left me in Chicago."

The End

Write a Book Review

Book reviews help other readers decide if a particular book is right for them. They also help writers by providing practical feedback on what you liked about the book. If you enjoyed this book, please take a moment to write down a few words describing what you liked about Raildogs at your favourite book retailer or at Goodreads.com, and help spread the word.

About the Author

Rejean Giguere is an avid outdoorsman, adventurer, photographer and artist. He enjoys fishing, hockey, golf, tennis, skiing and snowmobiling, his V-Max motorcycle and vintage Corvette.

He grew up in Canada and Europe, and enjoyed a business career in Toronto and Ottawa.

Visit his website at www.rejeangiguere.com

Enjoy the sample of my novel Jackfish Reborn on the following pages.

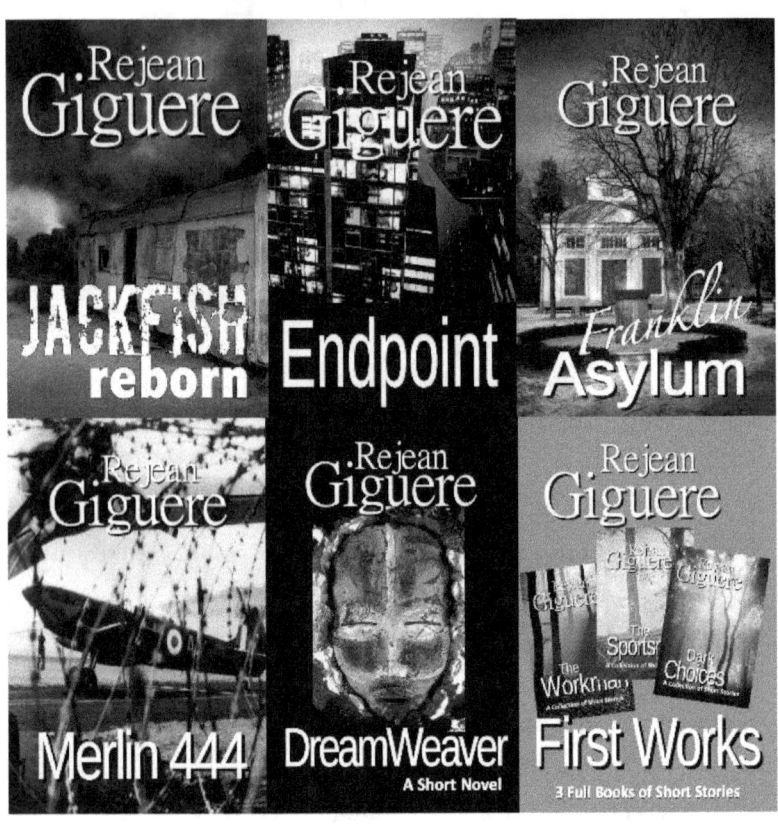

PROLOGUE

China, 2010

Chang "Dragon" Long sat across from his grand-mother. He couldn't understand the direction this conversation was taking. It seemed he was missing something.

His grandmother was one of those strong, intelligent women who helped advance a family's fortunes. In fact, he'd never known his great-grandfather who had disappeared in North America, so he'd received most of his wisdom from her.

Now he could tell she was waiting patiently for him to catch up. Dragon stared down at the box of items that she had handed him. Apparently they were from his great-grandfather and she clearly wanted him to see them.

The odd assortment of papers meant nothing to him, but when she asked him to read it all again he knew he was supposed to find something. She was a smart one, and obviously she had a reason, so he went through the papers one last time trying to understand what was written there.

Some of the papers appeared to be contracts, and he understood some of the maps. They were all related to the businesses his family was involved in, drug running and mining. Nothing stood out, but he was left with one piece of paper in his hand that he couldn't place. He knew it was the right one as he watched his grandmother smile.

The sheet of paper made no sense. It was like a riddle or a code;

Come to the land of tree and rock,
Simple people, land of riches, a fish named Jack.
Big tongue in the water, protected by two,
Walking steel eyes into the late day sun, past the two,
Leaving the ocean, finding the other side of three,
Wealth and prosperity, awaits in eights, the white lightning

He kept returning to the eights because he knew the number meant good luck. When he looked up, the confusion on his face clearly evident, his grandmother took a deep breath and leaned forward. "It is time eldest grandson. It is time to learn about your destiny."

Book 1
A Riddle

CHAPTER 1

China, 2012

Dragon Chang was twenty-four years old. Strong from years in the trade, he paced quietly along the mountain path. This would be his last trip leading the opium shipments from inside Burma to his home province of Yunnan, in southwest China. He would ensure the cargo made it from the jungle bases in Burma, where the processed opium originated, along the well-travelled routes through his territory, to the distributers in Macau.

His family had been associated with the TeoChiew, or TC triad, for generations. Relatives had even moved to Burma and Thailand to become part of that end of the supply chain. Years later the opium was constantly on the move. He used this route every third or fourth run, choosing from the many available trails along the fourteen hundred miles of border between China and Burma.

Dragon stopped suddenly. His eyes squinted as he strained to hear something. Impossible to most people, he had an ability to hear in the rain and to sense the unexpected. Now he stood there with his eyes closed and let his flexing muscles transmit the threat which had brought him to a halt.

The two men travelling with him ahead of the mule train had used this route many times and knew the land well. Dragon turned to the first one. "Return to the train, get it off the trail until we come back for you."

There was no answer as the man hurried back to meet the cargo.

To the other he said, "The valley opens up close to here, we'll find high ground."

Dragon headed off the trail towards a rising hill. In the west of the province it was all steep hills and valleys running north and south. It was beautiful unless you had to climb the hills. Today their route worked its way up a canyon beside a raging river. He knew that this side of the valley would give him a clear view of the trail that wound its way along the other side.

Intensity mixed with the rain on his face, not from the fear of what might be ahead, but in anticipation of what was to come.

Who would make the mistake of hitting one of his trains? These guys weren't the first ones to try, but like others before them, their first attempt would be the last.

This was Dragon's last shipment. It had taken him over a year to convince his father to let him follow his dream and take his place in expanding the family business.

For generations the family had followed the same pattern. One generation kept the supply routes running and promoted their legitimate businesses. The next generation spread out to new territory, expanding the family fortunes.

Dragon's father was very influential, he hardly ever saw the man who was constantly on the move in the mountains while running the trade. His father's generation the one entrusted to stay in the mountains, keeping routes open, keeping things flowing. He knew his father took this responsibility seriously and was doing whatever was required to keep the family fortune protected.

It was his father who showed him the routes and introduced him to their contacts. He'd also been the first to show Dragon the lengths required to protect the family business.

The memory of these brutal lessons brought him back to his immediate concern. His anger was inching closer to the surface, and he hadn't even seen the danger yet. It might just be simple peasant women out on a supply run. Still, he ground his teeth at the thought it could be something else.

Dragon had grown up exercising a level of power, even when he was young he could tell his family was dangerous. He himself had never been weakened by fear, but excelled at creating it in others. He wrinkled his nose in disgust at the thought and shook the rain off his head momentarily. After climbing twenty yards up the hill, he got down and crawled the last ten feet to a ledge where he could look down into the valley. The other man crawled up beside him.

He was sure someone was out there, coming up the trail. His instincts had never been wrong before. He was patient, which was something he didn't learn from his father, but from his grandmother. It had been two years since the day she had given him his great-grandfather's papers and explained that she didn't think the old man had died in vain.

Chang "Tiger" Cheng was supposed to expand the family, and had taken advantage of an opportunity to sail the far seas. He had ended up in Canada at a time it was a virgin land that had hardly been explored. It had always been assumed that

Tiger died there sometime around 1885. The cryptic riddle in his final letters home had contained references to wealth and prosperity, but had meant nothing to anyone in the family.

His grandmother reminded him that he had an obligation to move away and expand the family business.

Suddenly, a nudge from his partner made Dragon dial in on what was going on down in the valley. It took a moment to find them through the falling rain and drifting fog that hung between the mountains. Once he spotted them he went completely still, staring like a hawk. The outlines of four strangers walked up and over a knoll before their trail disappeared back behind a large bank of rock.

He closed his eyes briefly, enjoying the feel of adrenaline working its way into his system. It was his only drug. He waited for the intruders to cross a larger open area. A slight smile spread across his face.

Now that they were out in the open and he was sure they were alone, he thought to himself, four of you, that's a bad number, it means death. Two of us is a good number, good things come in pairs. He smiled widely. "Li, we'll take them out from here."

From this distance he wasn't really sure who they were. They could be soldiers, police, or another gang. Either way, it wasn't someone who ruled in this area, because that fell to him and his family. Dragon took the bag off his shoulder and hunched over to create a rain-stop while he unloaded the M99 sniper rifle. His father always believed in having the right equipment for the job. Even though the family looked like struggling miners to everyone else, they were highly efficient and deadly in the mountains. One thing they never had was a shortage of money and connections.

The rifle was more than he really needed, the fifty-calibre bullets could punch holes through armoured vests. He settled over the stock, feeling the wet metal against his jaw. He knew how far it was across the valley and adjusted the scope slightly. Aiming at the next knoll along the trail he waited for them to appear.

How many times had he fought in these hills? It was personal to him that he was successful on his last run, and it pissed him off that these intruders were even here. It was time though, he looked through the scope entering into another world.

Everything around him evaporated, he stopped listening and let his eye take over. The path was enlarged in the scope. He was always amazed at the distance you could kill from. He was picking out the individual pebbles on the trail when he saw the first figure step out into the open.

The sight of combat fatigues was enough, and Dragon flipped off the safety, still watching through the scope. He let the first two men cross his field of view and waited for the third one appear. The third one was his first target. Surprise was everything. Taking the rain into account, he gently pulled the trigger. A slight correction and he was onto number two who had almost made his way across the opening. He pulled the trigger a second time.

The two cracks of the rifle could be heard through the rain, and the remaining men scattered. The first guy went forward, the last one went back, spreading them apart. His two kills were laid out like broken rag dolls on the trail. Dragon's eye never left the scope, he swung back towards the last knoll the intruders had crossed and waited. On cue, his next victim peeked out from behind the top of the knoll before trying to retreat across the open space.

Dragon had been waiting for that move and the trigger moved slightly. The man wasn't any better off than his buddies, the round slammed him sideways and he landed in a heap. Lowering the rifle, he stood up and relaxed slightly. "Li, you take the last one and get the bodies off the trail. I'll get the train."

*****

The Chinese gangster went to ground when the first rifle shots rang out. He was in someone else's territory. They had known that, and been prepared to negotiate an arrangement with whoever ran this area in order to smuggle drugs from Burma. Obviously these people weren't interested and now two of his comrades were dead.

Another shot let him know that his third friend had indeed tried to run back down the trail. He was terrified. He had to stay hidden, but had to get moving. Looking around he crawled up to a rock ledge that was between him and the shooter, turning to stand with his back against it. He didn't get much time to think.

The figure dropping onto the trail from above, landed in front of him. A machete sliced into his shoulder on the way past, driving him to the ground with the force of the blow. Looking up, he could see arms holding the blade, everything else was blocked out. There was only a silhouette of the man in the pouring rain. All he was able to focus on were the tattoos running up the two arms as they jerked the blade free.

He held back a scream, even with his arm hanging away from his body. But as he was grabbed and dragged to the river's edge he began to yell. His only thought as his screams hit the rushing water was that he'd never learnt to swim.

*****

Dragon's pack train continued along the ancient trail until they came to one of the changeover camps. Here the bundles were unloaded from the mules and transferred into small vehicles. They would make their way overland through Guangxi and Guangdong provinces towards the chaos of Macau.

Dragon had been to the end of the route a number of times back when he began his training. His father wanted him to see the product all the way to the docks and the ships that would take it away. He usually turned around here with the mules and let his men take it the rest of the way. The load was secure and the most dangerous part was over now that the product was moving in vehicles.

He thought back to his first runs. He could laugh at it now. How their connections must have looked at him as he came down the trail with one bundle and one mule. Dragon had thought he was a major player while his father had let him get his footing.

Now the trains were huge, this one had twenty mules and one hundred bundles. It would take three vehicles to carry it all. This shipment alone would generate huge profits. Paying the farmer one thousand for the raw opium, they would refine the product and move it to North America where it sold for one hundred and fifty thousand. Even he realized this was an exceptional return.

This time Dragon would be riding with these bundles to the end of the line. He was going to the docks with his right hand man Li. They would catch a ride on one of the ships and pursue the dream his great-grandfather had begun.

It was hard to leave these hills and the comforts of family. Bouncing along the small goat paths in one of the vehicles, Dragon thought about his great-grandfather's riddle. He had spent a lot of time turning it over in his head in doing as much research as he could. In the end he knew he would have to trace his great-grandfather's travels to piece it together.

It was when Dragon studied the construction route of the Canadian Pacific Railroad where the family assumed his great-grandfather had died, that he hit the jackpot. A ghost town along the north shore of Lake Superior called Jackfish. It was a long shot that this was the, fish named Jack, at beginning of the riddle, but he was going to have to start somewhere.

This intrigued Dragon the most. If his hunch was correct, then Tiger left them clues to a place that was now a ghost town. What did that mean? Was there any significance? He was putting a lot of faith in this place Jackfish.

He couldn't figure out anything else from the riddle his grandmother had given him, but it seemed that he that this was the place to start. Dragon knew he was really just a mountain miner and part-time gangster. Even with his piles of money, he was unfamiliar with the rest of the world. This trip to another continent was going to take all the skill and courage he had. He looked at Li sitting beside him and smiled. He'd need all the muscle he could get.

CHAPTER 2

Hours later the small convoy crawled towards the populated section of the coast along the South China Sea. Soon they were crossing the bridge over the Xi river, turning off the highway towards the hustle of the tight streets and bright lights of Macau. Compared to his place in the mountains Dragon loved this city. He had to sacrifice the comfort he found in the silence of the mountain nights, but was excited by the noise and nightlife of the city.

The small convoy headed down Shihua East Road towards the container port. Circling around the freight and customs warehouses, his driver pulled up to the back gate of the trucking yard where the triad controlled things. Waved through quickly, the cars headed along the busy docks to a ship anchored near the end. Without many words the deck hands and smugglers began hauling the bundles up the gangway. This ship was bound for Vancouver in the morning. Dragon and Li were going on a second freighter also leaving the next day. That gave the men some time to enjoy a bit of the nightlife.

Dragon had to be careful. As much as he ruled his area of the mountains, and he would be welcome in any TC Triad's bar or restaurant, Macau was a major centre for distribution, prostitution and gambling. The other triads were active here as well. He would have to make sure he didn't cross any hidden boundaries.

He felt a huge weight on his shoulders. Would he make it back to China, or was he leaving for the first and last time? Once their product was loaded onto the ship they all piled into the vehicles and headed out to get drunk.

The bar was just a few steps off the trendy Sun Yat Sen Avenue. The dark and run down exterior of the gang hangout of local TC Triad members was a hundred years apart from the imitation Miami dance clubs lining the avenue. Dragon was enjoying his beer and unwinding a little. The life of a drug runner was intense and he had spent the last couple weeks in a heightened state of alert.

Li sat beside him. Close calls and scrapes had brought them close. Li's family had worked for his since before both of them were born. Dragon looked at him as an equal and as a friend.

He lifted his beer. "Our last run together Li. May our luck be as good in the new world."

"Cheers to the new world." Li tipped his beer in salute.

His answer wasn't that enthusiastic. All along Dragon's planning assumed that Li would want to come. Now he wondered if he had it wrong. "You don't sound that excited Li. You don't have to take this trip if it doesn't suit you."

"It's the uncertainty of the trip. I'm not sure where we are going or what we are trying to do." Li took a drink from his beer, "besides when will we see a smooth Chinese woman again?"

Dragon burst out laughing. "That is all you ever think of, but you do raise a serious issue." Dragon hadn't thought about it, and the way Li said it really got him thinking. "Maybe we better find some girls tonight Li, it could be our last chance."

He waved over their local connection, who had brought them to the bar, instructing him to take them where they could find some women. The five men ended up in the red-light end of town outside a strip club. Dragon let his contact do the talking at the door, then followed him inside.

The interior was a stark contrast to the rundown neon-lit exterior. Inside flashing strobe lights swirled, casting beams through the cigarette smoke. Dragon felt the bass of the music punch against his chest as if he had run into a wall.

Li stopped, just staring. There were more naked women that either of them had ever seen in one place before. On the stage, carrying drinks, dancing in front of men at their tables, the gorgeous women were clearly available for a good time.

Dragon noticed curtained booths set off to one side. He let their contact know he wanted one of those, where he could have more privacy and less scrutiny. Once a little money changed hands they were inside their own space.

When the first waitress came in to take their orders, Dragon pulled her aside, "Can you get seven or eight women to join us for the night." He flashed some of the money he had tucked into his inner jacket. "Girls who want to have fun," he said with a smile.

Soon the little curtained booth was rocking. He threw some money down on the table, welcoming the women for the evening. The dancers were ecstatic as they divvied up their shares of more money than they might ordinarily earn in a month, settling in to have some fun.

Dragon watched over the scene for a bit as Li and the three other men indulged themselves with the naked women. Never shy in public, Li wasted no time, and quickly was thrusting himself into a woman in the corner.

Once word got around the bar about the generous flow of money, other women approached, asking if they could join the party. Over the next hour Dragon stayed alert and ensured the other men had their fun.

When he could tell Li was finally done with his third woman, he settled back to enjoy himself. Two of their local contacts were leaving, one behind staying to keep him and Li company. Dragon let a few new girls into the booth and encouraged the rest of the others to leave. He wanted it a little less crowded.

Finally he leaned back against the booth and pointed at his lap. One of the women straddled his legs, facing him. He felt his pants open and the zipper go down. She reached in and pulled him out.

Dragon looked her in the eye as she stroked him. Rising up, she held his gaze as she moved closer, dropping down, taking him all at once. He leaned his head back and let the woman move on him. She closed her eyes, slowly sliding up and down.

When a menacing looking young gangster suddenly burst through the curtain, Li jumped up to confront him. The woman on top of Dragon froze momentarily, until he put his hands on her waist and started her moving slowly again.

"Li, wait." Dragon's voice was calm. He could see the intruder clearly from his position and knew he was a threat. "Who the fuck are you?"

That seemed to have caught the young man off guard, he'd probably expected the men to fear him, but it was obvious they didn't.

"Who the fuck am I? Who the fuck, are you?" The gangster took a few steps forward, vibrating with anger. He couldn't believe the balls of this guy, who just kept the woman going up and down as if he wasn't concerned at all. "You got yourself a serious problem here and you don't even understand it."

The gangster kept his right arm turned forward like he wanted them to see his 14K triad tattoo. He obviously wanted them to know that he was beyond the reach of police and the authorities. He seemed to think he could do whatever he wanted.

Dragon had two choices. Let Li make quick work of the guy, which would mean they would have to fight their way out. Or, he could use the negotiating skills his father had taught him and the patience his grandmother had taken the time to instil in him.

He wanted, without a doubt, to mess this asshole up. It would have been a sure thing if they were in the mountains, but one did have to adjust in the city. He looked at the woman who had started to speed up her movements and again used his hands to slow her down.

Raising his right hand, he pointed at the young gangster. "You better get your boss, because you've made a big mistake."

Now the guy was losing his momentum, bosses meant upper-level triad members, and he obviously wasn't anywhere near that point yet. Dragon watched him struggle with the thought that this might be a friend of his bosses and perhaps he was in over his head. He could see the moment when the young gangster decided he wasn't letting it go, he'd heard about the money floating around and was going to get some if these guys weren't protected.

"I'll get my boss asshole, just so he can watch me screw you guys up."

Dragon never even looked up. He was starting to really enjoy the woman's movements and kept his focus on her. "We'll be waiting I'm sure. Now go get someone boy." He knew that would really piss the kid off. After all, Dragon wasn't much older than he was, but he continued to ignore him as he steamed out of the booth.

"Okay woman, it's time." Finally he let her speed up, rising higher and higher until she brought him to a satisfying release. That was the way he wanted to remember his women. He had business to deal with now and he quickly lifted her off his lap and pointed to the door. She seemed relieved to get out of there, he was sure she knew the shit was coming.

Street level gangsters were at each other constantly, fighting for space, but he also knew that the triads operated together at the highest levels to ensure everything ran smoothly. He would let that be his card out of here. "Li, calm is required. I will let you know if I need your help."

The curtain flew open a second time and in walked the young gangster with one of his bosses. This one was older and rounder, and moved with purpose. He was covered in tattoos, his 14K symbol out in the open. He looked briefly at Li before settling on Dragon. "This is the man you speak of? Where is the woman he used while he threatened you?"

"She was here," was all the youngster replied.

The boss continued to stare at Dragon. "You bring trouble to one of my bars? And to one of my men?"

"I came in to enjoy some liquor and women. We took a booth to be private and considerate to the other patrons. This useless man of yours interrupted us and has been rude and insulting." Dragon stood up and faced the older gangster head on. "Which I hold against you. The question is, will this end here, or is it going to escalate?" Dragon took off his coat and rolled up his sleeves. He made sure his own tattoo was clearly visible.

All tattoos said something to those who knew what to look for. The gangster would see the TeoChiew triad symbol represented by the TC, but it was the symbol above it that would get his attention.

Anyone affiliated with the triads had a symbol saying so. If the symbol was below the triad tattoo, it meant that they were under the triads control and reported to them. If it was beside the triad tattoo, it meant that they were in partnership with the triad, as equals.

When the symbol was above the triad tattoo, like Dragon's, it meant the person was integral to the triad's profits and highly respected. Someone that was to be protected at all times. Dragon watched the gangster as he put it together.

The man could still take a shot at them. He was a gangster from another triad and might get away with it; but he'd be wondering if it was allowed. Look at the mistake his soldier had already made.

The man was in an uncomfortable position, he couldn't believe this young tough-looking kid was attached to the higher levels. It was all about saving face now. "My apologies for the rudeness of a simple soldier. We will leave you to your evening."

"Just make sure that there are no more incidents tonight," Dragon let that hang a second. "Are we clear?"

The gangster nodded as he pushed his soldier out through the curtain. Dragon and Li had another drink and decided they needed to get out of there. Their contact, who had been quiet and uninvolved through the entire hassle, was still with them. He was providing a bed to stay that night, so the three of them left the club, heading for his place.

The contact took two steps onto the sidewalk before he was swarmed. *Shit,* Dragon had known it was still a possibility. If that boss was a hothead he might have been embarrassed and wanting to do something about it. As long as his bosses didn't find out, there would be no consequences.

Big mistake. The gangster should have been worrying about Dragon's group instead of his own bosses. As their contact went down, Li jumped forward. He pulled his machete from the back sling hidden under his coat and went to work.

Swinging the deadly blade in an X pattern in front of him, Li walked into the group, taking off outstretched arms or legs as they presented themselves. Dragon looked at faces until he found the boss he had spoken to. He could see the man was shocked at the sudden explosion of flying body parts as Li began to wreak havoc. The man started to back up, separating himself from the group.

Dragon surged towards the boss who saw him coming at the last second. As the man tried to maneuver out of the way, he was hit hard and driven backwards onto the ground. Dragon landed hard on top of him and quickly gained the upper hand. Now he had the gangster pinned.

He took a quick moment to turn and check the others. Their contact was getting up off the pavement and there wasn't a group of attackers left. Those uninjured by Li's initial assault were running in every direction. The rest were screaming, crawling or stumbling away from the viscous attack.

Dragon looked down at the gangster again and made sure the man saw the anger on his face.

"You've made a mistake Mr. Big Boss, and now you are going to pay."

Before the gangster had a chance to wonder what was coming, Dragon drove his head downward, smashing it into the guy's face. There was an awful crack. He pulled back and watched the face explode with blood from a broken nose that was now bent over to the left.

"You'll have a memory of this night forever."

The boss was struggling to breathe as the blood running down the back of this throat was starting to make him cough. Dragon slammed his head down again, making sure he connected forehead to forehead. He cut himself in the process, as he battered the gangster, causing the skin above the man's eye to flap open.

"Every time you see the scars in the mirror, or someone asks about them, I am sure you will lie and tell a story; but deep inside you will know you are a piece of shit who was beaten like an old woman."

The gangster was close to passing out from the second blow. He tried to focus his eyes through the blood and pick out his attacker's face. Dragon drove his head down a third time, connecting with the man's jaw. The eerie noise caused him to look down to see the man's jawbone had shifted to one side.

Dragon jumped to his feet. "We're out of here. We don't need any more problems tonight."

The three men stepped over the bodies littering the road and started to run down the street. Dragon was feeling the booze, laughing as he remembered the fight and the woman. Tomorrow was the eighth of the month, the number eight was a good omen and good luck. He felt the energy roaring through his veins and he looked over at Li as they ran. "China – why would we ever leave?"

CHAPTER 3

Marathon, Ontario, Canada. East of Jackfish, 1883

"The ground is alive. It eats the rail overnight."

The worker's comment rang true. Tiger couldn't believe it himself. They would lay track one day and the earth would devour it by the next. If it wasn't the rain and rivers washing it away, the steel simply sank below the surface.

This was the mess he was in. Somewhere near a town that would eventually be called Marathon, in Canada's north. The delays didn't stop the madness though, the men continued laying the rails that were supposed to link this massive land. They blasted and moved rock, levelling the mountains, filling the swamps and flattening the valleys to keep the track level.

He and the other Chinese workers were kept away from the locals. They camped together in tents, working ahead of the main crews, doing the most dangerous work. Tiger didn't mind, it worked in his favor.

He didn't know how long his family had been in the crime business, but it went way back. His father had worked the poppy routes, affiliated with the triads like previous generations.

Tiger thought he had it made and had settled down with a nice bride, only to have the family history of "secure and expand" explained to him. This was the way that the Chang family would continue to grow and prosper. His destiny was to spread the family's influence by moving to another country. He picked North America based on talks he'd had with ship captains. They said the place was, "a country the size of China with no one living there. A place full of mountains, rivers, and endless wilderness."

Well, he had sure found the wilderness endless. For over a year he had been working this rail, and he couldn't believe how big the country was. They had been laboring along the north side of a large lake called Superior for over four months now. Whenever they climbed a hill with enough height that they could see the big water, Tiger always took the time to sit and ponder its size.

"This is just a lake Bao, can you believe it?"

His trusted lieutenant was equally amazed by its size. "They say that there are other lakes to the south just as big."

Tiger nodded, he really wanted to get off the damned railroad and get on with the family business. He almost left a few times, but kept working the next section. Right now he had too much going his way here in the middle of nowhere.

He had been in Canada a year before they started bringing laborers from China to work as crews on the railroad. He'd been quick to see an opportunity. When the first crews arrived in the eastern province to start working westward, he was in place and quickly found ways to put himself in an influential position.

Finding some men who were not leaders, but who liked the respect they received as feared soldiers, he quickly organized them into a group. Hearing that Chinese workers were getting beat up on nights when drunken local men were wandering around looking for trouble was the opportunity he was seeking. This would be where he gained the trust of his people.

*****

The fire had been stoked with large logs up to a foot wide. The flames jumped high into the night air, creating a bright, warm circle in the cold dark night. The Chinese workers were laughing and getting drunk. Tiger and his men watched from the woods surrounding the clearing.

On one hand his men should be sleeping and getting the rest needed to just survive the heavy work. On the other hand, he could understand their desire to unwind and escape the harshness of a backbreaking job. As long as they worked the next day, he had no issues.

Tiger hoped that this weekend would bring them the trouble he was looking for. He was getting tired of listening to his own men getting drunk and carrying on, if the locals didn't show up soon he was going to do something to somebody, one way or the other.

After two hours huddled in the cold dark inside the tree line, they heard people coming through the woods towards the fire. He silently waved his men down, low to the ground.

"Come on guys, they're over here!"

The *gwei lo*, white devils, were making just as much noise as the celebrating Chinese, egging each other on. It seemed they were trying to keep their courage up.

"Let's get in there before they try to run."

A short loudmouth led three tough looking men into the opening. Tiger watched the drinking workers jump up and move to the other side of the fire, clumping up like a herd of scared sheep. Not one of them moved forward to confront the intruders.

The smallest white man was first to speak. "Well, what have we got here? Looks like a bunch of little boys all huddled together."

The three big guys laughed and started flexing their muscles, trying to look tough. One of them punched his fist into his palm a few times which seemed to intimidate the intoxicated Chinese.

Tiger could see the intoxicated workers were clearly not interested in defending themselves, which was fine with him. He'd hoped they wouldn't.

Without a word, he got up and stepped into the clearing. Bao and three others ranged out beside him. In a line they walked towards the locals. The intruders heard the murmurs of the Chinese huddled on the other side of the fire and turned to see Tiger and his group. Initially, the white men didn't see any difference between these Chinese and those on the other side of the flames. Then they caught the glint of a knife and heard the unmistakable sound of metal on metal as a machete was pulled from it's sheathe.

The three big men lost a bit of their courage at the sight of the unknown arrivals, these clearly weren't the pushovers they were looking for, but the smallest one was still cocky. "Look here boys, we got us some Chinamen with balls." His smile looked like a snarl.

Tiger knew this was his intended target. "So you think it is fun to beat up on men from my country. Well here I am." He spread his hands open in from of him as he moved towards the smaller man. "Let's have some fun."

Tiger watched the sudden spike of fear as the gang's leader looked around at his men for help.

"Are you not man enough to fight your own battles?" The question brought laughter from Tiger's own group and some of the drunken men around the fire who could understand English.

The fear started to change to anger in the eyes of the other man. He was being called out in front of witnesses. He appeared to be calculating his odds and trying to gauge the difficulties this Chinese was going to bring.

Tiger stepped closer as everyone else moved away. His men backed up while the three big men, unsure what to do, created some separation from their boss.

Fighting was something that Tiger had learned in the mountains protecting the family's smuggling routes. The only way to fight was to stay on the offensive and be as brutal as possible. As he lunged forward, the white man tried to move away. Tiger hit him square in the chest and kept pushing backwards. He didn't care what they hit or fell on, just that the local was below him.

Tiger kept pushing the man, warding off his blows until they slammed up against a tree. As the air rushed out of his opponent's lungs, he pulled him away from the tree and threw him towards the fire. The man landed on his side and rolled a few times before coming to a stop dangerously close to the flames. He quickly tried to lever himself up out of the dirt, but Tiger was already beside him, kicking him hard in the ribs.

Now all the intoxicated Chinese were yelling and cheering, excited to see the local being beaten. The three tough guys weren't running away, but they weren't hurrying to their leader's defence either. The man curled up in a defensive position as Tiger kicked him in the side again, he was sure he felt ribs give way.

He leaned over his victim. "You mentioned a bunch of boys. I only see one here." Reaching down he grabbed the man's arm, stretching it towards the fire. Sliding his hands back to the guy's elbow, Tiger thrust the hand into the heat.

He'd expected his victim's sudden struggle to pull the hand out of the fire and braced himself, keeping the hand against the coals for a few moments. Stepping back Tiger let go of the man's arm and the leader jerked it out of the fire, staring in shock at his melted flesh.

"You can't do that!" One of the big tough guys found his courage.

Tiger ignored him. He turned to his countrymen still huddled on the other side of the fire. "What's wrong with you? Have you no pride in yourself or your country?" He asked in Chinese.

Again, there were murmurs in the drunken crowd.

"You are scared of men like this?" He kicked the contorted man on the ground. "You cannot let this happen, or you will be slaves in this country. Stand up for yourselves and protect your own."

Tiger turned and nodded. His lieutenant jumped forward, straight into the big man who had finally stepped out to protect his boss. Bao swung his machete, aiming the back side of the blade for the big man's knee. Everyone in the clearing heard the impact as the man's leg buckled and he toppled over sideways, landing on his back.

An overhead swing, still using the back of the blade, came down hard on the other leg just missing the knee.

"Jesus Christ," the man yelled as he jerked upright, trying to protect his legs with his arms.

Bao brought the butt end of the machete down on the man's head, the hardened steel splitting his scalp open, the force of the blow flattening him back out on the ground.

"Look what a Chinese can do!" Tiger yelled at his countrymen who were getting more enraged and vocal.

"I took one man. Bao here took down this big one by himself." He let his voice go quiet as everyone listened. "Can't you men take care of these other two by yourselves?" He swung his arm around to indicate the remaining tough guys.

The crowd started to yell, moving together around the fire pit.

The two tough guys hadn't understood the conversation, but could tell things had taken a bad turn. They started to back up, trying to retreat. The crowd surged from behind the fire and spread out, surrounding the men.

Tiger, Bao, and his men stood back and let the mob go. Blows rained down and the mass of men surrounding the tough guys kept beating until the men had fallen, huddling on the ground in self-defence. Tiger led his group away, certain that his reputation had been established and that word would spread throughout the rest of the Chinese workers.

*****

There were twelve thousand men and five thousand horses working out of the makeshift town at Marathon. The five hundred Chinese workers were no longer having any problems with the locals. They were left alone and kept to themselves.

Tiger had strengthened his grip on the Chinese workers by getting supplies, better food rations, providing protection, and then strong-arming them all for small payments to keep things running smoothly. He became the go-between for the workers and the railroad's big bosses.

The last thing he did cemented his leadership and gave him complete control. He managed to get the bosses off the work-site. Management showed up for morning and evening inspections, but otherwise the Chinese were left alone to get their work done.

When Tiger introduced a system where twenty different workers were excused from the work detail each day to rest, their appreciation multiplied as did their health and the crew's moral. Each day a handful of men were sent to hide and rest in the woods, out of sight in case someone came by.

As Tiger walked along the rail inspecting the work in progress, he turned to Bao. "Why are we still on this damned railroad?"

"Because it is profitable." The answer was simple, but exact. Tiger was putting away a nice sum every month, as were his soldiers.

"Yes, but isn't this living in hell out here? I'm sick of it."

"They say that they will put it a siding forty miles ahead at a place that they are calling Jackfish. There will be room for better accommodations and we will work from that camp for a period of time."

Tiger was silent while Bao continued, "Maybe we should wait until then, things may be better there."

He'd heard it before, the next place, the next place. That carrot was working well. He would continue to this new place and decide what to do once he got there. Tiger yelled down at a group of workers carrying rocks down into a hole that required filling. The fools couldn't even do a simple task.

He didn't work hard himself, but his presence was always felt as he did the organization and planning, or strong-arming as required. With his men as crew leaders directing the workers and Bao at his side, Tiger was now the uncontested leader.